DREAM CRUSHER

IONA ROSE

AUTHOR'S NOTE

Hey there!

Thank you for choosing my book. I sure hope that you love it. I'd hate to part ways once you're done though. So how about we stay in touch?

My newsletter is a great way to discover more about me and my books. Where you'll find frequent exclusive give-aways, sneak previews of new releases and be first to see new cover reveals.

And as a HUGE thank you for joining, you'll receive a FREE book on me!

With love,

Iona

Get Your FREE Book Here:

https://dl.bookfunnel.com/v9yit8b3f7

DREAM CRUSHER

Publisher: Some Books

1

LANE

When I graduated high school, I was voted 'Most Likely to Succeed'. My classmates who voted for me probably meant it as an insult. Because when you're seventeen, it's not cool to be ambitious. It's much more socially acceptable to live in the moment having fun and partying. Which was probably why I never had any interest in hanging out with the cool crowd anyway.

Working was more my thing... and being involved with every club and organization that would look good on my college applications. Even as a teenager, I had a laser focus set on succeeding and proving others wrong.

So when our senior yearbooks came out, and everyone in my class laughed as they congratulated me on my superlative, it didn't bother me as much as it would have bothered other girls.

As my grandma used to say; living well is the best revenge. One day, I will have the last laugh. I just hoped it wouldn't take too much longer to finally earn just a little bit of success. I need to achieve something before it's too late to matter.

This is the goal that motivates me every morning. And when I'm motivated, everyone had better look out.

"Is my two o'clock here yet?" I ask our receptionist as I come sprinting around the corner of the lobby of the bank where I work, and nearly collide with a large potted plant. My heels click on the polished marble floor and echo through the massive three story entryway.

"Not yet." Janice reassures me with a smile.

Phew, I think to myself. I have another jam packed day of back to back meetings, and haven't had a chance to eat yet.

"Thank goodness, I'm just going to run out to grab a sandwich. When they get here do you mind...?"

"Stalling?" Janice asks, reading my mind. "Not at all. Take your time."

"Thank you." I say, giving Janice a wave as I make a run for the door.

Just as I'm turning, I smack into something that feels like a brick wall. It sends me flying backwards, and it's all I can do to maintain my balance in the four inch heels I'm wearing. I let out a small startled scream, but just as I'm about to topple over a hard hand lands on my elbow and pulls me upright. I look up, and meet a pair of piercing ice-blue eyes.

"I'm sorry, are you ok?" blue eyes asks, as if he were the one who ran into me. We both knew it was very much the other way around.

"Yeah, I'm sorry."

Regaining my balance, I look down at his hand that is still on my elbow and back up to his chiseled face. He smiles suavely before letting go. I take a moment to scan this man up and down, savoring every detail. He's well over six feet, and I can tell from the way it felt to run into his chest that he is built very, very, very solidly.

"Can I help you?" Janice asks him. It's only then I realize I am still staring at him and haven't said a word.

"Yes, I'm here for a meeting," he answers Janice, but his eyes are still locked on mine.

"Yes, you must be Mr. Dunkirk. Let me show you to the elevator. They are waiting for you up on the fortieth floor."

I watch stupidly as he follows Janice. To my great embarrassment, he turns and gives me a quick smile before he reaches the elevator bank. Awkwardly, I offer a small wave, then totally check out his ass until he disappears from my sight. I lean against Janice's desk and stare into space.

"Nice looking, isn't he?" she comments approvingly when she returns.

"What? I mean, maybe." I say, doing my best to hide the fact that I'm still trying to picture what he looks like with his shirt off. I practically salivate as I remember how hard his stomach felt when my hand briefly brushed up against it. He had at least an eight pack, and rock hard biceps.

"What did you say his name was?"

"Chris Dunkirk. He's meeting with the commercial lenders upstairs." Janice says as she motions towards the set of fancy elevators in the back of the lobby. To get a meeting up on the fortieth floor, you have to have serious money to invest. Unlike the personal banking clients I met with that were looking for money for a car or a small line of credit, the banks commercial clients are the big players. The exact kind I hoped to one day be.

"Did you say Dunekirk? Like Richard Dunekirk?"

I shake my head to keep my mind from going to places it doesn't belong as I think more and more about Chris.

"Probably."

I roll my eyes, and feel stupid for checking him out so hard. Richard Dunekirk owned half of the buildings in Philadelphia. He was practically royalty. If the guy with the blue eyes was his son, no matter how hot he was, it wasn't worth my time even thinking about him. He was probably just here using his dad's money and pretending to be a big shot and enjoying having his ass kissed. There is no bigger turn off than a guy who is handed every opportunity in life, and who didn't know what it meant to struggle.

"Oh well, I should get going. I'll be back in ten minutes tops." I say as I feel my stomach growling.

As I grab the cold brass handle of the revolving door and it begins to move, I see my next appointment entering the building with a huge smile on his face.

"Hi Lane, sorry I was running a little late."

I look at the massive clock above the reception desk, and see its 2:03pm.

"No, don't apologize." I say, doing my best to not sound disappointed. I already know this is going to be a long meeting, and my three o'clock will probably already be waiting by the time we are done. So much for lunch.

"Come on, let's go." My client, Louis, and I head off towards my small office in the back of the first floor. It's the third in a long line of other small offices that contain flimsy plastic desks that look more like folding tables.

I sit down in my desk chair and gesture to Louis to take a seat in one of the chairs on the opposite side of my desk. This is the third time Louis has been in my office, and he already told me on the phone he is hoping to add to his line of credit. With any luck, he'll be borrowing at least as much as he did the last time he came in. And with my commission structure, I stand to make a couple of hundred dollars from this one hour meeting.

Not a bad payday at all for sixty minutes of work. Unless you factor in the first three months I worked at the bank, where I did nothing but make cold calls and didn't earn a penny until I finally landed my first client. It was beyond discouraging, and most of the other new hires I started with gave up and quit. But I didn't. And little by little, it was starting to pay off. My climb to the top of the corporate ladder was much slower than I ever could have imagined. Which was why I really needed to find a way out of personal banking, and into something that paid a hell of a lot better.

I feel a familiar mix of jealousy and annoyance when I think of how the guys up on the 40th floor will probably make more in a one hour meeting with Richard's son than I do in an entire year. It was extremely unfair, but I have to remember that I am paying my dues. One day all the hard work I'm doing now will pay off big time. And my success will be all the sweeter since I know what it means to struggle.

"All right Louis, what can I do for you today?" I switch into game mode, and smile at him as I ignore the sharp hunger pains in my stomach. When I have my mind set on something I can ignore everything else.

A skill that one day I will have to thank for all of my success.

2

CHRIS

When I arrive outside the boardroom I take a deep breath in an attempt to steady my nerves. I peer inside the room through the glass door, and see a twelve foot table filled with men in expensive suits making small talk while waiting for me.

I straighten my suit jacket, tuck my pad folio under my arm, and open the doors a confident smile on my face. I was going to get what I came for or I was not leaving.

"Afternoon gentlemen." I say, effectively commanding the attention of everyone in the room as I enter.

All eyes are on me as I find my spot at the front of the room. I instantly feel a sense of calmness wash over my body when I see my pitch deck up on the SMART Board on the wall. I stand up straight, and make solid eye contact with the man seated closest to me at the front of the table. He shoots me a grin and nods his head.

"Thank you for being here today," I begin.

Everyone in the room grabs the set of financials that are already in front of them on the table and begin flipping through the pages of spreadsheets.

This is the moment I have been preparing for months. I know every number in my pitch deck like the back of my hand. I've spent countless hours projecting cash flows and running every scenario possible. My business plan is rock solid. And once these bankers give me the go ahead today it will finally be time to execute my plan.

"So Chris Dunkirk, any relation to Richard?" one of the men in the back of the room asks me.

I do my best not to swear. I'm used to this question, I must get in at least once a week. And its getting harder and harder not to let my irritation show.

Richard Dunekirk is the biggest real estate developer in Philadelphia. He made a killing when the first tax abatement was passed nearly twenty years ago. Since then he has completely transformed the city, and brought back countless jobs by creating modern apartments and condos that have brought young people flocking to the city.

And while I admire him tremendously and know that our last names sound similar, these guys should know that his last name is spelled differently than mine.

"No, he's Dunekirk with an e." I respectfully point out, and hold my breath as I wait for what is going to come next.

Everyone at the table looks at each other. I feel a twinge of anxiety . Clearly the only reason I was given this meeting was because they thought I was related to Richard. I feel my big opportunity slipping away, and I try to think of everything possible I can do to hold onto it.

"But I am a huge fan of Richard's career. Not many people know he actually started off in residential real estate. And there is still tremendous opportunity and demand for luxury housing in Center City Philadelphia. The job market is as strong as it's ever been, and those who work in the city want to live in the city. Naturally, they want to do it in style."

I go right into my pitch before anyone has the chance to think anymore about Richard Dunekirk. Even though he's one of the most successful real estate developers today, there was a time when he was just a young guy full of hope just like me. He was probably once in a room begging investors for money, just like I am today. Everyone has to start somewhere. And I'd be shocked if his first business plan was even half as elaborate as mine.

"So Chris, it says here you plan to invest up to thirty percent of your own assets?" the leader of the team at the head of the table asks, lowering his glasses as he studies my spreadsheets.

"Yes, I want to have as much skin in the game as possible."

Two of the other men nod at each other. I have been saving every penny since I was a teenager to have enough to qualify for a small business loan. I know not many guys in their thirties can say they have anywhere close to what I have saved up. It wasn't easy saving over half of my salary every year and living with my dad all throughout my twenties. But it will all be worth it if it shows these guys just how serious I am. This isn't a game to me, it's everything. I am betting everything I have on myself, because I know I won't fail.

"Impressive. It sounds like you have done your research. We are going to pre-approve you for the full amount. We will get an official letter to you this afternoon." the team leader announces as he stands and comes to shake my hand.

I feel frozen as I raise my hand and shake his. *The full amount,* the words echo in my head as my brain does its best to comprehend the fact that my dream has just come true.

"Fuck yes." I whisper to myself once they're all gone and I'm alone. Then I grab my phone, and call the only other person on this planet who will be as happy as I am, my father.

As I think back to all of the sacrifices he has made to get me to where I am today, it makes me feel like the luckiest guy on the planet to be able to share this news with him.

"Dad, they gave me the full amount. Let's start our search." I yell into the phone when he answers.

"I knew it, Chris. I've already started pulling listings for you."

My dad is not only my biggest supporter, but also a kick ass realtor. He knows exactly what I'm looking for, and I know he has something that would be perfect for me. This is the beginning of something huge. I can feel it.

3

LANE

When six finally rolls around, I am only half way done with my paperwork for the day. The rest of the office is empty, since most of my co-workers leave by five. It's no wonder I kick all of their asses each month when the earnings report comes in. I work at least an extra three hours later than everyone, and get twice as much done.

Today, I decide to treat myself and head home early since I can catch up over the weekend. I pack up my bag, switch off the lights, and wave to the night guard as I leave the building.

It's a beautiful spring evening and the first day of the year when the temperature has hit seventy degrees. It's about a mile walk from my office to the row home I live in, and I use the twenty minutes to unwind as I make my way down the crowded sidewalks of the city. It still never gets old seeing the tall office buildings and everyone milling about in their business suits.

Most days, I still can't believe that I am lucky enough to live in Center City and that I have the luxury of walking to work. When I first moved to the city after college with my roommates, the only thing we could afford was in a very sketchy part of town. Not to mention we were miles away from any nightlife, which was one of the main reasons my roommates wanted to live in the city. For me, it was all about the job opportunities, and being close to the financial district. All my life I dreamed of wearing a suit and working in a big impressive office building. Little did I know that I should have been more specific with my dreams. Even though I technically was living it, I know I still have a very long way to go.

As I arrive on my block, I see my neighbor Lindsay frantically pounding on the door of the house that I live in with my two best friends, Ashley and Heidi.

"Everything ok, Lindsay?" I ask.

"There you are." Lindsay turns in the direction of my voice, and flails her hands in the air as she talks. "The kitchen sink is all backed up and leaking again. I didn't think you were home yet, so I tried to tighten the pipe myself..."

"Oh God." I scream, already knowing this can't be good.

I jam my keys into the lock, fling the door open, and grab my tool box from the front hallway. The only reason we are able to afford the rent on our place is because I also work as the property manager for the six row homes in our complex that are all owned by our landlord Howard. It was extremely generous of him to offer me the job and the reduction in rent, because when we first made the deal, I didn't know a thing about old homes or how to even change a lightbulb. Thank goodness for the internet. You can learn almost anything from video tutorials. Four years later, there hasn't been a repair or a problem that I haven't been able to handle. And my roommates and I sure have made the most of city life.

"Come on, let's go." I say to Lindsay as I take off my heels and my suit jacket.

We both run to Lindsay's house next door. I hear the sound of water rushing as I enter through her small living room. And sure enough, I see several inches of water on the beautiful, original hardwood kitchen floors. I know I have to stop the leak fast and get my wet vac before any more damage occurs.

"What were you doing Lindsay?" I say as I get on my back and take a look under the sink. This is always a difficult fit for me, since I have to make sure my massive chest doesn't get stuck as I try to fit in the small cabinet space. I know everyone thinks I'm lucky to be a 32DD, but most of the time it's just annoying having huge tits.

"Just dishes. There's something wrong. This is the third time this month it's done this."

I quickly spot the source of the leak, and reach for a wrench from my tool box. After a few turns, I hear the sweet sound of the running water stop.

I exhale loudly as I come out from under the sink, and wipe the drops of stray water from my face.

"I'll talk to Howard about having someone come out and maybe replacing some of the plumbing, but in the meantime, just try and be careful."

"Careful? I was just washing dishes. Tell Howard that I'm not giving him another penny until he fixes this."

I nod, and am just about to tell Lindsay that she's right when I stop myself. My intense loyalty to Howard won't allow me to say anything bad about him. Howard has been the most amazing landlord, and I know there's no way I could ever afford to live in the city without his generosity.

But the last few months he's really been hard to get a hold of, and even tighter when it comes to money for repairs. This isn't like him, but I'm sure if we sit down together and have a talk I can convince him to do what needs to be done.

Howard has been renting these homes for over 40 years. Every dollar he gets in rent is pure profit to him at this point. The least he could do was protect his investment.

"Anything else?" I ask Lindsay, who shakes her head.

I take my toolbox home and call Howard repeatedly to see what he wants me to do about Lindsay's sink. I'm in the middle of my second voicemail when my roommate Ashley comes home.

"Everything ok?" she asks, looking at my white cotton dress shirt and pencil skirt that are still wet and plastered to my skin.

"Yeah, Lindsay's sink again. Might be time to call in a professional." I tell Ashley as I research local plumbers on my phone.

"Nothing you can do about that tonight. Come on, it's Friday, let's go get a drink."

Drinking, going to a bar and being hit on by a bunch of drunk guys is the last thing I want to do right now, and most nights really. But I have a feeling Ashley isn't going to take no for an answer. It's been over a month since we've had a girls night, and since Ashley broke up with her last serious boyfriend Tom a few months back, going out is the only thing that seems to make her happy.

"Ok, but I can't be out late."

Ashley jumps up and down and claps her hands in excitement.

"Yes! I just bought this new dress I've been dying to wear, I just hope it's not too fancy. What are you going to wear?"

I look down at the outfit I'm still wearing from work. I

pull on the front of my shirt, and try to decide if I need to change or not. But the fabric remains stuck to my chest, and I know I can' t go out like this.

"I'll just go put on something dry."

"Ok, as long as it's not another one of those manly looking shirts. Don't you own anything besides work and gym clothes?"

It's a fair question, and I actually have to think before answering Ashley. The truth is, on the rare occasions I do go out, I prefer to wear a nice suit. I like everyone knowing that I am a professional. And the men that do approach me usually end up asking me what I do for a living when they see me in my suit, which is my favorite thing to talk about.

"I'll see what I can do."

I walk upstairs to my room, and grab a silk blouse from my closet that I save for my most important meetings. I also grab another black pencil skirt that fits me like a glove. I throw my heels back on and a fresh coat of lip gloss.

"How's this?" I ask, doing a twirl as I await Ashley's verdict.

"Better I guess, but still kind of professional."

"Perfect!" I exclaim as I grab my purse and head out the door.

Dressing the part is good enough for now.

4

LANE

The next morning, I wake at eight with a throbbing headache. I drag myself out of bed, and search through the kitchen cabinets for an aspirin as I wait for a pot of coffee to brew.

"Morning." I say to my roommate Heidi as she enters the kitchen in her robe and fuzzy slippers.

"Why are you always up so early?" she asks as she yawns.

"It's not early, it's after eight."

The truth is sleeping till eight on the weekends is considered sleeping in to me. During the week I'm up by five every morning. I've just always found that if I sleep in too much on the weekends, I pay for it Monday morning. Which are usually my busiest days.

"I let Ashley convince me to go out last night, and now I think I might have a hangover." I tell Heidi as I grab my favorite coffee cup.

"Well, if you slept till noon like a normal person, you would be over it by the time you got up."

"Unlikely, my head is killing me." I say, rubbing my temples.

"How many drinks did you have?"

"Maybe two glasses of wine? But they were big, and filled to the top."

My head throbs just thinking about it.

"Must be nice to be such a lightweight." Heidi says.

"Well not everyone can drink all night like you can. What did you end up doing last night?"

Heidi smiles as she takes a seat at our small round kitchen table.

"Well, I went out with some of the guys after work."

I pull out a chair, already knowing this is going to be good, when a knock at the door interrupts us.

"What?" I yell even though I'm aware there's no way someone standing outside our door can hear me. They knock again, so I get up to answer.

"Howard!" I say when I see our seventy year old landlord on our front steps. "There you are, I've been trying to get a hold of you."

"Yes, I got your messages. Sorry I was out of town."

"Again? Weren't you just in Florida?"

"Yes, I went back. Becky had another baby, grandbaby number four. You should see him, such a bug guy."

Howard reaches for his phone and begins scrolling through his camera roll. I do my best to suppress the urge to drum my fingertips on the door handle as I hope he hurries. Even though his grandkids are cute, I've seen a lot of pictures of them, and there are more pressing matters we need to discuss.

"Cute." I say taking a quick glance at the image of a small baby wrapped in a hospital blanket with a blue stripe.

I hope by answering quickly I can discourage him from showing me any more pictures.

"Yeah, even named him Howard, after me." Howard continues to stare at his phone screen and silently shakes his head as he sighs.

"That's kind of an old fashioned name for a baby, don't you think?"

Howard looks up at me, his eyes narrow. I decide it's a good idea to change the topic.

"Anyway, Lindsay's sink. There's got to be something wrong with the sewer since this keeps happening. I'll make some calls this morning."

"Let's maybe hold off on that for now."

I'm so busy scrolling through the list of local plumbers I have made in the notes section of my phone that I almost don't hear what he just said.

"Hold off till when? Her entire house floods?"

Howard scratches the back of his head and looks down at the doormat.

"I have some news I've been meaning to tell you."

I can tell by his tone it's something serious. My mind races as I try to guess what life threatening illness he could have been diagnosed with.

"I'm moving." He finally tells me. I let out a huge breath that I didn't even realize I was holding.

"Moving? Ok, it shouldn't be a problem to find a renter for your unit. And of course, I'll be here so I can handle things when you're gone."

I smile at Howard to reassure him that I will be fine. But instead of smiling back, Howard's face remains serious.

"The thing is, I'm moving to Florida. And it's too far away if anything goes wrong."

"Ok, Florida is far, but I'm here. I can handle anything. Haven't I shown you that you can trust me?"

Howard puts a hand on my shoulder and pats me.

"You have been wonderful, but I'm old. I need to enjoy my life and be with my grandkids. I'm sorry Lane. I have to sell all the units."

Sell all of the units. The words echo in my head as I think of Howard selling these houses to someone else, and what the chances are that the new one will give me the same reduction on rent as Howard has all these years. I quickly determine they are not good to say the least.

Even the rent that Howard charges Lindsay is still a bargain compared to most of the houses in Center City. And I know we couldn't even afford that. Looks like our dream city life is over. *Unless.*

My brain shifts into overdrive as I think of how much money the new owner will make, while doing nothing but collecting rent each month. All that person will need is money, and then they will have a fantastic investment that will set them up for life.

"I want to buy them. All six." I tell Howard. He pats my shoulder again, and exhales loudly.

"I've already found a realtor, this is a very desirable area now. He thinks they'll go quickly, and for a lot of money."

"I know, I will take out a loan. I work for a bank you know. I can rent out the other units, and bring in more than enough to cover the costs of living here. And I'll be building equity, and not to mention the tax deductions."

My mind races to work out all the details, but I already know this is my big break. The one I have been waiting for my whole life. It was all starting to make sense why my job at the bank was the only one I could find when I first graduated from college. At the time, it seemed like a waste of my talent, like I'd never get to where I wanted to be. But now I realize I found that job, because it was destiny. That job has taught me everything I needed to know to make this opportunity work.

"Well, you'd need to talk to the bank fast. They're hitting the market next week. Already have a few showings lined up for this weekend."

"Ok. I'm sure I can get a meeting on Monday. Just please Howard, give me a chance."

I never thought I'd stoop so low as to beg, but after everything I have done for Howard, I deserved a chance. I wasn't asking him to give me a discount, I didn't need charity. Just time.

"Of course Lane. But I hope you won't be offended if we show it until you can get an offer together."

"No, I'm not afraid of some competition." I say, feeling so excited that nothing can phase me. Then I realize the last thing I want is to get into a bidding war with someone with deep pockets. I try to think of a way that I can nicely hint to anyone that shows up to view these homes that they need some major TLC. That might be enough to scare any potential buyers off.

"Here's my realtor's name." Howard says, handing me a business card. Just get in touch when you have an offer."

"I will, thank you!" I grab the card from his hand, and race back towards the kitchen.

"Anyway, so we went to this great place last night." Heidi picks up where she left off in her story, but I can't even remember what we were talking about. And I no longer care.

"I'm sorry, I have to go into my office." I tell Heidi, as I grab my travel mug and fill in with steaming hot coffee. It's only now I realize my head is no longer throbbing. The thrill of finally being given my big break is enough that I can block out all distractions. Nothing is going to stop me now.

"Work? On a Saturday? Must be an important client."

"It is. Me."

I can tell from the way Heidi's jaw drops that she is about to ask me to explain. But I don't have time to waste. I have to get to my work computer, and gather my own financial information the same way I do for all of my clients. It shouldn't take too long, since I don't have very many assets at the moment. I think of all the information I gather when someone comes into the bank looking for a loan. I always start by asking what their salary is, for all of their bank statements, and for them to tell me about their experience and expertise.

Hmm, as I think about my current salary and my small checking account, I can't help but realize that I am lacking greatly in both departments.. If I was the person in charge or reviewing myself, it would be a firm no. As I think of how unimpressive I look on paper, it's almost enough to stop me. Getting a small business loan that would be enough to buy all six units was a long shot at best.

But I take a deep breath, and push all of the negativity aside. This is not the time for self doubt. No one is going to believe in me unless I believe in myself. And believing in myself when no one else has is one of the things I am best at. Since I've done it a lot over the last twenty-six years.

5

CHRIS

As my dad pulls into a tiny side street and the robotic voice of the GPS notifies us we have arrived at our destination, I double check to make sure we have the address right.

"These?" I say, looking at the six almost identical homes that fill the entire block. This was not what I had in mind when I told my dad I was looking for luxury rental properties. The brick fronts of the homes are covered with a layer of dirt so thick I can't tell if they are made of real brick, or some awful fake vinyl siding. The second stories all have window AC units sticking out, which are real eyesore. A very good indication that they don't have central air.

"Yes, there are six units I've been telling you about. They all just need a little bit of cosmetic changes, and you'll be able to sell them for twice as much as they are asking now."

Dad and I get out of the car, and climb the concrete steps to the front door which are uneven and cracked.

"They're just so old. You know most buyers are looking for something modern."

"You can make them modern, and make a killing if you want to sell them after. Let's at least see the inside."

Flipping wasn't what I had in mind when I told my dad I wanted to invest in real estate. I was looking for something with less risk that was more long term. But if my dad thought there was potential here, I needed to at least hear him out.

Dad puts the code into the lock box, and I follow him. When we step inside, I'm surprised to see twelve foot ceilings and a large sliding door that leads to a courtyard complete with a fire pit and trees. Not something you usually see in the city.

"Can you imagine what buyers will think once we redo these kitchens? New appliances, some quartz countertops. We won't have to change the floor plan at all, since it's already open. That's what gets really costly."

The wooden floorboards creak as I take a step towards the kitchen.

"Yeah, and new floors. Something more durable like laminates." I say.

"That we can fix. But these yards, look at them. Who wouldn't want their own outdoor space in the city?"

As we open the sliding door, I think I hear a knock at the front door. I look at my dad, not sure if it's our place to open it or not. He shrugs, and motions for me to follow him into the backyard. I have one foot out the door when I hear a female's voice.

"Anyone in here?" The voice calls out.

"Uh yeah." I answer, not sure what else to do.

"Sorry to interrupt." I hear the sound of high heels clicking as the woman makes her way across the living room. " I just wanted to introduce myself in case you had any questions. I am Lane, the property manager here."

The woman keeps walking until she is about three feet from my dad and me. Then she stops, and her eyes widen, gorgeous, gold-flecked, hazel eyes I could recognize anywhere.

"Hi Lane, nice to see you again."

Lane bites her bottom lip, as she looks back at the front door she just came from.

"Funny running into you again," she finally says.

I laugh at her choice of words, and remember in vivid detail how she ran right into my chest at the bank last week. Her cheeks flush slightly, as if she feels embarrassed remembering. Little does she know how much I enjoyed the feel of her huge tits pressed up against me. I feel my cock twitch in my pants as I look at her long toned legs in her super high heels.

"I didn't get a chance to introduce myself properly. I'm Chris."

I take another step towards Lane, and steal a glimpse of her magnificent chest. The button of her white shirt looks like it might pop off at any second from the strain of being stretching so tightly over her breasts.

Lane follows my gaze and folds her arms over her chest as she clears her throat.

"Chris, you said. Sorry, I didn't mean to interrupt."

"No not at all." I look to my dad, who arches his brows. I know he wants me to get this girl to leave so we can finish the tour. Even though my dad has never dated anyone since my mom left, and tells me how women are a waste of time, I know there isn't a chance he doesn't notice how smoking hot this girl in front of us is.

"So, as I said, I've been the property manager for the last four years. I can tell you every repair we've had to make, and there've been quite a few." She places an extra emphasis on the last few words of her sentence and shakes her head.

"Thanks, I appreciate you coming here to tell me, but I'm not surprised given the age of the properties."

Lane presses her lips together. I get an intense sudden visual of what it would look like to have her mouth on my dick. The thought is so distracting I have to check to make sure my cock hasn't just ripped through the front of my pants.

Lane catches me as I am staring at my crotch and wrinkles her nose. I know she's trying to discourage me, but she looks even cuter to me now.

"Yeah they need a lot of work. Probably a new sewer which you may or may not know, most insurance companies won't cover." Lane continues as she brushes a large piece of soft brown hair out of her face.

"Thank you Lane, but I'm sure the owner will cover all of that in the disclosures. It's required by law." my dad says, gesturing towards the front door.

I turn around to look at him, hoping he'll give me a minute with Lane. But instead of excusing himself outside, he remains in the kitchen.

"Oh yeah. Just making sure." Lane turns as if she's about to head for the door. But I don't want her to leave just yet. I haven't been able to stop thinking about her since I saw her at the bank, and now here she is right in front of me.

"Thanks Lane, so you said you're the property manager?" I ask, walking till I'm standing directly in front of her. Lane looks up at me, and even in her heels, I can see the top of her head. I'd guess she is about five foot three, which is perfect.

"Yes, I handle everything. So if you want to know about any issues..." Lane says, taking a step backwards.

"Yes, I'd love to hear. Tell me everything."

Lane smiles, and walks towards the brick fireplace that is in the center of the living room.

"Well, for starters, this chimney is clogged. Can't even use this, since there's no ventilation."

Lane turns the handle of the flute, and it hardly budges. She tries once more, and suddenly we hear chirping, and a noise that sounds like something is tumbling down.

Lane screams and jumps as a bird comes flying out the front of the fireplace.

"Oh my god." She screams.

The small sparrow flies around frantically, squeaking loudly and looking for a way out. I look at Lane and laugh, but she seems genuinely terrified.

"Get out. " I yell at the bird, opening the front door. It continues to fly around, bumping into the ceiling repeatedly. I grab a broom that is propped up against the hall closet, and jab it up towards the ceiling to get the bird to fly in the direction of the open door. I'm careful not to make contact with the bird and accidentally hurt it. I continue to coax it out, until it finally flies right through the doorway and outside.

"Thank you for that." Lane says, finally bringing her hands down that were covering her head. It's funny and kind of cute that she thought a small frightened bird was going to attack her.

"Sure."

"So I guess it's not blocked anymore." I say with a laugh. Lane doesn't seem amused.

"You should also know we had mice in the basement last year." Lane shutters at the thought.

"Not unusual for the city."

Lane shoots me a dirty look. It's like she expects me to

be more upset by what she is telling me. I decide to play along, anything to keep her talking and here with me.

"You should also know that in unit three, there's something very wrong with the sink. It keeps backing up."

"Good to know. So tell me, do you live nearby?" I ask, hoping to change the subject and get to know a little bit more about Lane.

Lane places her hands on her hips and exhales loudly.

"Yeah, I'm in unit two. I've lived here for four years." She says matter of factly.

"That's great. We'd be neighbors."

"Yeah great." She mutters.

Lane heads up the stairs, and points out a floor board that she replaced last year. She also tells me about a leaky toilet.

"Can you show me?" I ask, dying to see what her ass will look like bent over.

"Sure."

Much to my delight, Lane bends over and takes the back off of the toilet. I pretend to listen intently as she explains proudly how she replaced the entire thing herself. I have no idea what she is talking about, since I've never really done any home repairs myself, but I do everything possible to encourage her to keep talking. And remain bent over just like she is.

"Impressive." I say.

"Thanks. And we haven't had any issues since."

Lane grunts as she tries to lift the heavy lid to the back of the toilet off of the ground.

"Let me." I say, picking it up with one hand and sliding it back into place.

Just when I thought it wasn't possible for Lane to look any more beautiful, she smiles. As the corners of her mouth turn up, her eyes seem to sparkle, and I notice a small dimple in one of her cheeks.

"I really appreciate all your help." I tell her, which makes her smile even wider.

Our eyes remain locked on each other, and for a minute, it feels like she is thinking the exact same thing I am. It's all I can do to not put my hand on the back of her neck, pull her towards me, and crush my mouth down on top of her pink full lips.

I search her expression, looking for any indication that she wants me as much as I want her. I lift my arm up, but she looks away and exits the bathroom.

I follow her back downstairs, and Lane heads to the front door.

"Would it be ok if I grabbed your number. You know, in case I have any more questions."

I take my phone out from my pocket, ready to take down her digits. Lane hesitates, but gives them to me.

"Thanks again, Lane, I'll text you." Lane turns to me once more, and opens her mouth to say something, but instead closes it and leaves.

"Well that was totally unprofessional." My dad says the minutes she's gone.

"What? She was just trying to help."

"Yeah. What she said might help with negotiations. I'm just surprised she would be so up front with you."

I chuckle, already pretty sure I know why she was so helpful. She clearly wants to jump my bones just as much as I wanted to jump hers. That's the only logical explanation. I waste no time and send a text message to Lane.

'Great seeing you today. Thank you for your help. I'd love to thank you by taking you to dinner this weekend. Anywhere you'd like. How's Saturday night? :)'

I hit the send button, and do my best to listen as my dad shows me the rest of the house. But I keep checking my phone, waiting to see where Lane wants to go to dinner. By the time we're finished, I still haven't heard back from her.

Looks like Lane is playing hard to get.

6

LANE

My alarm beeps, and I look out the window and see that it is still dark. It's only four am, and my tired body begs me to hit the snooze button. But I know I can't, since this is the morning of my big meeting. I throw back the covers and leap out of bed as the excitement of what might happen today fills my body with adrenaline.

As I brush my teeth, I review my pitch in my head for the millionth time. I know that if I don't get approved for a loan immediately, I will lose my chance to buy these houses from Howard. Twelve different people came and saw the properties over the weekend, so there was a very good chance that Howard would be getting an offer today.

I did my best to scare off as many potential buyers as I could, but most of the time when their realtors saw me coming, they wouldn't even let me in the house. Chris was the only one who even seemed to care what I had to say.

I cringe as I think of Chris, and how he might be asking his dad right now to write him a big fat check. He probably feels so important and powerful, having the means to buy six houses at his age. Even if it is only because of his dad.

I can already tell that he's the type that would totally get off from the power that comes with being a landlord. The thought of writing him a rent check each month or asking him to approve a repair turns my stomach. He'd enjoy that way too much.

And even though it is no surprise that someone who grew up with a rich father would be completely entitled, it was so wrong the way he asked me for my number. I only gave it to him because he pretended like he was only going to use it for professional reasons. And then he had the nerve to ask me out on a date. He is as delusional as they come.

Ok, as much as I know that it's wrong, there was a small chance that maybe he picked up on the fact that I do find him physically attractive. Any woman who would say differently is a fucking liar.

As much as I wish I could stop it, I know that my body wants him. But I also have a brain, one that's smart enough to tell me to stay the hell away from Chris.

It took everything I had not to write him back and to him and tell him to fuck off. As much as he deserved that, I still need to play nice. In case we end up in a bidding war, I need him on my good side. It was obvious even before he asked me out that he has a thing for me. So I need to use every advantage I have.

Even though I am used to getting male attention, it still isn't awful knowing that someone who looks like Chris wants to sleep with me. I feel my nipples tighten against the cool silk fabric of my bra as I imagine what it would be like to rip his clothes off of him. And not just because I know he would look really good naked. I laugh as I picture myself tearing his expensive, custom looking dress shirt to shreds.

As if it would actually bother him if I destroyed one of his shirts. He probably has a whole closet full of clothes.

I finish getting dressed and head off for work. I attempt to block all thoughts of Chris from my mind during my walk. I do my best to catch up on a few items in my office before my meeting, but I literally can't sit still. My leg bounces up and down as I try to type an email. I decide to take a walk before it's time to head into my boss's office.

When I called my boss Nick on Saturday morning to tell him about my terrific opportunity, I expected him to be a little more excited. Even though he is the president of the entire personal banking department, he can't sign off on a loan this size. I still will need to meet with the commercial guys on the fortieth floor.

But it made sense in a way that as my boss, Nick wanted me to present to him first. Most likely he wanted to make sure I was prepared, and do everything in his power to help me hit this out of the park. Even though it would be a huge loss to Nick to lose me, given I have been his top performer for the last three years straight, I know a part of him just wants to see me succeed. He knows firsthand how hard I've worked. And it's not like I can stay and work here forever.

I arrive outside of Nick's office door at nine thirty sharp. I take a deep breath, and am just about to knock when I see he's on the phone. I use the time it takes for him to hang up to give myself a quick pep talk. In the next half hour, my entire life will change. I just needed to push all my nerves and doubts aside.

"Sorry about that, come in, Lane."

Nick gestures to the chair on the other side of his desk, and I take a seat.

"So, I hope you have had enough time to review my numbers."

"I took a quick look."

Quick. I tried not to be insulted that he didn't devote a little bit more time to something this important.

"Ok, well here's a copy of my plan. I can walk you through it line by line."

I slide a copy of my excel sheet to Nick. He looks down at the paper briefly, and then back up at me.

"Lane, I appreciate you being so prepared. But this is a lot of money we are talking about."

"It is. But real estate is a collateralized and low risk loan. All of the units currently have tenants, and the cash flow is enough..."

Nick shakes his head as I talk.

"That's great Lane, but things happen. You could get into costly repairs, or someone could fall behind on their rent. I don't want you to be in a position where you're over-stretched."

"That's what I do. I thrive on pressure, you see how hard I work."

"Yes, but for the bank to make this kind of loan, we'd need to see a larger down payment. And is your checking account all you have?"

My cheeks redden. I know it's not much, but if there was ever a time to make an exception, this was it. Nick knows what I was capable of.

"Yes, I'm still waiting on a settlement from another venture of mine. I was an investor of a company that recently went bankrupt."

Nick puts his head in his hands.

"Not that dog clothing company, I told you not to give that guy any money. It was a horrible idea."

"Well hindsight is always twenty twenty."

Clearly, giving money to a guy who the bank didn't deem

worthy of a loan was not one of the smartest things I had ever done. But the guy was so passionate, and he needed a break. Not to mention, had it been successful, I would have earned a very good return. At the time, it seemed like my big break. And as much as it stung when that company went under, and I lost all of my savings, I still never gave up hope. I knew something bigger and better was out there. And when Howard told me the news that he was selling, it all made sense to me. This was my big break. And I wasn't sure how many more opportunities the universe was going to throw my way.

"Well, even if you get all of your money back, which is highly unlikely, that would give you about three percent the asking price? And you'd need the bank to finance the rest? That's a lot of exposure for the bank."

I try to speak, but feel a lump in my throat. I swallow hard to clear it away.

"I know it's a risk. But I need you to take a chance on me. I know I can do this."

"I have faith in you, and wish I could. But I'm also pretty sure I heard the guys up on the fortieth floor are already closing a deal for the properties you are interested in."

I feel my blood boil as I imagine someone else closing the deal that should have been mine.

"Do you know the client's name? Is it Chris?"

Nick looks at his computer screen, and scrolls through his emails.

"As a matter of fact, yes."

My hands clench into fist, and I squeeze so tightly that I feel my nails cutting into my skin. I have never been a violent person, but the thought of Chris owning the house I live in was making me feel like an actual crazy person. I keep seeing his face, and imagining his neck between my hands. The thought of actually strangling him is the only thing keeping me from losing my mind.

"Actually, it looks like they're re-doing all the paperwork this morning. Seems like this Chris is asking for a lot of cash back. Apparently he somehow found a lot of repairs that were done in the last couple of years that the seller didn't disclose. He must have one hell of an inspector, he's going to be getting himself a great deal."

My heart nearly stops when I realize where Chris probably got his information from... me. I try and kick myself under the desk without Nick noticing as I realize just how stupid I was. I told him everything he needed to force Howard into lowering the price. I helped Chris, and most likely screwed Howard over in the process. How could I have been so stupid.

My face must look as pale as it feels because when Nick finally looks over at me, his eyes widen in shock.

"I'm sorry Lane." Nick says, his voice full of pity.

That is the last thing I need is pity. I am used to tough breaks, and having to work my ass off. I still have everything going for me. Proving my boss wrong will only add to my desire. One day he would see he was wrong.

"Don't be. I understand and appreciate your time."

I stand from the desk, and leave before he can see the small tear that somehow just escaped from my eye. I don't want to give him the satisfaction of knowing I am upset. I run to the ladies room, splash some cold water on my face, and return to my office. Back to work. This is not what I expected for myself this morning.

7

CHRIS

It has only been two weeks since my father and I first saw the six row homes that were for sale. And now, we are having dinner at the most exclusive restaurant in all of Philadelphia to celebrate the fact that we just closed the deal. Life at the top is good.

"Right this way Mr. Dunkirk." The hostess dressed in a short black dress says as her bright red lips twist into a mischievous grin. She looks me up and down, and it's pretty obvious from the way her eyes linger she likes what she sees.

So I return the favor, and look her up and down as well. She's petite and brunette with a gorgeous smile, which makes her my type. But something about the way she's checking me out so blatantly is a real turn off tonight. A girl this desperate isn't the type of girl I can see myself with. That doesn't mean I wouldn't be opposed to taking her home and fucking her later, which is what I'd normally do. But I'm with my dad tonight, and I know he will do everything in his power to try and cock block me. He knows I don't have time for any distractions, as fun as it might be.

"After you." I tell the hostess, shifting my tone to convey that I'm in a hurry.

She nods her head, and shows us to the only open table in the far right corner of the restaurant. The lights are dim, and all the tables have white covers and candles. It's a mix of couples on romantic dates and men in suits closing deals and entertaining clients. I feel like I fit right in with the latter, wearing the custom suit and shirt my dad bought for me when I graduated college and had my first interview. The outfit he picked for me was timeless and best quality. You can tell a lot about a guy from his suit, I have heard many times in my life. And I wanted the world to know I am unstoppable. And that's exactly how I feel tonight.

The moment we are seated, a waiter with a white shirt and tie appears at our table. My father grabs the wine list and orders the most expensive bottle of red on the menu. I am about to stop him and tell him that beer would be fine, but the proud look on his face stops me.

My dad was very good at what he did, and one of the top residential realtors in the city. But I knew he didn't have the kind of money to go to dinners like this very often. This was a true celebration, and proof that he was proud of me.

"To all your hard work finally paying off Chris."

We both swirl the wine in the glass and inhale deeply before taking our first sip. The Cabernet is smooth and rich, and it goes down very easily.

"It's all thanks to you dad, I wouldn't be where I was today without you."

It still doesn't seem real that I am now the owner of six houses in Center City Philadelphia. And not to mention I am Lane's new landlord. You would think once she heard the news that I closed the deal, she'd at least have the decency to text me back. We are going to be neighbors that share a wall. Never has a girl I asked out blown me off before. Even when I was just a broke kid in college failing all of my classes and partying my ass off, women always threw themselves at me.

And now, I was something. I have successfully executed a plan I've been working on for over ten years now. There is no telling how far I will go in real estate investing if this project is a success. As much as most women enjoyed sleeping with men that were good looking, they liked men with power and money even more. So the fact that Lane would ignore me still didn't make sense. Maybe owning six houses wasn't enough to impress a girl like Lane, but this was just the beginning for me. Once she sees what I am capable of, she will regret not taking me up on my very generous offer to take her out. She will regret it big time.

"So I know it's a lot of work, but you can do it. You just have to keep yourself focused in the game."

My dad points to his temple to emphasize his point as he pours the rest of the wine into my glass and motions for the waiter to bring us another bottle. I know exactly what he is referring to, and I know I have to do everything in my power to not make the same mistake I did in college. disappointing my father again is not an option.

As I sip my wine, I feel my entire body relaxing. Instead of worrying about how I'm going to get all of my new properties in tip top shape, all I can think about is how good it will feel when it's all over. And when the next owner writes me a big fat check that I can use to move on to an even bigger project.

"Dessert this evening?" The waiter asks.

My dad looks at me and I shake my head.

"No, just the check."

The waiter nods and leaves the table.

"Dad, I think I'm going to head over there tonight."

Even though I wasn't moving all of my stuff into my new house until the next day, I still had to see it tonight to make sure this was all really happening. The first unit in the complex was the largest, and the one the previous owner lived in himself. So that was the one I was going to be living in. Being on site during the renovation meant I would be there to oversee it all, and make sure nothing went wrong. I had already quit my old job, since the only reason I worked for someone else over the last ten years was to save enough money for this. I had what I needed now, and enough to live on until the units were sold. As long as we stuck to the budget and timeline.

"Ok son." My dad says, intercepting the bill from the waiter. As he signs the check, I chug the entire glass of wine that is left in my glass. I know it costs my dad a fortune, and even though I'm already pretty buzzed, I don't want to waste it.

The room spins as I stand from the table, but I don't care. I exit the restaurant, and tell the first cab driver I spot to take me home.

When I arrive at my new house, I have to try three times before I am able to slide my key into the hole on the door knob. The two bottles of wine we drank at dinner seem to have affected my coordination. I feel my body swaying as I turn the key, but the knob finally moves and the door flies open.

The lights are on inside. It takes several seconds for my Cabernet soaked brain to realize this isn't right. The previous owner Howard moved out last week, so there shouldn't be any lights on. Or furniture for that matter.

Holy fuck. I realize I am in the wrong unit just as I hear footsteps on the stairs. I turn and run for the door, but it's too late. I hear a woman scream, and I know I have to explain to her that I'm not here to rob her before she has a heart attack.

"I'm so sorry. It's ok, I can explain." I say, turning around with my hands in the air to show her I'm not here to do her any harm.

I see Lane in a short silk nightgown holding a broom like it's a weapon. I laugh as I think of her hitting someone my size and the plastic handle breaking off. She's lucky it's just me, and not an actual intruder.

"What the fuck?" Lane screams waving the broom in the air. I can see her chest rising and falling as she tries to steady her breathing. I feel awful seeing her so frightened.

"It was an accident. We closed today, a few hours ago. I just wanted to stop by and see the place. I'm moving in tomorrow actually..."

Lane stares at me and I can see all the muscles in her jaw are tightly clenched. Her fingers tighten around the handle of the broom.

"Well good for you, but that doesn't mean you can just walk in here like..."

"What? Like I own the place? Because now I do."

Lane clutches the broom even tighter. I take a few steps towards her, expecting her to step backwards. But she holds her ground, maintaining intense eye contact. I'm not sure what to do next, but I reach up and grab the broom out of her hands and throw it onto the floor.

"You don't need this anymore." She gasps as the broom falls to the ground.

"Look, I am sorry I scared you. As your landlord, I want to apologize. And also remind you that you only have six months on your lease left."

"Well as the landlord, you should know that you have to

give your tenants at least twenty four hours notice to come into their house."

Lane places her hands on her hips, and this causes the short silk nightgown she is wearing to travel even further up her toned thighs. The hem of the skirt is now dangerously close to giving me a little peak of her underwear. All I can think about is how to keep pushing her buttons. It's like I am causing her to lose her mind. Maybe I can make her lose even more than that.

"We'll in that case, how about I come back tomorrow night? That's twenty four hours from now right?"

I'm not even sure if what I just said made any sense, but from the way Lane narrows her eyes at me, I can tell I am striking a nerve.

"Fine, I'll just make sure I'm not here. So I don't have to look at your face."

Lane's hands fly up from her hips, and she holds them in front of her face about six inches apart and pushes them together. It's like she's squeezing something that's invisible, like someone's neck. Probably mine, I realize with a laugh. The thought of Lane attacking me is more adorable than scary.

"Ok, so I clearly fucked up tonight. And I'm sorry. But I don't know why you hate me so much."

Lane glares at me like I've just asked the stupidest question ever. And it's definitely not calming her down.

"Let's start over again. I am Chris..." I take a step towards Lane, silently asking her for permission with my eyes after each step I take. Lane remains where she is standing, and even nods her head. So I keep going, but stop when I'm within arms length of her. I reach my hand out to her to offer a handshake. She stares at my outstretched hand, and makes no attempt to place hers in mind. I try to imagine what her skin would feel like, and I'm overcome with the desire to feel her touch me.

"Ok, what would make you feel better? You want to punch me? Here take your best shot." I thump my chest like some sort of caveman, indicating where she should place her blow. If she hit me anywhere on my pectorals, I know it won't hurt me a bit. And it might make her feel better.

Lane looks at my chest, and I can tell she's thinking about it. But it looks like she needs some reassurance that my offer is real.

"Come on, right here." I loosen my tie so I can get to the buttons on my shirt. I undo the first three, and open my shirt wide enough so she can see the skin of my chest. I squeeze the muscles in my chest, so that they look even more pronounced than usual. This is a move I have practiced in the mirror a time or two, and I know just how to make my muscles pop.

As I look down at my chest, I am relieved that I shaved it the other night. The last thing I needed was a bunch of hair getting in the way of what I work so hard every night at the gym to achieve.

Lane licks her lips as she stares at my chest. I am pretty sure she's no longer thinking about how much she hates my guts, which is encouraging. I undo another button, and another until my shirt is completely open. I watch as her eyes travel down my torso, and stop right above my pants. I know most women love how pronounced the ridges of my hip bones are. I love the fact they're like an arrow pointing to my cock.

"It's all yours. Take your best shot." I say to Lane, with the hint of a challenge in my voice.

Lane finally reaches one hand up, and I close my eyes as I wait to feel her fingertips on my skin. Instead, I feel my head being jerked downward by my neck. My eyes fly open, and I see Lanes hand wrapped around my tie.

I guess I look pretty shocked, because when Lane's eyes meet me, she lets go of my tie. Her cheeks redden as she takes a step backwards.

"No it's ok. That didn't hurt. I kind of liked it." I say to Lane, and she finally cracks a smile. Then she shoots me another deadly serious look and grabs me by the tie once again.

"This way." She instructs me, as she leads me to the couch by my neck.

Once we're in front of the black leather sofa, she presses down on my shoulders. I eagerly drop to my knees right in front of her. I am practically salivating as she sits down on the couch in front of me. I am eye level with her knees, which she keeps firmly pressed together as she lowers herself. Once she's seated, she tugs me by my tie once again, bringing my face towards her legs. My cock throbs as I wait for what's next.

"Go down on me." Lane says as she finally spreads her legs wide open.

My heart hammers in my chest as I take in the sight of her slick, pink pussy. She is completely bare, no panties and not a hair on the delicate creamy skin surrounding her slit. Her lips glisten with wetness, and it gives me the ultimate pleasure knowing that I am the one who made her wet.

I dig my hands into the flesh or her meaty and toned thighs, and pull her towards the edge of the couch. She gasps as she falls backwards.

"I got you." I say, taking one last deep breath before I bury my face between her legs.

Lane lets out a loud scream the minute my tongue touches her. I start off slowly, licking the area around her swollen clit first. I savor the taste of her as I once again feel her pulling me in closer by the tie around my neck. She moans each time I make contact with my tongue. I take a break to look up at her face, and her eyes are tightly closed. She looks completely lost in the moment. I watch as her pulse quickens as she waits for what's next. Suddenly, I get the idea to tease her and make her wait.

So I remain where I am and just continue to look at her beautiful face. After about twenty seconds, her eyes open wide. She shoots me another pissed off look.

"You want me to continue?" I ask with a mischievous grin.

"Yes please." Lane says in a sweet voice, before she closes her eyes again. She shifts on the sofa, literally squirming for my touch.

"Ok, since you asked nicely." I say in a mocking tone.

Then I grab a hold of her legs once more and dive right back into her pussy headfirst. She wraps her legs around my head, pushing me further and further until all I can smell and see is her.

She bucks her hips wildly and moans as I swirl my tongue over her bud. She's dripping now, and it's all I can do to keep my tongue from slipping off as I continue to rub my tongue all over her clit. Lane moans, encouraging me to keep going.

I slip my tongue right into her slit, and she screams. Her hands find their way into my hair, and she pulls a fistful. I don't even care that it feels like she's about to rip a chunk out. I am too absorbed in making her lose control.

"Yeah just like that, but harder." Lane screams as she moves her hips and tries to drive my tongue even deeper inside of her.

I keep going, thrusting in and out of her. I also reach my

hand around, and stroke her clit with two fingers as I continue to fuck her with my mouth. I can tell by the way her body is trembling and how loud her moans have become that she is getting close. So I pick up my pace, and wait for her to explode all over me.

"Yes, yes."

Lane yells so hard her voice starts to sound horse as she finally climaxes. Her pussy gushes, and all the muscles inside of her vagina clench one last time before her body goes completely limp. Lane falls backwards into the couch, and her legs are dead weight on my shoulders.

I carefully guide her legs down until her feet touch the floor as she lays gasping for breath.

"Was that good?" I ask rhetorically.

Lane simply nods her head and continues to breath heavily. I slide onto the sofa next to her, and place my arm around her shoulders. Her head falls onto my chest, and I give her a kiss on the top of her head. I am just about to close my eyes and enjoy the moment when Lane jumps up and pulls away from me. Her movements are so sudden and jarring that I stand up too.

"I think you should leave now." Lane says, pulling the hem of her nightgown down as far as she can until she's once again covered her pussy. I don't even care that I can no longer see it, because I know there is no way I will ever forget how magnificent her more intimate parts are. I have seen a lot of naked women in my life, but none of them were even half as spectacular as Lane is.

I remain on the couch, and adjust the front of my pants to accommodate my massive hard on. I look at Lane, expecting to see some indication that she knows the effect she is having on me. I think of how amazing it would be right now if she were to return the favor and give me a mind blowing orgasm too. One even half as intense as the one I just gave her would be incredible.

"What about me?" I ask.

Lane exhales loudly, and once again reaches for my tie. She pulls me to my feet, and I am so turned on, I'm afraid I may explode at any second. Just the thought of her touching me is that much of a turn on.

"Get out." Lane yells as she tries to drag me to the door. Trying to pull me is completely useless. Her bare feet slip in place on the wood floors as she tries to dig them into the ground to gain traction. She yanks again and groans, but I still don't move even an inch.

Lane looks tired, and gives up as she lets go of my tie.

"Please, get out." Her voice once again is soft and timid. And I don't have it in me to upset her.

"Ok, I'll go."

I take a minute and button my shirt and adjust my tie. I look to Lane once more with my hand on the doorknob, hoping she's come to her senses now and will beg me to stay and screw her senseless. It isn't possible that she couldn't be just a little bit curious about what else I can do to her.

"Bye." Lane says as she comes up behind me, grabs the door and opens it wide.

Instead of begging me to stay, she practically pushes me through the doorway and slams the door shut. I stare at the door, and try to figure out what the hell just happened.

I know one thing for sure, I have just rocked Lane's world. And even though her mind was telling her to hate me, her body was telling her something much different. And it was only a matter of time before her body won.

8

LANE

It's been completely exhausting spending the entire week avoiding Chris like the plague that he is. As dramatic as I know it sounds, he is just like a disgusting deadly disease. The way he showed up at my house late at night was most unwelcome. He completely ravaged my body and has been invading all of my thoughts ever since. But I have to remember that he is dangerous and must be kept at arm's length at all times. He's already taken my dream and soon, he'll be taking my house from me. I might even be homeless all because of him. My roommates and I have been looking for a new place to live practically non-stop and have had no luck. Everything we've looked at has been twice as much and half as nice. We haven't yet accepted the fact we might have to look outside of the city, since that would be a huge step backwards to us. And it's all because of Chris.

So the real question is *why the hell did I let him go down on me*? He is the last guy on earth I should be hooking up with. It was completely irresponsible, I remind myself once again as I beg my body to control itself. But I feel my pussy getting wet as I think about Chris unbuttoning his shirt. He looked like some super sexy caveman the way he was beating on his rock hard chest and telling me to let him have it. Any girl in my position would have done the exact same thing, right? Ok, maybe they wouldn't have tried to choke him, and halfway through decided it would be better to just ask him to eat my pussy. But at the time it seemed like a much more enjoyable punishment. I shiver as a chill travels up my spine. I want to blame it on the weather, but it's almost eighty degrees out today.

"Screw him." I yell to myself as I walk home from work. This is my time to clear my mind, and relax. And instead I'm wasting this time thinking about Chris.

I'm so close to my house now that I can see the last unit of the complex. I think for a minute about continuing to walk, maybe going up to the Italian market and grabbing something for dinner. I'm just about to cut up a different side street and over to Washington Ave when I hear a man talking loudly on his cell phone.

I stop in my tracks when I recognize the voice. It's none other than my new landlord Chris. I'm just about to sprint up the side street when his eyes meet mine.

"Look, I know it's Friday evening, but I need someone out here..." Chris stops when he sees me, and lowers the phone from his ear. I remain where I am on the corner with my hand tightly clutching my work bag.

"You know what, I'll call you back." Chris says into his phone before jabbing his index finger into the screen and tucking it back into his pants pocket.

I know there's no way I can run away from him now. But I can buy myself some time to think about what to say next if I remain where I am.

Chris continues to look in my direction without saying a

word. He probably assumes I'd come running over to him once he ended his call. But I don't want to give him that satisfaction. He can come to me.

After about thirty seconds of us just staring at each other, Chris finally begins to walk in my direction. With his hands in his pockets, he takes a few slow steps until he's only about three feet in front of me.

"Lane, good to see you again."

I actually bite my tongue to keep myself from saying something nasty. I'm trying to think of something to say that won't make me sound like a total bitch, but isn't a complete lie. I can't think of a thing, and fortunately we're interrupted by a buzzing noise from Chris' pants pocket. He reaches for his phone again.

"Excuse me, I have to take this."

I nod, happy for a chance to escape and make a run for my front door. I'm about to sprint inside and deadbolt the door behind me when I hear Chris talking.

"No, I tried that, and the waters still running everywhere. It's a mess."

"Fuck." I mutter under my breath, when I realize that I'm not a big enough asshole to just run into my house and not offer to help when I know that I can fix the problem. Not to mention I am still the property manager here, and the sooner I stop the leak the less I will have to clean up.

"Can you send someone over tonight? By tomorrow the whole house might be flooded."

I walk over to Chris whose back is turned towards me with his phone still up to his ear. I tap him on the shoulder to get his attention, and he practically jumps out of his skin.

"Hold on." He says to the person on the other end as he turns to face me.

"Did you try turning the water off?" I ask, doing my best

not to let him see how pissed off I am that he didn't think to try that in the first place.

"I looked everywhere, but I can't find where to do that."

"It's in the basement. The pipes actually run along the ceiling. When these houses were first built..." I'm just about to give Chris a brief lesson on nineteenth century row homes when the blank look on Chris' face stops me.

"Come on, I'll show you."

Chris races to the steps of his house, and throws the door open. He gestures for me to enter first. I immediately hear the sound of running water, and know this isn't some minor leak. This is almost identical to the problem we keep having in Lindsay's house.

I run to the basement steps, and take a brief look at the standing water in the kitchen. I grab onto the railing, not wanting to slip in my high heels I am still wearing from work. I go right to the water valve, and do my best to reach it on the ceiling. But it's not working, even in my four inch heels I'm still a few inches short of the valve.

"Where's your ladder?" I ask looking around.

"Uh I don't have one."

I roll my eyes at the thought of a grown man not having such a basic piece of equipment. As I am looking around for something to stand on, Chris appears beside me.

"It's this one?" He points towards the knob.

"Yes."

He reaches it effortlessly and gives it a few twists. We both exhale loudly when we hear the sound of the water shutting off.

"Thank you."

"Yeah, let me grab my wet vac before the water gets under the floorboards."

"No, that's ok, we're replacing those soon."

I feel my jaw drop and I am almost too stunned to speak.

"Ok, you know those floors are solid wood, and almost one hundred years old."

"Yeah, that's why we are replacing them with waterproof vinyl."

I feel my nose scrunch as I imagine those tacky, cheap, synthetic floors. Chris laughs, which only aggravates me more.

"I really appreciate your help."

"Well it's my job. I don't know if Howard told you, but the reason our rent is so low is because I work as the property manager. So for the next six months while we're here, I'm happy to keep working for you."

A wicked smile comes over Chris's face, and I suddenly regret offering to do anything for this man. But a deal is a deal, and I always see all of my obligations through until the end. I have never quit a job before in my life, and I was not going to start.

"I have a crew starting the renovations on unit three next week once the tenant moves out. So I think they can handle whatever comes up."

My chest felt heavy as I remembered that Lindsay's lease was expiring next week, and how Chris refused to renew it. Lindsay has lived in that house for almost ten years, and has been a perfect tenant. The fact that Chris didn't even consider letting her stay was so cold.

"So what is this crew going to be doing?" My hand involuntarily flies to my hip as I await his response.

"We're practically gutting all the units. New kitchens, bathrooms, floors. These houses looked like they haven't been touched in fifty years."

"No, they have had a lot of work done by me." I practically scream as I recount all the repairs I've done during my time as property manager.

"Sorry I didn't mean that. It's just that most buyers nowadays want modern."

I roll my eyes as I think of how most people nowadays all have the same crappy taste. They think just because something is new that it's somehow better than something that has been around for the last one hundred years. If they only knew how cheap new construction is compared to the way things were done when these homes were first built.

"Some people like character."

"You know that's just realtor talk for old." Chris says with a laugh.

"Well I like character. I would never live in one of those ultra modern lofts or any other building in the city. They're just all the same, so impersonal."

I leave out the part about not being able to afford the rent, since even a one bedroom in Center City would be about three times what I pay now.

"Well, I respect that. But that's not what most buyers want."

"Buyers? So you are planning to do what? Fix the homes up and turn around and sell them?"

"Yeah that's the plan."

A surge of adrenaline fills my veins as I think about what Chris just said. He didn't buy these homes so he could live here and rent them out like Howard had all these years. He only saw dollar signs, and a chance to make a quick buck. And he was going to destroy a huge piece of Philadelphia history in the process.

"Well, that's a really stupid idea."

Chris' eyebrows arch, and I can tell he's not used to anyone telling him what they really think of him. He probably surrounds himself with people all on his father's payroll, who only tell him yes. Which is probably why he's such an entitled prick.

"So, I guess you won't be needing me. I'd better get home."

I take a step towards the stairs just as Chris shifts his body towards the right, blocking my path. I try the other side and he shifts once again. I feel a frustration building inside of me, and place my hands on his chest to push him out of the way. But before I am able to shove him, his hands come up and gently push mine out of the way.

"Lane, I'm sorry. I don't know what I did to make you so angry, but I'd like for us to talk and clear the air. Can I take you to dinner or something?"

"Ugh." I thought I was saying this inside of my own head, but from the way Chris' eyes widen I have a good feeling I accidentally said this out loud.

The more I think about it, the more I realize he deserves to hear how I truly feel. It's beyond insulting that he thinks a free meal is enough to make me want to prolong being in the presence of his company. I have a job and money that I actually earn on my own. If I wanted to go out to dinner, I didn't need him to take me.

"I really don't know what I did to make you so angry." He says as he tries to put his hand on my shoulder.

I feel my hands clenching into fists again at my sides. It was beyond infuriating the way he was playing dumb. I wasn't going to fall for it. I have no problem reminding him of what he did.

"Well I didn't appreciate the way you used the information I gave you in confidence to screw Howard over."

Chris narrows his eyebrows until they are practically touching.

"What are you talking about? You mean what you told me that day I first saw the property?"

All of his stupid questions are only making me madder by the second.

"Yes, that's what I am talking about!"

"Why did you tell me all of that if you weren't trying to help me?"

Help him, HA! I want to scream. That was the last thing I was trying to do. He was supposed to be scared off by all the work that needed to be done and run away. How was I supposed to know that my plan was going to end up back-firing on me?

"Well I didn't expect you to use what I told you against me!"

I stomp my foot like a small child having a temper tantrum. I don't even care how immature I look. It feels like if I don't do something, I might explode.

"Against you?" He asks, taking a step in my direction.

My cheeks feel like they're on fire when I realize that Chris probably never knew that I was trying to get financing to buy the houses. I don't want to give him the satisfaction of knowing that he has done what I couldn't. And that he crushed my dream in the process.

"I have to go. Please get out of my way." I raise my fists again, and am just about to hit him in the chest when he steps out of the way.

"I'm sorry."

I race up the stairs and out of his house. My blood pressure feels sky high when I finally sit down on my couch. I blame it on the fact that I just ran up a flight of stairs in heels, and that I am pissed off. Until my nipples once again harden. I take a deep breath, and do everything in my power to block all thoughts of Chris from my mind. Even though

I'm facing a temporary setback, I still have a lot of work to do to reach my goals. And sitting here thinking about Chris isn't going to get me anywhere.

I feel my heart rate slowing as I realize that I am sitting in the exact same spot on the couch as I was the other night when Chris went down on me. I can picture the way he looked on his knees, with his shirt open and his tie still wrapped around his neck. As the image of him floods my brain, I can almost feel his tongue on my pussy.

I close my eyes and slide to the edge of the couch. I even spread my legs, which helps me remember in even greater detail just how good it felt when he went down on me. My pussy drips and begs me for a release. I tell myself this may be the only way to get him out of my system. So I close my eyes, and reach up through my skirt with my fingers. My clit is hard and swollen, so I stoke it as I picture Chris once again. It takes only a few seconds till my body explodes in an orgasm. I scream into a pillow and pray that none of my roommates are home.

When it's over, I feel a sudden clarity wash over my body. I remember that it's a Friday evening and that I sort of made plans with Ashley and Heidi. And that tomorrow I have spin class at nine , and all of the meetings I have to prepare for Monday morning. My head is no longer clouded with thoughts of the biggest asshole on the planet. I smile as I realize; I am back.

9

CHRIS

As soon as Lane runs out my front door, I feel a hard on so massive I know a cold shower is the only way I will be able to concentrate on anything else. I grab a beer from the fridge, and head up to my bedroom. I take off my suit, and hang it back in my closet and strip off the rest of my clothes and throw them in the hamper.

I look at myself in the mirror on the back of my bathroom door to make sure I haven't suddenly become some sort of fat slob. The last couple of weeks have been so busy with closing on these houses and moving that I've only made it to the gym maybe four nights a week. To some, that may seem like a lot, but I feel like I'm slacking when I do my daily workouts. I've done my best to make up for the skipped workouts by making the time I do spend in the gym count. During my workouts last week, I pushed myself mercilessly for over two hour. So it doesn't seem possible that I could have lost any significant amount of muscle mass.

As I turn around to look at my legs and butt in the

mirror, I see my calf and hamstring muscles are as pronounced as ever. And as cocky as it sounds, most women go crazy when they see me at the gym. Or at work, or a bar, or even the grocery store. Practically everywhere I went I was used to women admiring the way I looked. Except for Lane. She was the one woman who seemed totally indifferent. That was probably the reason I wanted her so badly.

I reach for the shower and turn the knob to cold and wait. But nothing happens, so I turn it again. I feel like a total idiot when I realize we just turned off the water.

I grab a towel and wrap it around my lower half before heading down stairs back to the water valve. I'm about to turn the water back on when I remember if I do that, the leaky sink in the kitchen will once again erupt. But it's not like I can spend the entire weekend without any running water. I have no idea what to do, but I know who will.

I tip toe in my bare feet and knock on Lane's door which is luckily right next to me. I look around as I wait, hoping no one will notice that I'm outside wearing nothing but a towel. I see a couple walking their dog heading in my direction. I knock again harder this time, hoping Lane will hurry before they get too close.

I press my ear to the door and hear the sound of women laughing inside, and then footsteps heading towards the door. When it opens, I'm just about to beg Lane to not slam it in my face when I see a woman I have never met before.

"Why hello." She says with a snicker as she looks at the towel wrapped around me.

"Hey, sorry to bother you, but I need to talk to Lane."

"Tell him I'm not here." I hear Lane shout from inside the house.

"Excuse me, one moment." Lane's roommate leaves the door open with only a small crack as she goes back in to talk to Lane. I can't hear most of their conversations, but the parts I am able to make out are pretty entertaining.

"Are you sure, have you seen him without a shirt?" I hear the roommate ask Lane. It's a nice reassurance to hear that I still have that effect on Lane's roommate.

"Just go talk to him. I have a feeling he won't take no for an answer." She says again. I hear a loud dramatic sigh, and the next thing I know Lane is opening the door.

"What?" She demands. Her eyes travel down to the towel I'm holding with one hand, and she takes a long and deliberate breath.

"Sorry to bother you again, but is there a way you can turn on the water so I can take a shower? You know without my entire house flooding?"

"Fine." Lane grabs a large bag filled with hammers and other tools, and it's the sexiest thing I have ever seen. The only thing that would have been better would be if she was still wearing her high heels. But she is barefoot, and slips on a pair of pink rubber rain boots before coming outside and following me back to my house.

When we arrive at my door, I reach for the handle so quickly that I almost forget that my hand is the only thing holding up my towel. It flies open only about an inch before I grab it and close it with my left hand. I'm attempting to tuck one side of the towel over the top so it will stay in place when Lane decides to reach for the door herself. I stop her just as she is trying to transfer the heavy tool bag to one hand so she can reach for the door with the other.

"No, I got it." I reach for the door, and am able to get it wide open before my towel falls all the way down.

Lane wades through the water on the kitchen floor, and I realize now why she put on boots. The top of the pink rubber boots hit her right below the knee and several inches from the hem of her skin tight shirt. The way she looks in her boots is somehow even sexier than the shiny black pointy heels she was wearing before.

Lane opens the cabinet under the sink, and scoots herself under on her back. Her huge tits scrap the top of the cabinet as she shimmies herself into the tight space. She plants her feet on the floor in front of her to give herself traction. As I watch her, I feel like I am having a damn heart attack from the way she moves her legs ever so slightly to the sides and wiggles the rest of her body.

"Ok, I just have to tighten this." Lane grunts as she twists her wrench so hard that her butt actually lifts up. I catch a quick glimpse of hot pink lace between her legs before she presses her thighs together tightly. Just the sight of her panties is making my dick so hard it practically hurts. I can't get into that cold shower quickly enough.

Lane emerges from under the sink, and brushes a piece of hair out of her face with the back of her hand and smears a bit of grease onto her cheeks. Then she looks down at her white cotton shirt that is wet from the residual water that was still dripping from the pipe.

"You should be good to turn the water back on." She says.

I try to offer her my hand to pull her to her feet, but she stops me.

"You've got your hands full already."

I look down at the front of my towel and see the large bulge of my dick. Lane is standing now, and trying to brush the front of her shirt off. Her tits bounce ever so slightly.

"Ok, I'm going to run downstairs and turn it back on."

Lane nods, and I hope that the fact that she doesn't move towards the door means she's planning to stick around for a little while. I race down the stairs, turn the water back on, and fly back up the steps. But by the time I make it back to the kitchen, I don't see Lane.

So I head upstairs once again, ready to give taking a shower another try. When I reach the bathroom door, I finally remove the towel from around my waist. As I open the door to the bathroom, I hear a gasp.

"What the fuck?" Lane says, bent over the side of the tub.

"What are you doing here?" I bark, and immediately regret.

"You said you were going to take a shower, so I wanted to make sure the bathroom wouldn't flood if you did."

"Ok yeah."

I reach around Lane, and turn the water on in the shower. I place my hand inside, to get a feel for the water temperature. Lane's eyes remain glued on mine, and I know she's doing everything possible to not look down at my cock.

"Looks good," I say, as I step under the shower head. The cool water spills over my body, and I start to feel a bit of relief. But the ice cold water is too jarring on the rest of my body, so I turn the handle to the right, until steam begins to come out.

"Ahh much better." I step back under the water and run my hands through my wet hair. My back is to Lane, and I haven't heard her leave so I can only assume she's watching. So I have to make this good.

I reach for my bottle of shampoo, and lather my scalp well, until suds drip down my body. I turn around ever so slightly to rinse the shampoo from the back of my body, when I see Lane with her mouth wide open.

"Water feels great if you'd like to join me. No offense, but you kind of look like you could use a shower."

Lane scrunches her nose but looks into the mirror above

the sink. Her fingers touch the grease that is smeared over her cheek. I let out a laugh, and Lane turns and shoots me a glare.

"Come on, I've got soap." I tell her, holding up a bottle of body wash.

Lane looks at herself one last time in the mirror with her lips pressed tightly together. She takes one look at the door, and another right back at me as the steamy shower water runs over my body.

Without a word, Lane reaches up and takes the elastic out of her hair that was holding it in a tight bun. I watch as light brown waves fall over her shoulders. I can't understand why any woman, let alone anyone that looked like her, would ever want to pull their hair back. The way her brown locks were tumbling over her neck was so damn sexy.

I hold my breath as I wait for what's coming next. It's a miracle I don't pass out before she finally begins to unbutton her shirt. She has to pull the fabric covering her chest together before she has enough room to unhook the buttons that cover her breasts.

Once she's undone the first few buttons, I watch as her lace covered breasts pop out of the opening in her shirt. The hot pink fabric of her bra is identical to what I saw earlier between her legs. I pray that she leaves her bra on while she takes off her skirt. I want to see her in just her panties and bra for a second before she finishes stripping naked.

After the buttons are all undone, Lane stops for a few seconds before moving the shoulders of her shirt down and off of her arms. I feel like I'm watching the slowest, and sexiest strip tease I have ever seen in my life. Except Lane isn't even trying to be sexy. It's like this is the way she undresses every night, and I just happen to be in the room.

Could she really have no idea what this is doing to me? I

look down at my cock again, and it's rock hard. I know I need some release soon.

As her shirt hits the ground, Lane kicks her boots off one at a time. The waist of her skirt is up almost to her belly button, and is making the curves of her hips look irresistible. I barely have time to take it all in before she reaches around towards the back, and I hear the sweet sound of a zipper. Two seconds later, the skirt is around her ankles. She reaches up onto her tip toes as she steps over it, and closer to me.

I want to grab her, and drag her into the shower with me. But part of me also kind of wants to see what she's going to do next. Lane doesn't disappoint me, as she reaches around to unhook her bra. The way her back arches makes her breasts look even more gigantic than usual. My eyes remain glued on her as the hot pink lace straps fall down off of her shoulders, and the bra hits the floor. But right before I am able to see her gorgeous breasts, her arms come up and she covers herself.

"Let me see you." I say, not able to wait a second longer. Lane bites her lips and looks down at the arm she is still holding across her chest.

I finally reach out of the shower, and grab her arm that is still by her side around the wrist. I pull her lightly, and she takes another step towards the shower. Before stepping in she shimmies out of her panties.

I take a step to the right and out of the way of the shower head, so that Lane can have a turn under it. She positions herself right under the heavy flow of hot steamy water. I watch as beads of water trickle first down her face, and as her hair becomes plastered to the side of her face. I know it's only a matter of time before she has to reach up. And sure enough, the arm that was covering her breast finally moves up towards her eyes. I see two large pink nipples that are as hard as rocks. The water runs over them, like boulders parting a stream. I exhale so loudly, that Lane looks over at me.

"Sorry." Is all I can think to say, as I watch as she turns her back towards me. Even though her backside is amazing, I want to see her tits again. I take a step towards her, and gently press my body against her back. My cock digs into her back, and even that is almost enough to make me explode.

"Want me to wash your hair?" I ask, suddenly overcome with the desire to run my finger through her locks.

Lane nods, so I grab the bottle of shampoo and hold it upside and squeeze a fistful of it into my hand. I run it over her head, starting in the center and watching as the lather covers all of her hair. I begin to massage her scalp as the clean smell of the tea tree shampoo fills my nostrils. Lane starts to moan when I place my second hand on her head and really dig in.

"Hmm, don't stop." I hear her say as she leans backwards into my chest.

I watch her chest rise and fall, and her nipples look like they could cut glass, even though the water is scalding. I reach one of my hands down, and run my finger tips over them. I roll her nipple between my fingers, and she moans again, eager for me to continue.

My other hand travels down her stomach and parts her legs. It takes me no time at all to find her clit. Lane gasps as I begin to stroke it. I use the same even rhythm as I did the other night, tracing small circles around it with my finger tips. Next, I insert two of my fingers inside of her, and swirl them around. Lane's body practically goes limp in my arms, but it's no trouble at all to hold her up as I continue.

"That a girl." I whisper into her ear. She's pressed up against me so hard I'm afraid I might impale her with my cock. I feel her shift ever so slightly, and almost don't believe it when I feel her hand wrap around the base of my cock.

"Fuck yeah." I whisper into her ear. I bring my fingers back out from inside of her, and continue to rub her clit. My knees feel weak as Lane runs her hand up and down my dick. I just hope I can make her cum before I lose it.

"Just like that." She commands, and I hold my pace firm and steady. I feel her body tremble, and her breathing growing heavier by the minute. I press down even more firmly on her clit, and move my fingers a little faster. Her pussy gushes, and I know what's coming next.

She falls back into my arms after she explodes. I pick her up, and put one of my arms under her knees. I carry her towards my bedroom, not even caring that we are both still dripping with water.

I lay her on top of the down comforter and watch as she sinks into it and closes her eyes. I am hoping after a quick rest she'll be able to finish what she started with me. My cock twitches as I think about how good her hand felt wrapped around me.

"You need anything?" I ask Lane. She doesn't answer.

So I place one of my knees on the bed, as I crawl to lay down next to her. Just as I am about to slide in beside her, she sits up.

"The kitchen. I have to get my wet vac. If we don't get that water cleaned up-"

I put a finger on Lane's lips to stop her.

"Don't worry about that now." I push lightly on her shoulders to get her to lay back down, but Lane stiffens her back and remains sitting up. So I place my arm around her shoulder, and pull her head on my chest.

"I can think of other things more fun to do than cleaning up a mess."

Lane lifts her head to look at me, and I see the unmistakable look of lust in her eyes.

"Oh yeah?" she asks with a half smile.

I move my hand down onto my cock, and squeeze hard enough that you can see every vein in my bulging cock. Lane looks down with huge eyes.

I see her hands clenching into fists, as if she's trying to talk herself out of it. So I look at her intensely, doing my best to beg her with my eyes. Lane's tongue darts out of her mouth, and her lower lip glistens with saliva. I can almost feel her lips wrapped around my cock. The thought of it is almost too much. I want to grab her by the back of the neck, and push her down on top of my throbbing dick. But I have a strong feeling Lane doesn't like to be told what to do. So all I can do is sit here and wait, and hope it doesn't kill me.

Lane finally unclenches her fist, and moves one hand towards me. When it finally lands on my cock I suck in a deep breath. Lane's eyes lock with mine as she runs her hand up and down along the shaft of my cock. She moves in a perfect rhythm, and the room starts to spin.

I can almost feel myself exploding. Talk about premature. I have never had that problem in the past and know it would make me look like a real amature. I have to think of a way to stop it from happening, I must do everything and anything to prolong this feeling.

"I want to fuck you." I blurt out.

Lane's hand freezes and her gaze falls to the floor.

"Let me fuck you." I tell her, and wait for Lane to lie on her back so I can climb on top of her. But she stays sitting up right where she is and her hand falls off my cock. The second it's gone I regret my decision and miss the feeling of her. Even though the thought of burying my cock in Lane's tight pussy would be the ultimate pleasure, a hand job would have been better than the nothing I was getting now.

"I'm sorry, if you don't want to." I say as Lane stands up.

"This was a mistake, I have to get going."

"Stop." I try to grab her by the arm, but she dodges me and heads to the door. I fall backwards onto the bed, feeling like the world's biggest idiot. As much as I want to chase after her, I know if I don't take care of business soon, I'm going to have a real problem.

So I grab myself, and imagine just how amazing Lane would feel from the inside. I imagine my hand is her pussy, but know full well it can't feel even a fraction as good as the walls of her tight slit.

When I finally explode, I imagine I am blowing my load all over Lane's amazing tits. Then I run to the bathroom to see if she's still there getting dressed. But all of her clothes are gone. I search the rest of the house and don't find her. Lane is gone again, and I am all alone trying to figure out what the hell just happened.

10

LANE

I have officially lost my mind. After what happened with Chris last night, it's clear I cannot be trusted around him. And it's also super obvious I need to find someone else to fulfill my needs physically. Luckily I know just the girl to help me find such a man; my roommate Ashley.

"You almost ready?" I yell up the stairs to Ashley.

I check the time and it's almost eight thirty at night. A full half hour past the time she told me we'd be leaving. I've been up since six, so it's already going to be hard to stay up till ten. Which is the time most people are just starting their nights. So the chances of finding a guy, being able to have a conversation with him before inviting him back to my place and getting to sleep at a reasonable hour weren't looking very good.

"Yes, I'm ready." Ashley says as she starts walking down the stairs. Her long, light brown hair hangs over her shoulder in loose glossy curls. Her lips are shiny and pink, and her legs look about ten miles long in the wedges she's wearing.

"Oh, I thought you were going to change..." She says as she looks at me.

"Let me guess, you don't like my outfit?"

I look down at the cotton blouse and black dress pants I am wearing. I know most girls don't wear their work clothes to a bar on a Saturday night, but these are the clothes I feel the most confident in.

"It's a Saturday night, you're trying to get laid right? Not promoted."

I try to think up a clever story that would explain why I'm wearing my work clothes on a Saturday night, but nothing good comes to mind.

"Do you have something I could maybe borrow?"

Ashley's eyes light up, and she runs down the rest of the stairs and throws her arms around me.

"Yes, I'd thought you'd never ask."

She leads me by the hand up to her room. She throws open the double doors to her closet, and we both stand back and admire the racks of beautiful designer clothing. Ashley works for an online clothing store, and working in fashion comes with a lot of perks. Which is probably the reason Ashley chose the field she did.

Everything in Ashley's closet is organized by season. I watch as she flips through her collection of summer clothes. She stops abruptly and brings what looks like a sports bra over to me.

"This." She says, holding the small top made of only a few pieces of black cotton strips.

"What should I wear over it?"

"It's like 80 degrees out. Doubt you'll need a jacket."

I grab the hanger out of Ashley's hands and continue to examine it.

"You're telling me this is a top?"

Ashley rolls her eyes.

"Yes, a crop top. Come on. With abs like yours this will be perfect!"

I look down at my stomach and run my hand over it. Even though I had pizza for dinner, it still feels mostly flat. Maybe this won't look so bad after all.

"Ok, I guess I can try it on."

I unbutton my cotton dress shirt and slide it off. At least I'm already wearing a black bra, so even if the straps did slide out from under the straps of the top, they shouldn't be too noticeable.

Ashley eagerly holds up the top, and I stick my arms through the openings and slide the straps up into place. Ashley moves around back of me to help me zip. I walk to the full length mirror on the back of the door not knowing what to expect. I take a deep breath before I look at myself.

"Ashley, I am half naked."

I cover my stomach with my arms and feel completely exposed.

"No, you look amazing."

Ashley comes up from behind me and pulls my arms from my stomach. I look again in the mirror, and notice that when I turn, you can actually see some of the definition in the sides of my stomach. All the crunches and planks I do at the gym seem to be paying off.

"Well you definitely can't wear a top like that with those pants."

Ashley brings her hand up to her mouth to try and hide her laughter. I look at the flared, black polyester pants I have on, and realize they have to go.

"Ok, maybe some jeans?" I ask.

"No. Let's try some shorts."

Ashley goes over to her dresser and digs around in her

drawers until she finds a pair of jeans shorts that are no bigger than a pair of panties.

"No." I say, holding my hands in front of me as she walks in my direction.

"Just try them, please."

Knowing I don't have a choice, I take my pants off and step into the shorts. Even though Ashley is a size four just like me, I have to jump up and down to get the shorts up over my hips. I start to worry I'm doing something wrong when the waist band comes up almost to my belly button.

"They're high waisted." Ashley tells me.

Once they're zipped, I take another look in the mirror. The high waist doesn't look nearly as bad as I thought. They hug my hips in just the right place, and leave only a few inches of my stomach showing. Having only the narrowest part of my waist exposed makes me look even curvier than normal. I stand tall when I imagine the attention I will be getting tonight in this outfit. It will for sure speed up the process of trying to get laid.

"Ok, you were right. I like it."

Ashley jumps up and down and squeals with delight.

"You look amazing! The guys will be lining up to fuck you."

I just hope she is right.

After we're dressed, Ashley and I head into the kitchen and pour two shots of tequila as we wait for our Uber to arrive.

"To getting laid." Ashley says as we clink our shot glasses and throw the alcohol down our throats. I grab a wedge of lime to suck as my eyes water.

The minute the tequila hits my stomach, I feel myself relaxing. A night out to most girls was exciting, but to me, it just felt like a waste of time. I normally can't justify spending so much money and energy just trying to meet a man. But with how horny I've been feeling lately, it seems necessary.

"Our ride is here." Ashley says as her phone pings.

She races out the front door to flag our driver down. I have to grab my purse, and do my best to try to catch up to her once I have it. I'm on the first step of our porch when I see Ashley opening the door to a white SUV. I run so I won't have to keep them waiting. But as I take a step, a sharp pain radiates through my ankle. In my hurry, I seem to have rolled it in the four inch heels I am wearing. I grab a hold of the railing just in time, and let out a surprised scream as I catch myself. Ashley stops where she is and looks at me.

"I'm fine, let's go." I assure her.

"Are you sure?" I hear a man voice asking.

Before I even get a chance to look and see who it is, I realize it's Chris. I debate running to the car and hopping in before I have to say anything to him, but I don't want to actually fall this time and break my neck.

"Wait, let me help you."

He appears at the bottom of the steps and holds out his hand to me. I know I'm capable of making it down the stairs myself, since I've done it hundreds of times in the past without any issues.

"I've got this. But thanks."

I wait to see if Chris is going to leave, but he remains on the step, blocking my way once again. His hand is still raised in my direction, and he seems to be genuinely concerned that I might break my neck.

"Ok thanks." I say with a heavy sigh. Chris races up the stairs and grabs my hand. I feel like some little old lady that needs help crossing the road.

Once we make it down the steps I pull my hand from

Chris'. I know I should say something, but I already thanked him. I hope he doesn't expect a medal for walking me down three steps.

"You look nice." Chris says as he looks me up and down.

I cover my stomach again, and yank at the hem of my shorts in a ridiculous attempt to try and cover more of my upper thighs.

"Where are you ladies heading tonight?" Chris asks Ashley who is still waiting for me at the car.

"Just out for drinks. You know, trying to get laid."

"Ashley." I scream as I shoot her a dirty look.

I can't even bring myself to look at Chris. The last thing I need is for him to know how horny I've been lately. It will only encourage him.

"Uh, let's get going Ashley."

I climb into the backseat of the car and tell our driver that we're ready.

When we arrive at the first bar, all eyes are on Ashley and me as we walk in. I hold onto Ashley's elbow and try to smile at the guys we pass. I do my best to determine if they are cute enough to talk to, but it's so dark inside that it's hard to see everyone's face from far away.

"Can I buy you ladies a drink?" A guy asks the minute we find a spot at the bar.

I look him over before answering. He's close to six feet tall I guess. He has nice hair, and seems friendly.

"Sure." Ashley says.

The guy smiles and flags the bartender down.

"A round of shots." He says. I look at Ashley, not sure how to tell the guy I don't want a shot. But Ashley just smiles and mouths 'come on' to me.

"Here you ladies are."

My stomach turns as I look at the small glass in front of

me. I don't even know what it is, and I am already feeling buzzed from the shot we did at home. I have a good feeling I will be paying for this tomorrow morning,

Ashley and the guy each grab their drinks, and take the entire shot in one sip. I know if I refuse mine Ashley will never let me hear the end of it. So I reluctantly grab my drink.

"Cheers." I say, already shivering before my first sip.

Luckily, it's not as bad as I thought. It tastes kind of sweet. I am able to drink the whole thing in two manageable sips. I don't even need a chaser.

"That wasn't bad." I tell the guy who bought the shots for us.

"You want another?"

"No, not right now."

"Come on." The guy puts his arm around my shoulder, and pulls me into his side ever so gently.

I feel my entire body cringing as my shoulder touches his chest. He isn't in bad shape, it's just his chest feels a lot less hard compared to Chris. Brushing up against Chris' chest feels like running into a mountain. And this guy feels more like bumping into a kitchen chair.

"I said I'm good." I say, sitting up straight in my chair until there is at least a foot of room between me and this guy.

"Ok then." He says with his hand up in the air. "Let's start over. I'm Craig."

Craig sticks his hand out for a shake and I just stare at it.

"Lane."

We slip into silence. Craig looks around for his friend as I look for Ashley. She was directly behind me just a second ago, but knowing her she probably ran into someone else she knew. I spot her across the room, talking to a guy that she seems to know. He must be telling her something funny, because Ashley is laughing with her head all the way back. I debate for a minute going over there, but I don't want to interrupt. I decide to give Craig another chance.

"So, what do you do?" I ask him.

Craig takes a sip of beer before answering.

"It's boring stuff. I trade commodities."

Cha Ching. All I can see in my head are dollar signs. I know for most girls, when they find a wealthy man, they fantasize about marrying him and spending all of his money. But for me, all I want is information. Commodities traders make big bucks. If I can get Craig to tell me exactly how he got his start, maybe I can become a trader as well. This could be my big break.

"No, I would love to hear all about it."

I shift in my seat till I'm facing him directly. Craig laughs and takes another sip of his beer.

"Well, it's pretty complicated stuff."

I feel my lips curling in disgust. It's obvious he doesn't think I'd be able to understand. It is a good thing he didn't try and mansplain it to me, otherwise he'd be wearing the rest of his beer. *What an asshole.* I spin in my chair again until I'm facing the opposite direction. But Craig is so stupid that he walks all the way around me until he's standing directly in front of me again.

"I'd rather hear about you. Tell me what you do to keep this tight body of yours looking so good."

I slap his hand before it lands on my knee and jump out of my seat. I grab my purse off the top of the bar and run to where I saw Ashley last. She's still talking to the same guy and his hand is on her shoulders. I don't want to interrupt, so I scan the room to try and find another guy to talk to. Maybe one a little better looking and far less forward.

As I look from one guy to the next, I see a few that are no doubt attractive, but something inside of me already feels disappointed. I realize that somewhere in the back of my mind, I keep comparing each guy I see to Chris. It's like I can almost see him, towering over these guys and flexing his huge biceps. Every guy in here is literally falling short when I compare them to Chris.

Maybe this was a bad idea. I can't picture myself sleeping with any of these guys. They're all strangers. I decide that I'd better go home before I do anything else stupid. So I go outside and flag down the first cab that I see.

The temperature must have dropped about ten degrees since I first arrived. A breeze kicks up, and I feel a shiver run through my body. I rub my hands up and down my arms to warm myself up. Luckily it's a short ride back to my house.

"Thanks." I tell the driver when he drops me off.

I look inside the widow that is at the front of our house to see if Heidi is home yet. There are no lights on, so I assume she's still out. I do my best to convince my body that it's time to go home and go to bed. But for some reason instead of climbing up my stoop and opening my door, I look at Chris' house next to ours. I see the white glow of a TV screen through the widow. And light from the kitchen. It looks like Chris is home.

My body is pulled towards his house like it has a mind of its own. The next thing I know, I'm on the second step of his stoop. I know I need to figure out what I'm going to say when he answers the door, since it won't take long for him to open it once I knock.

Hey neighbor, I was just passing by and saw the light on, I practice in my head. I laugh a little too hard at how stupid that sounds. That second shot I took at the bar seems to have made me a little tipsy. Funny I didn't notice it sooner.

Normally I would be able to come up with something better to say to Chris. Maybe I should just be honest, and tell him that I'm horny as fuck for him.

No, that is way too desperate, the sober part of my mind screams at me. I take one step backwards, until I feel one foot on the sidewalk. I need to get home fast. As I bring my other foot down, my purse suddenly feels like it weighs fifty pounds. I pull harder, until I realize it's stuck on the railing.

"Come on." I scream at my purse.

I hear a sound at the door that can only be one thing; Chris undoing the deadbolt. I have about ten seconds till he sees me. I have no choice but to run. I let go of my purse and leave it hanging from the bottom of his front porch railing and run up my steps as fast as my legs can carry me. I'm already at my door, about to open my purse for my keys when I realize that I don't have it anymore. I let out a groan just as I hear Chris' door open.

"Lane?" He says. "Is that you?"

"Hey neighbor."

I giggle as I remember how stupid that sounded moments before when I was practicing what to say to Chris in my head.

"Are you ok? I thought I heard someone."

"Uh yeah, sorry I had the wrong door. Funny how that happens."

Chris looks me over from head to toe, totally fucking me with his eyes. Even though just moments before I was about to ask him to fuck me, I feel offended by how obvious he is acting now.

"You're home early. And alone."

"Yeah I have stuff to do tomorrow." I say as I cross my arms over my stomach.

Chris looks down his steps and immediately spots my

handbag hanging at the end of his railing. I wince as he walks down to take a closer look.

"Is this yours?" He says after he's unhooked my purse from the railing and is holding it towards me.

"Umm yeah. Thanks. I was looking everywhere for it."

Chris' eyes narrow, and I race over to grab my purse before he has the chance to ask me any more questions. I am totally aware that what I just said to him made almost no sense, and I can't for the life of me come up with any sort of logical explanation for leaving my purse on his porch.

"I'll take that."

I lunge for my purse, and Chris playfully lifts it up just out of my reach. My hand collides with the hard muscles of his stomach as I grasp for it.

"Are you sure everything is ok Lane?" He asks with a straight face.

"Yeah, I just happened to see your light on, and I thought..."

Chris's face lights up as he waits for me to finish.

"I thought...."

I reach once again for my purse and lose my train of thought. Chris moves it even higher out of my reach, and I jump in an attempt to reach it. The minute my feet are off the ground I reach my arms forward and fall face first into Chris.

His intoxicating scent fills my nostrils. I try to figure out what it is that smells so good. It's not as obvious as the scent of cologne. Maybe his soap? I inhale a little deeper as I try to figure it out.

"Sorry, you can have this back."

I feel Chris' arms coming down, and I look up at him with one cheek still pressed up against his chest. His lips begin to part and start to form into a smile. One of his hands lands on my back, and begins rubbing it slowly up and down.

"Just wanted to make sure you were ok."

"Oh yeah, never better. I just..."

I squeeze my eyes tight as the overwhelming urge to press my mouth to his overtakes me. I can almost taste him on my lips. I already know the things his tongue is capable of when it comes to my pussy, but we haven't kissed yet. If he's even half as good at kissing as he is at eating pussy, it might be worth giving it a try.

With my eyes still closed, I do my best to stand on my tiptoes even though I'm wearing heels. I am only able to gain about an extra inch, so I wrap a hand around the back of Chris' neck and lower his face towards me. It's not easy to find his neck without being able to see, but I know if I open my eyes and see the look on his face I might lose my nerve.

I finally find his neck, and he lowers his head as my hand guides him downward. Right when I can feel his breath on my lips, I pause in an attempt to review one more time in my head whether this is a good idea or not. But before I can run through all of the reasons why I shouldn't be making out with Chris, his mouth crushes down on mine. The force is so strong it nearly knocks me backwards. I only move about an inch before Chris' hand finds my back once again, and pulls me towards him. His tongue ravages my mouth, and I have to gasp for breath.

"Too much?" He breaks the contact of our mouths and his other hand strokes my cheek.

"No."

"Good, because I wouldn't know how to slow down anyway."

Chris' hand travels down to my neck, and he brings my mouth to his and our lips lock again. His tongue darts in and out of my mouth and each time it disappears I want to cry out for more.

"Get a room." Someone shouts from the other side of the street. Both Chris and I look up, and give a dirty look at the young guy walking his dog down our street.

"Mind your own fucking business." Chris yells as he holds up his middle finger.

I giggle at his assertiveness, and watch as the stranger hurries away with his head down. At least he recognizes he's no match for Chris. I shiver as I imagine what someone Chris' size would do to him if it came down to a fist fight.

"Let's take this inside. Fewer interruptions."

Before I have a chance to answer, Chris wraps one arm around my lower back, bends down and places his other arm under the back of my knees. He scoops me up effortlessly and heads into his house. The second he kicks the door closed behind him, his mouth once again finds mine. I reach up towards his neck to pull his mouth towards me and deepen our kiss, even though his tongue is so far into my mouth I'd probably choke if he stuck it in any farther.

"Ahhh." I scream.

I open my eyes when I have the distinct sensation that I am falling. I let out a sign of relief when I realize I'm laying in the middle of Chris' black leather couch. Chris is standing over me, his eyes narrow and his lips pressed together as he attempts to stroke himself through his pants.

"You look so fucking hot right now."

I look down and see the tops of my breasts are spilling over the plunging neckline of my crop top. My shorts have also ridden all the way up my thighs.

"Thank you." I say stupidly.

Chris lunges for me, and I'm grateful I don't have to think of anything else to say as we continue to make out. His hands find my breasts, and he strokes them through my shirt.

"I can't believe you came home alone looking like this."

I don't know how to respond. I don't want to kill the mood by telling him it wasn't because I couldn't find anyone, but only because I have high standards.

"Well, it was one of those nights."

Chris' hand moves to the top of my jean shorts, and I feel instantly wet as I imagine his fingers on me.

"Well that's good for me. I don't know what I would have done if I had seen you come home with someone else..."

Chris leans in to kiss me again, but I push him away in the middle of his chest.

"What do you mean?"

Chris looks me directly in the eyes.

"You know what I mean."

Even though I do know what he meant, something about the way he said it so casually is sending off alarm bells in my head. Chris isn't my boyfriend, he is my neighbor. We have only fooled around a couple of times, we haven't even had sex yet. Why was he already jealous? This isn't a good sign.

"I should get going." I prop myself up on my elbows, and Chris straddles my legs pinning me to the couch.

"What? You think I want to see you with another guy when I want to be the one who fucks you?"

I wasn't sure, but I knew that I didn't want to be having this conversation.

"I said I need to go."

Chris looks at me, and I hold his stare without blinking. He gets up, and offers his hand to pull me to my feet.

"Look, we keep getting off on the wrong foot... maybe we should try getting dinner, or a drink one night?"

"I'm kind of busy."

I leap off the couch and head to the door, grabbing my purse as I step outside. I find my keys, and jab them into the lock. As much as I want to look and see if Chris followed me outside, I can't bring myself to check. I know that if I catch a glimpse of him, I'll lose the little bit of will power I have left.

So I fling my front door open, run inside and slam it shut. I can hardly hear anything else over the hammering of my heart inside my chest. I inhale deeply, and remind myself I need to focus. It was time to go back to my original plan, which was to stay the hell away from Chris. Which would be a whole lot easier, if he didn't live right next door.

11

CHRIS

It's been a week since we started renovations, and nothing has gone according to plan. Nothing, not a single thing. So when my general contractor called this morning and told me there was a problem with something called a sub floor, you wouldn't think it would have come as any surprise to me. But I'm so fucking angry I can hardly see straight. The sexual frustration isn't helping either. It's been almost two weeks since Lane showed up at my door late at night, half dressed and tipsy. There's only one reason a girl would do that, and instead of just admit that she wanted to fuck me, she did everything in her power to deny it. It's a real shame, because if we had gotten started, there is no way she would have ever wanted to stop. But she made her decision, and I have no choice but to respect it. I just keep replaying that night over and over again in my head, and imagining what would have happened if she had just given into her own desires. I know she thinks she's strong, but you can only deny your own body for so long. Sooner or later she was going to come back to my door, begging me for more. Because I sure as hell wasn't going to give her the chance to tell me no again.

"So we can either go with this option, which will run us about an extra ten grand, or this one, which will be more like twenty." My general contractor says to me, interrupting my thoughts about Lane.

Even if I had been listening, I wouldn't have understood a word he said. Except when it comes to numbers and dollars. Those I understood all too well. So I have no idea how to make this kind of decision.

"I just need this installed. Now." I tell him grabbing a piece of the laminate floors from a box and snapping it in half with my bare hands.

"Wish we could boss, but with all the water damage...."

"Fuck." I say as I think of all the water I left on my kitchen floor that night Lane and I took a shower together.

Lane told me it needed to be cleaned up, and that she even had some sort of vacuum that could do it. But instead, I chose to shower with her and to give her another orgasm. The score was still two for Lane, and a whopping zero for me. And it was going to stop there. As much as I hated the fact that I was losing in the orgasm department, I needed to stop. Being with Lane and losing track of what really mattered was going to cost me a lot of money. I couldn't afford any more distractions; literally.

I spin around as I notice a woman in a trench coat and sunglasses lurking once again in the alley at the end of my last unit. As crazy as it sounds, I'm pretty sure I heard her laugh when I snapped the board. *Who the fuck was this girl?* I take one step to get a closer look, but she notices me and hurries off again. So creepy, but I don't have time to deal with any more shit.

"So tell me again, what are my two options?" I ask Carl.

I rub my temples in a useless attempt to stop the massive tension headache I feel forming and do my best to focus on what my contractor is telling me. Even though I can hear and understand the individual words he is saying, I am at a total loss as to what they mean. Or how to use them to make a decision.

"So it really comes down to durability or..." He continues.

"Just go with whatever you think is best." I turn to head back into the house, already sensing that this isn't over.

"That's the thing, one isn't really better than the other. You have to decide."

I pace back and forth on the small sidewalk in front of my house. I turn each time I reach Lane's front steps, and resist the urge to see if the TV is still on in the living room. I noticed the glow of a screen earlier, which means that someone was home. Maybe Lane. I shake my head to force out all thoughts of her from my brain. No more distractions.

I have a huge project in front of me that needs every ounce of my attention. I try to refocus my thoughts on the decision at hand, even though I have no idea how to make it. I'm very much over my head. Real estate, that I understood, but not how to conduct an entire six unit renovation. I should have never let my dad talk me into this when I didn't even know the first thing about home repairs. Neither did my dad for that matter, even though my first thought was to call him and ask. There was only one person I can think of who would know what to do; the same person that rejected me the last time we were together. I vowed I would never go crawling back to her, but this isn't for sex. This is business. I also know that if I am going to get her to agree to help, I have to make it worth her while.

"I'll be right back." I say to my contractor, handing him the two pieces of the floor I just ripped in half.

I walk directly to Lane's door, and bring my hand up to knock when something stops me. I take a few minutes to review in my head the pros and cons of asking Lane to help me with the renovation. I start with the pros:

1.) Lane knows a lot

2.) She seems oddly determined

3.) We would get to spend time together

I mentally put a line through number three on my list. That kind of thinking would not do me well in my business. I need to be rational. Time to think of the cons.

1.) Lane hates me

2.) There's a good chance she might actually choke me the next time she sees me

I'm still trying to come up with a third item for my con list when the door in front of me flies open. This time, it's another woman I have never seen before. She's tall and blonde, and she is wearing a ton of makeup, stretchy workout pants and a tank top. Her eyes that are rimmed with really long lashes and tons of brown shimmery stuff open wide when she sees me on the porch. This must be Lane's other roommate. I know from the lease agreement her name is Heidi.

"Sorry, I didn't realize we had company." She says as she looks me over from head to toe.

"It's ok, I was just-"

"You must be Chris."

Heidi extends her hand, and I shake it. After a few good pumps her hand remains in mine. I'm not sure what to do next. A few seconds pass until I hear Lane approach. She's wearing a skin tight pair of tiny spandex shorts, a thin workout tank top with bright red straps sticking out on her shoulders. Her face looks different, and I quickly realize it's because she doesn't have any make-up. Her hair is also pulled back in a tight ponytail, but it looks perfect with the rest of her outfit. It looks like the two roommates were heading to the gym. I should have known Lane worked out. It was the only way to explain how her body was so perfect. She was definitely lean and sculpted, but not overly so. She still had curves in all the right places, but was also fit and strong. My favorite type of woman.

"Alright I'm ready."

Lane freezes when she sees me and her face goes pale. Heidi's hand is still in mine, so I drop it like it is on fire.

"Lane." I say, feeling guilty for some stupid reason.

Lane looks at Heidi and back at me with her lips pressed tightly together. If it weren't for the fact that I knew she hated me so much, I'd say she was jealous.

"What do you want?" Lane says as she folds her arms over her chest.

"I was... uh. Hoping we could talk."

"Don't worry about me, I'll leave you two alone." Heidi says with a wink before stepping outside the door.

I try to move to give her space next to me on the step to leave, but it's so narrow that my only option is to step inside their house. Lane looks less than thrilled as she rolls her eyes, but she closes the door once I'm inside the house.

"My spin class starts in ten minutes, so make it quick."

Lane heads into the kitchen which is on the other side of the tiny living room. She's still in my sight as she grabs a water bottle and begins filling it up from the dispenser in the refrigerator. The last thing I want is to make her late for the gym. I can already picture her riding a spin bike, dripping in sweat as she jumps up and down on the bike seat.

Damn it Chris, the rational part of my brain yells at me. *Stay focused.*

"So, we're starting the renovation on my unit first. But we keep running into issues, it seems there is some damage..."

Lane pulls the water bottle from the fridge and slams it down onto the counter top, spilling some of the water over the top.

"Look, I did the best I could as the property manager. But everything had to be run past Howard that costs money, so if you're trying to blame me..."

"No, not at all."

I wave my hands in the air in front of me, to emphasize the point that I am not blaming her in any way. In fact, her being honest about all the existing problems with the houses was one of the reasons we got the seller to drop the price as much as he did. It was immensely helpful, and freed up enough money for me to do all the work that needed to be done.

"You know so much about repairs, and these historic houses. I was wondering if you wanted to be involved in the renovations."

Lane turns to grab a towel and starts wiping up the water she spilled from her bottle, then takes her time screwing the cap on tightly. I am about to repeat myself to make sure she heard me when she finally looks up and her eyes meet mine.

"Help how?"

"Well, you could be like the project manager. My general contractor has some questions, so you could be the point person. As long as you stay within the budget, which shouldn't be a problem right? Given you work in banking."

Lane smiles and moves her head from side to side.

"I really couldn't think of anyone more qualified for the job, Lane. Truly."

Lane smiles again, and I know I am on to something. You wouldn't think a girl with as much going for her as Lane did would need anyone to point out something so obvious. But every time I compliment her abilities, she really seems to light up. I want to keep complimenting her, anything to keep her smiling.

"And I know you are busy, and it would be a lot of work. But how about you stay in your house for the next six months rent free."

Lane inhales loudly, and I can't tell if I said something wrong or she is just lost for words by my generosity. To tell you the truth, I'm a little surprised myself. I hadn't really planned on offering her that. She was already getting almost a 50% reduction in rent, which is more than fair. But I know that I have to make her an offer she can't refuse.

Lane drums her fingertips on the counter top, and stares at the clock above the stove. I try to search her face for any indication that she is considering my offer.

"So we don't owe you any rent at all for the rest of our lease?" Lane asks.

This is my chance to change my mind, but I know I can't go back now.

"No. That is, if you help me."

"So why do you need my help?"

"I want to be there every step of the way, but I just need your expertise when it comes to the more technical matters."

Lane's eyebrows arch. I don't want her to think this is more than she can handle, when I already know she can do it. But I also don't want her to know how stupid I am when it comes to home repairs.

“Do you know what a sub floor is?”

Lane stares at me before answering to make sure I’m for real. At least she wasn’t laughing at me.

“Yes, its underneath-”

“Ok, perfect. I need you to help me pick one out. Now actually if you can.”

“Well that really depends on if you want something that’s durable, or…”

Lane stops when she sees me rubbing my forehead as I once again feel a tension headache forming.

“I know you have spin class, but can you just come talk to my guy out front? It should really only take a few minutes.”

Lane looks at the time again, grabs her water bottle and walks towards the front door.

“Sure.”

“Thank you.” I run towards Lane, and wrap my arms around her and hug her so tightly I accidentally lift her off the floor. Her body remains stiff, but at least she doesn’t push me away.

“Let’s make it quick, I have plans, you know.” Lane almost elbows me right in the stomach in her hurry to reach for the door.

“Excuse me.” I say as I jump out of her way. Lane rolls her eyes.

I am just about to tell Lane not to worry, and that we can make this as fast as she would like when I realize something. Even though she is helping me, the fact that I am letting her live rent free for six months is more than enough to pay someone to do this job. So it's not like she is doing me a favor out of the kindness of her heart. I am paying her very well for her time, which makes me her boss. And bosses deserve respect.

Lane is opening the door, when I reach over top of her and slam it shut. Lane looks up at me stunned.

"One last thing I forgot to mention; if you are working for me, you'd have to drop this attitude. I am your boss, and you need to treat me with respect or else."

I stare Lane directly in the eyes as I speak. She surprises me by not looking away even for a second, or blinking for that matter.

"Or else what?" Lane asks reaching for the door handle again.

"Or else I will fire you."

Lane almost rolls her eyes but catches herself and stops.

"Do we have a deal?" I ask, extending my hand for a shake.

Lane hesitates before placing her hand in mine. Her hand looks so tiny in the palm of my much larger hand. I wrap my fingers around hers as I savor the feeling of her skin on mine.

"Ok it's a deal. But if you think I'm going to call you the boss, or sir or anything like that you're mistaken."

Lane looks down at her hand that is still in mind, but surprisingly doesn't try to pull away.

"No that would be stupid. Mr. Dunkirk is just fine." I do my best to keep my face straight so she thinks I'm serious. She tries to pull her hand from mine as the corners of her mouth turn up. I wrap my fingers around hers even tighter to hold it in place.

"I'm kidding of course. Chris is perfect."

Lane nodes her head and even begins to crack a smile.

"Ok Chris."

The sound of my name on her lips is enough to cause my cock to twitch. It's crazy how sexy something as simple as my name sounds when she says it. Maybe it wasn't the fact she said my name, as much as the fact that she actually listened to what I said. The thought of Lane obeying me, and not being such a pain in the ass was a very exciting idea. I was going to have a good time given her orders.

"Ok, let's go and try to get the sub floors picked out." I open the door, and motion in the direction of my general contractor who is still in front of my house.

"Carl, this is Lane. She's been the property manager here for a number of years, and has just agreed to take over as the project manager. You can now direct any questions you have to her."

Lane stands up tall and proud as I make the introductions. Carl's tongue is practically handing out of his mouth as he looks Lane over head to toe. I shoot Carl a look to let him know that he needs to treat Lane with respect, but Lane beats me to it.

"Carl, nice to meet you. Chris was telling me that you needed me to help you pick out some new sub floors?"

"Yes, right this way. I have a couple options to show you."

Lane follows Carl in the direction of my unit, but stops when she spots the open box of laminate flooring in the back of Carl's truck.

"What is this?" she asks, holding up and inspecting one of the gray floor boards.

"New floors. Going to run them through the entire first floor." Carl says matter of factly.

Lane turns the board over in the hand. The look of disapproval on her face is palpable.

"These have already been chosen. It's the underneath part you have questions about, right Carl?" I say in an attempt to stop what I know is coming.

"Well, these need to go back. How much to refinish and patch the original floors?"

Lane looks directly at Carl, as if I wasn't even there.

"Refinish? That's a lot of work. Would probably be easier to just replace them at this point." Carl says scratching his head.

"I didn't ask what would be easier. I know it's more labor intensive, but those floors are a hell of a lot nicer than this crap."

Carl looks at me, but I look to Lane before answering. Her eyes are narrow, and her jaw is tightly clenched. I have a feeling she isn't going to take no for an answer.

"Is that an option Carl?" I ask.

"It could be. I'd have to hire some more guys."

Lane smiles and practically jumps up and down.

"I know you can figure that out Carl, we have faith in you."

"But I know you'll have to replace some of the boards in the kitchen near the sink. And it probably makes sense to replace the sub floors while we're at it. I think it's all concrete underneath."

Carl leads Lane towards the house, and the two spend the next ten minutes discussing the various options. I do my best to keep up, but the questions Lane asks reassures me I made the right decision putting Lane in charge. She decides quickly, and Carl seems very satisfied with her decision.

"Alright Lane, we'll get everything ordered. And we'll send the laminates back."

The two shake hands before Lane excuses herself for the spin class.

"I'll be back this afternoon if you need me for anything else." She says as she places her ear buds on and heads to the gym.

I watch Lane's ass sway from side to side in her shorts until she disappears around the corner. And I guess I wasn't the only one watching her, because I hear the guys behind me carrying on like a bunch of horny frat boys.

"Shake it girl." One of the guys from the construction team says as he whistles.

"Going to enjoy coming to work a lot more with her to look at." Another guy says as his buddy gives him a high five.

I feel my blood boil as I imagine the vile thoughts they are probably having about Lane right now. Even though I'm thinking of very similar things, I can't stand the thought of anyone else picturing Lane naked.

"What did you say?" I get right up in one of the guy's faces as I talk, so close our foreheads are practically touching. He knows I heard him, but I have to make it perfectly clear that talking about Lane in that way is not going to happen. Not if he or the rest of the guys value their jobs. Or their teeth.

"Sorry boss, is she your girl or something?"

I know that if I tell him the truth, it would be very hard to explain the reaction I am having. And a lot more likely they will keep up the cat calling when I'm not around to do anything about it.

"Yes, she's my girlfriend."

The guys look at each other, and nod their heads with envy. Lane is a catch, there's no doubt about that.

"You are one lucky son of a bitch." The guy whose face I almost just smashed in says as he pats me on the shoulder. I feel a goofy ass grin spreading over my entire face as I imagine what it would be like to go somewhere with Lane on my arm. I can see the look of envy on everyone's face as I introduce her as my girlfriend. I could get used to being envied. And to having Lane on my arm.

12

LANE

It's been a week since Chris showed up at my house and asked me to be his project manager. At first, it seemed like a terrible idea working with someone I couldn't stand. But I'm so glad I was wrong. Working on the renovation has made me feel more alive than I have in a long time. Not going to lie, it's been a nice boost to my ego finding yet another skill that I didn't know I possessed. I am killing the project manager role. Maybe flipping houses could be just the big break I need.

"Come on, it's a Saturday night, are you really going to stay home and work?" My roommate Heidi asks as she sits down next to me on the sofa with a glass of wine in her hand.

I finish updating my spreadsheet with the newest estimate for the refinishing of the floors that Carl just sent me before I answer my roommate.

"Yeah sorry, I told Chris I'd finish updating the budget this weekend. You wouldn't believe how much I just saved him by convincing him to keep the original floors instead of replacing them."

Heidi lets out a heavy sigh and rolls her eyes.

"Ok that's great. But come on, Lindsay is coming into the city tonight. We need to show her a good time and cheer her up. Apparently her new place in Manayunk isn't quite what she expected..."

My chest feels heavy as I think about how much I've missed our neighbor of over four years, Lindsay. We had so many fun nights out in the city together. Lindsay was like our fourth roommate, who just happened to live next store. Chris asked her to move out as soon as possible once he bought all of Howard's properties. Lindsay had to scramble like crazy to find somewhere to go, and the area just outside of the city called Manayunk was all she could afford. I hoped it wasn't as bad as Heidi was making it sound. Just in case we were forced to look there as well.

"Maybe we can grab brunch tomorrow after spin? I really don't want to mess this up. I think I could have a real future in project management or real estate. It pays a whole lot better than personal banking."

I look up from my computer screen and at Heidi. I was expecting a more enthusiastic reply from her, given how much she knows I'm enjoying my newest business venture. But instead of looking excited, she just stares at me like I'm crazy.

"Ok, if that's really more important than going out with your friends and having fun." Heidi says with her eyebrows raised. I knew better than to try and convince her otherwise.

"No I'm super bummed I can't make it out, but I have to get this done." I say with an exaggerated pout.

"That sucks. That boss of yours Chris is really riding you hard."

Heidi and I both burst into laughter. The sudden visual that pops into my head makes me forget where I was on my spreadsheet. Before I can regain my focus, we hear a knock on the door that I assumed is Lindsay. The least I could do is take a ten minute break to catch up with our former neighbor.

"Hello there stranger." Heidi says as she opens the door and her arms widen for a hug.

Lindsay steps into our house, and collapses into Heidi.

"Sorry it took forever to get here. My bus was late again. Public transportation is so unreliable. And not to mention disgusting." Lindsay pulls herself away from Heid and begins to dust off her shoulders. As if she was afraid there might actually be something stuck to jacket after a ride on the bus.

"No problem. Let's get you some wine before we head out. Take a seat."

Lindsay looks over at me on the couch with a half hearted smile.

"So how is life in Manayunk? Other than you know, the buses."

Lindsay takes off her jacket and throws it over the armrest of the sofa, then she sinks back with a heavy sigh.

"Well, my roommates are both still undergrads. So they basically go out every night of the week. Last Tuesday morning when I woke up the bathroom was covered in vomit."

I wrinkle my nose in disgust.

"Gross."

"Yeah. And it takes me like an hour to get into work each morning. When I lived here, it was like a five minute walk."

I nod silently to acknowledge that I feel Lindsays' pain. Life in Center City was pretty awesome. I remember the days of living in our college apartment that was a thirty minute ride outside of the city. What a nightmare that was. I just prayed we wouldn't be reliving it.

I'm doing my best to think of a way to change the conversation topic with Lindsay just as Heidi returns from the kitchen with two glasses of wine.

"So where are you guys going tonight?" I ask Heidi.

"Probably just dinner. I don't want to be out late. Don't forget, we're seeing that place by the art museum tomorrow at ten."

Crap. As much as I appreciated Heidi lining up showings for us, it was still kind of depressing how run down all the places were in our budget.

"Yeah, don't worry I won't forget."

"Anywhere by the art museum isn't bad. I would kill to have afforded anything there." Lindsay chimes in, reminding me it could be a lot worse.

Heidi looks to Lindsay and offers her a smile of support.

"My realtor also mentioned that there might be an opening in that new high rise, if we could just increase our budget even just a little." Heidi sticks out her lower lip as she holds her index finger and thumb about an inch apart.

I exhale loudly and roll my eyes. It was super annoying that Heidi was once again trying to convince me to go over budget again, when I had already agreed to stretch myself more than I felt comfortable.

"I just don't know that I want to live in a building. They're so crowded, and having to wait for an elevator each time you want to go somewhere..." I tell her.

"You do realize we only have four months to find something, right? It might be a little late to be so picky."

I sigh as I think of how daunting a process it is finding a new place. I know four months is not a lot of time and I normally like to be two steps ahead, but for some reason I just can't bring myself to face the facts. It was like my brain was in a state of denial. Or maybe I was just pushing the unpleasant thought of moving to the side so I could focus on the task at hand. Something I was very good at.

"How much is the place in the high rise?"

I feel my body stiffening as I ask. I know I am not going to like the answer.

"Well, Ashley and I were talking it over. And we know you're trying to save money, so we could cover the difference. It would be worth it if we can all still live together."

The thought of my roommates having to cover any of my part of our rent is like a punch to the gut. I know that Heidi and Ashley are both killing it at work and probably have a much higher budget than I do. I don't want to hold them back, but the thought of them covering any portion of my share of the rent was out of the question. I didn't need charity. But it was also not fair of me to ask them to live in a cheaper and crappy house all because I couldn't afford anything nicer. This was an unwinnable situation. The worst kind of problem to have.

"Ok, maybe we can take a look. And if we like it, maybe I could talk to my boss about a raise."

It wasn't very likely my boss would agree to a raise given I worked on commission. But maybe I could work a little later at night and come up with more money. I just needed to buy myself some time to figure it out.

Heidi shrieks and almost spills her wine as she leaps towards me for a hug. I try my best to smile, but my face doesn't seem to be cooperating.

"What's wrong?" Heidi asks me, sensing my disappointment.

"It's just going to be hard to leave this place..."

Heidi puts her hand on my shoulder and gives it a reassuring squeeze. Then she lets out a little giggle.

"What?" I ask her.

"I was just thinking, that maybe if you fucked Chris he'd let you stay. I mean, all it took was a shower with him to give us six months of free rent."

I slam the lid of my laptop shut.

"That's not why he chose me as project manager. I am good at what I do, and he knows I work hard."

"What? You're working for Chris?" Lindsay asks me with her hand over her chest. As if I was somehow betraying her by accepting the job from him. I just hoped she would understand that this was a big step for me, one that might really help launch my real estate career. And even if I had refused, it's not like it would have changed his mind about making her move out.

"Yeah, I'm just overseeing the budget for the renovation. You know, I was property manager here for so long. So it's kind of my job..."

Lindsay shakes her head and takes a big sip of her wine.

"But I would never sleep with him for rent. Or anyone for that matter." I say to Heidi, doing my best to convey the seriousness of what I am saying.

"No, I wasn't trying to imply that at all. I'm sorry, I was just kidding..."

Heidi waves her hands in front of her face in an attempt to take back what she has just said. As much as what she said was wrong, I also knew it wasn't right for me to get mad at her. I had known Heidi since I was eighteen years old and a freshman in college. We had been through a lot of crazy times together, and we told each other everything. No topic was off limits. So it shouldn't really be any surprise to me that she picked up on the fact that Chris wanted me bad. I mean, it was pretty obvious.

"I'm not saying you need to prostitute yourself, but come on, he's smoking hot." Heidi says as she lets out a huge giggle.

"What? No."

I move my head from side to side, knowing how hard it will be to convince Heidi I wasn't physically attracted to Chris. I feel my nipples harden as I think back to the shower we took together, and how he made me cum harder than I ever had in my whole life. I grin when I remember how he practically begged me to let him fuck me after. Not going to lie, I was very tempted, but luckily I was able to control myself. I have a very strong feeling that sleeping with Chris would come with strings. Being no stranger to the hook-up scene, I had met many guys that were just looking for sex. And they didn't look at me the way Chris did. And they certainly weren't as determined as Chris was to sleep with me. He was persistent, no doubt about it.

"Ok. If you say so..." Heidi presses her lips together hard as she tries to stop herself form laughing.

"So he's hot. But he's also really entitled. He's used to getting everything he wants without working for it."

"So you're doing him a favor by saying no to him?"

Maybe it didn't make a ton of sense when you say it out loud. But in my head it made perfect sense.

"He's just not my type. I want a guy that has worked in his life, who knows what it's like to struggle."

Heidi takes another sip of her wine, and I think about going into the kitchen and pouring myself a glass.

"So you're looking for the male version of yourself?" she finally asks.

"Maybe... more like where I see myself in the next five years."

"So like you but with money?" Lindsay says with a laugh.

Heidi and I both burst into laughter, and as funny as it is to me, I also hope it's not true. I really have spent my whole life trying to get to where I wanted to be. And that didn't leave a ton of time to sit around and daydream about what my future boyfriend would be like. I have just always assumed that when the time was right, the perfect guy would come along. And the timing sure wasn't right now.

Heidi and Lindsay start to discuss where they are going to grab dinner, so I turn my attention back to the spreadsheet in front of me. I scan the list of repairs one last time. The list is long, and seems complete. Until I remember one big item that I'm not seeing.

"Shit, that cheap ass..." I mutter under my breath.

"What did he do now?" Lindsay says, shifting on the couch until she's facing towards me and leaning in.

"He didn't budget any money for a new sewer line. They may not add a ton of value when it comes to resale, but there's no way we can just overlook a major problem. He's probably just hoping that the next buyer won't notice, and it will be their problem."

I feel my heart rate accelerating when I think back to all the times I had warned Chris over the last week that we needed to have the sewer looked at. He hired me because I knew more than him, and he always reassured me that he trusted my judgment. If that was all just to placate me, he had another thing coming.

"That bastard. The kitchen sink in my old unit flooded constantly. He's probably so used to having servants clean up all of his messes he doesn't realize what a hassle it is for a normal person. You should report him to the city!" Lindsay slams her hand onto her leg to emphasize her point and almost spills her wine.

"It would serve him right if I tipped off the city. You know, make an anonymous complaint to the inspectors. If they knew there could be a problem, they would force him to fix it."

My mind races as I consider what Lindsay said. While I wasn't sure if tipping off the city was the best thing to do, I know I can't just sit back and let him get away with ripping off the next buyer. Talk about the rich getting richer.

"Wow, you really want to do that? What if he found out? Wouldn't he be pissed?" Heidi asks.

"Well, I'd have to be careful."

While I wasn't entirely sure that there was a way to make an anonymous tip to the city, it sure was funny to think about. I giggled as I picture myself dressed in a trench coat with sunglasses placing the call while disguising my voice at some pay phone. The truth was, the city shouldn't really care who places the tip. I knew that if Chris found out it was me he would be pissed. But the thought of him losing his temper was amusing. I just hoped the next time he got mad he'd rip his shirt off, instead of undoing his buttons one by one. Or even better if he ripped off mine...

My giggle turns into an evil laugh as I think through my options.

"You ok over there?" Heidi asks.

"Oh yeah."

I wave my hand to fan my face as I feel my cheeks burning.

"Well, don't stay up all night working. Text us if you change your mind."

I nod as Lindsay and Heidi get up from the couch and head out for dinner. I stare at my spreadsheets once again, and decide I've done enough work for the night. The project is moving along so much quicker now that Chris has me working on it. I try to imagine the look on his face when I show him all the numbers that I've spent the last few days crunching. We are meeting at the end of the week to go over the budget. When he sees what I've done, he's going to realize that hiring me was the best decision he ever made.

13

CHRIS

Never in my life did I think overseeing a construction crew would be as much fun as it has been. Lane is coming over this morning at seven before she goes into work to review some numbers. When she first suggested a morning meeting, I almost said no. I've never been much of a morning person. Lane on the other hand is a workhorse. She never wants to stop. Never have I met someone who is as determined as she is. And another little bonus to our morning meetings is that when she comes over before work, she's always wearing one of her tight skirts. And one of those shirts with the buttons that always look like they're going to pop over her chest. It's hard to concentrate whenever Lane is around. Luckily, Lane has taken care of everything so far. Her judgement is spot on and I already trust her implicitly.

I feel sorry for every guy that works at the same bank as she does. They must walk around all day with hard-ons.The second I imagine how hard it must be for those guys, I wish I hadn't. But I know Lane knows how to tell a guy when to back the hell off. She takes shit from no one. I just hope one day to be the guy who changes all of that.

Right as the pot of coffee I put on to brew is finished, I hear a knock on the door.

"Morning." Lane greets me with a smile.

"Morning."

I hold the door open wide and gesture for Lane to enter. She saunters across my living room to the kitchen table. It's like she's intentionally making her ass sway from side to side as much as possible as she walks.

Lane takes a seat and fires up her laptop.

"Ok, so I've made some real progress here. So with the money we're saving by keeping the original floors and kitchen cabinets, we have almost enough in our contingency fund now in case we do need to have a new sewer line dug."

I am too busy picturing Lane naked and nodding my head that I almost miss the last part of her sentence. Lane takes my silence as agreement, and is already typing away at her keyboard once again.

"Wow who said we're keeping the cabinets? I don't think any buyer is going to be impressed with Oak."

Lane stops typing and looks over at me.

"We can paint them white, but they're in really good shape. New cabinets will cost a fortune."

"Well we haven't had any more problems with the plumbing in almost a month. With any luck, we can get these houses on the market before anything else goes wrong."

Lane shoots me a look like I just called her mother fat. As much as I appreciated her enthusiasm, it was still my decision to make. She was my project manager, but I was still in charge. I need to remind her of this and put her in her place.

"We are getting new cabinets. End of discussion."

Lane bites her lip like she's about to say something snippy back. As much as I kind of want to hear what she's thinking, I also am glad she knows I was serious about what I said the other day. She is working for me now, and I warned her about treating me with respect.

"Ok, we have enough to cover the costs of those, if you're fine with a smaller contingency. And if we do end up running into any issues, I'm sure you can just ask your family for some more money." Lane says matter of factly as she begins typing and furiously updating her spreadsheets.

"Woh, who said anything about asking my dad for money?"

Lane looks at me with her eyes wide, pretending not to know my question was rhetorical.

"We just have to hope for the best. I've put everything into this, no bank is going to loan me any more money, I'm sure you know that. But I'm not just going to ask my dad for money. He's already done so much for me."

I feel my head spinning as I try and imagine what I'd do if we ran out of money. It's not like I can just sell six houses half finished and make any sort of real profit. The only buyer's we'd be able to attach would be other investors, and they'd smell the blood in the water and low ball us big time. Running out of money wasn't an option. I was in far too deep. And even if my dad could help me out a little, I couldn't do that to him. It wouldn't be right.

"Ok, hoping for the best it is." Lane says with a cute smirk as she holds up two crossed fingers in the air.

The way Lane mentions asking my father for money so casually makes me question her judgement for the first time. It would sort of make sense that she would think nothing of it if she grew up with a rich father who gave her whatever she wanted. Except for the fact that she works her ass off. Nothing about her drive spelled privilege to me.

Lane shifts in her seat and looks me directly in the eye with a very serious look on her face.

"You really wouldn't ask your dad for money? Even if you were sure you'd be able to pay him back?"

"No. Would you?"

Lane lets out a small chuckle.

"No, because I know my parents hardly have any. My mom and dad are both elementary school teachers. They work really hard, but they barely get by. Ever since I was old enough to get a job baby-sitting, it was always up to me to work and save for what I wanted."

That made much more sense. And it was such a turn on that Lane never relied on anyone for anything.

"That explains why you work so hard."

Lane smiles and her cheeks turn pink as she looks down at her keyboard.

"That's funny, both of your parents were teachers. I actually taught middle school up until a few months ago when I quit to focus on real estate."

Lane's eyes widen and once they meet mine, she cracks a small smile.

"Really? Your dad made you work?"

That was a strange way to put it.

"No, he didn't make me. But I needed things like food. My dad even let me live with him so I could save as much money as possible. Every year I put away half my salary to save up for this project."

Lane nods her head as she stares into my eyes.

"That must have been nice."

"Living with my dad? It was ok. I am grateful for what he

did, so that I can chase my dreams. I just hope one day to be able to repay him."

Lane smiles again and her eyes light up.

"I'm grateful for all my parents did for me. I hope one day I'll be able to make enough money to be able to help them out if they ever need it."

"Well you are on your way, working at a bank."

Lane lets out a heavy sigh that causes the little wisp of brown hair in front of her face to float to the left. She reaches her hand up and brushes it behind her ear.

"Personal banking isn't really what I thought it would be. But it was the only job I could find right out of college. It's ok for now."

"For now?"

I put my elbows on the table and lean in towards Lane so that I can hear every detail. I really want to hear all about Lane's master plan.

"Yeah. I just always had this feeling that if I worked really hard, I'd get my big break. But it's taking longer than I thought..."

"I always felt that way too as a kid. I'd see people just working the same job day in and day out, and would wonder how they did it."

Lane's smile widens and she looks me dead in the eyes. I can tell she totally understands and has thought the exact same thing before. I've tried to explain this feeling to so many women in the past, and they all just looked at me like I'm crazy. But Lane totally gets it.

"So did your dad get you started in real estate?" Lane asks, resting her chin in her hands.

I think back to my childhood, and all the times my father warned me about the uncertainty of his chosen field.

He always tried to convince me to go to law school or medical school. Something that was safer and that came with a steady paycheck.

“Not exactly. It's funny, he always told me...”

A knock at the door stops me mid sentence. Lane looks to the door with her eyes wide and back to me. I know she wants to hear what I have to say. And all I want to do is continue having a real conversation with Lane. One that isn’t about the renovation, or filled with hostility. This was the first time since we met that I felt like I was finally starting to get somewhere with Lane. Even just ten more minutes of talking would probably be enough for me to crack through her rock hard exterior. I am more certain than ever there is an amazing and warm woman beneath Lane’s tough facade.

“I’m sorry about that, sure it's nothing important.”

The knock turns into an all out pounding.

“Boss you in there?”

I recognize the boss of my general contractor immediately. Carl always liked to get started early in the morning. And today was the day they were going to start sanding the floor in my house to determine if they were in fact salvageable as Lane claimed they were.

“Yeah, be right there.”

As I stand, I take a chance and reach for Lane’s hand that is outstretched on the top of the table. As my hand brushes up against hers, and she surprises me by not pulling it away immediately. I lower mine further until her hand is completely surrounded by mine, and I give it a gentle squeeze. Lane looks down at our hands as the pounding at the door continues.

“Hold your fucking horses.” I yell as I run to the door.

The entire construction crew is on my front step with their tools and hard hats. One guy is dragging something that looks like a huge mop out of the back of one of the vans. I know I have to let them into my house to get started.

"Didn't realize you had company." Carl says looking over at Lane who is busy packing up her computer.

Her back is turned to me and the guys as she's bending over to put her laptop back into her bag. I watch Lane as the skin tight fabric of her skirt shows off each curve of her magnificent back side. When I turn to look at Carl, I know he is staring at the exact same thing. I jab him on the arm to snap him out of it.

"I was just leaving." Lane says as she hoists her bag up over her shoulder.

"But we weren't finished. Can you come back this evening?" I ask Lane over the noise of the crew as they drag their equipment all over my living room.

Lane bites her lower lip and takes a step to the left as the guys start moving into the kitchen.

"Maybe. I really should try and get caught up at work... "

"Ok, just shoot me an email when you're done tonight. I'll be around."

Lane nods her head and walks to the front door. Her hand is on the knob, and just when I think she's going to leave she turns around and looks at me again.

"Ok, I'll let you know."

As much as I respected how hard Lane works, part of me also thinks that it's a little bit suspicious that Lane would have to work late on a Friday night. But Lane did love to work, so there is a chance that she is telling me the truth. If she did come back later, meeting with her on a Friday night was the chance I had been waiting for. We could finish up reviewing the budget and maybe I could even convince her to relax a little. Dinner on the couch with some wine, a good movie... that almost always leads to one thing I've wanted since the moment I laid eyes on Lane. It looks like my patience was finally going to be paying off.

14

LANE

I look at the large clock above the reception area as I enter the bank. It reads five after nine. This is officially the latest I have ever come into work. If I had come into work right after my meeting with Chris this morning, I would have been here about forty-five minutes ago. But I took the extra long way this morning, and even stopped for coffee and a bagel. My mind felt like it was going in a thousand different directions after I left Chris' place. I needed some extra time to try and clear my head. Funny it still feels like my brain is spinning inside of my head. A feeling I've experienced way too many times over the last couple of weeks.

"Morning." I say to one of my co-workers who is also just arriving.

As I walk past the rows of offices belonging to my other co-workers, only about half of them have the lights on. So I'm not officially late.

Normally coming in at this time would make my skin crawl. I have always prided myself on being the first into the office every morning, and the last to leave. But that was before I had my other more exciting job as a project manager.

Overseeing Chris' renovation has made me feel more alive than I have in a very long time. I finally understood what so many people meant when they've said things like 'do something you love for a living.'

Well, I love being in charge of a budget and making the hard decisions. And it was incredibly satisfying seeing the results of my efforts come to life so quickly. Working in real estate isn't anything I have ever really thought about before. But now I can see that this is what I was meant to do. Once I save enough money of my own, I am going to take the very same leap that Chris did. I am going to quit this job, and focus on building something that is my own. I'm far too good to work for someone else, and I was tired of watching everyone around me get rich off of my hard work. It was time I did something for myself.

"Morning Lane, did you just get in?" I look up from my desk as I am waiting for my computer to power up and see my boss Nick standing in the door of my office.

"Hi Nick, yes. Sorry I had a meeting this morning. You know, for the renovation I'm overseeing."

Nick holds his hands up to stop me from going into any further detail.

"The Miller's were here this morning at eight. I thought you were going to sit in on that meeting. They probably would have been very interested in hearing about how taking out a personal line of credit could have saved them some money..."

Crap. I lightly tap my forehead with the palm of my hand when I realize I completely forgot about the meeting. Even though the Miller's weren't exactly my clients, that meeting would have been a great opportunity to impress Nick, and maybe even his boss as well. But lately, it was becoming increasingly difficult to focus on banking, when I already knew that I wasn't going to have to be stuck in this job too much longer. There was finally a light at the end of the tunnel, and that was making it harder for me to see anything but that light.

"Sorry Nick, maybe I can give them a call later."

"That would be nice, if you're sure you're not too busy. I know it's not easy juggling two jobs at the same time."

I hear the sound of my computer powering on, and I quickly type in my password so that my emails will load. When I'm done, I look back at my doorway, expecting Nick to have left already. But he's still there.

"Yeah sorry, I will call the Millers this afternoon. But I have to leave a little early today. I have to take care of something..."

Nick nods his head, and takes two steps into my office until there's enough room to close my office door.

"You seem to really be enjoying the renovation you are working on." Nick says, pulling out the chair on the other side of my desk.

I look up at him and smile. Normally when Nick comes into my office, it's to talk about work. It was such a nice break that he finally wants to talk about the renovation. It was far more interesting than banking.

"Yes, did I tell you that we are completely redoing all six houses? The plan is to finish in six months, and get them on the market by spring. They'll sell in no time, and then Chris is going to find another project, maybe even a bigger one."

I feel butterflies in my stomach as I think about how there is a very good chance that if I hit this one out of the park, Chris might ask me to be the manager again for his next project. Working for him again would really help me jump start my own savings.

"So you really enjoy real estate?" Nick asks, crossing his left leg over the other.

"I do. The market is on fire right now. There's so much opportunity for those that have the capital to invest. That's what Chris says."

Nick nods his head.

"That's Chris Dunkirk?"

"Yes. But he's actually a really down to earth guy. He used to be a teacher, and he even saved up all the money that he used for the downpayment on his loan himself."

I nod to emphasize my point. Nick probably thought that just as I had that Chris' dad was bankrolling his project. I have a whole lot more respect for Chris now that I know he financed this all on his own. It couldn't have been easy for him to save all that money on a teacher's salary. His focus is almost as intense as mine.

"Good for you. That would be a very great family for you to marry into."

I turn my head around to look at Nick so quickly that I nearly fall out of my chair. Even though Nick is my boss, we do have the kind of relationship where we can talk about our personal lives. So the fact that he would talk about marriage wasn't that much of a surprise. It was the person he mentioned that was the real surprise. It was hard to understand how Nick was able to jump to the conclusion so quickly. I haven't even thought about marrying Chris. Not even just a little bit.

Before I can even think of anything to say, Nick stands up from his seat and gives me a pat on the shoulder.

"Just make sure you aren't taking on too much. I hate to see things start slipping through the cracks."

I smile and nod as Nick exits my office. I am really so lucky to have a boss as understanding as he is. I was afraid the fact that I have been slacking off a bit the last couple of weeks would make him upset, but he actually seems to understand that I have to follow my passion. I owe it to him to do the best I can, for as long as I am stuck at this job. Which should only be a year tops with any luck.

The rest of the day I do my best to get caught up on emails and make sure I am prepared for all of my meetings next week. I only have two on Monday, and the first one isn't even till eleven, so I decide that I can prepare for it that morning. I spend the rest of my time at work updating the budget for Chris. This morning when we met, I had planned to run a few things by him for his input. But we got interrupted before I had the chance to ask him about new light fixtures. It probably makes sense that I just go with the ones I had in mind, since Chris usually likes everything I pick anyway. So I plug in the numbers, and finish making a few more changes as well. By the time I'm finished, it's already four thirty, which is too late to really start anything work related. So I pack up my computer, and head home.

I decided to stop by my place first before I go back to Chris' to change into something a little bit more comfortable. Just as I am closing the front door, I almost jump out of my skin when I hear a voice from inside the kitchen.

"You're home early." My roommate Ashley says.

"So are you." I say as I clutch my chest. Ashley was never home at this time.

"Well I was going to surprise you, but guess who is coming over tonight? Remember that guy Paul I met last weekend when we were out?"

I had no idea who Paul is, but I know better than to

admit that to Ashley. She would most likely describe him in excruciating detail until I remembered who he was.

"Yeah sure."

"Well, we already had plans for tonight. But Paul totally forgot that his friend is coming into town tonight."

"Ashley no." I say as I feel my eyes rolling back so far into my head I am afraid I might get a headache.

While I was very used to being Ashley's wing man, this sounded more like a blind date. I wasn't anywhere near that desperate. Besides, I had already told Chris I'd be stopping over this evening. And who knows, maybe after we finished going over the budget tonight, one thing might lead to another...

"I sort of already told them both to come over. Please Lane, it would be super weird if you left me with both of them."

Ashley sticks out her lower lip and grabs onto my arm. She's been such an amazing friend to me over the last four years, I already know that I can't say no to her.

"Ok, fine. I'll hangout with you guys for a little bit. Let me just email Chris and see if he is around now."

I take out my phone and send Chris an email asking if he is at home so we can look at the budget. He writes back almost immediately telling me to stop by anytime after eight. He also says he would like to buy me dinner, and asks what my favorite take out place is. I close my eyes, and imagine us on his couch with some good Chinese food. That sounded like the perfect evening.

"Ashley, what time did you tell Paul?"

"They're coming around eight."

"Crap."

I flop down backwards onto the couch and grab my phone to write Chris back. But when I pull up my email and see that I have another message from Chris with an attachment. I open it, and see an invoice from an electrician. I scan the message until I get to the total at the bottom. The sight of the amount makes my blood run cold.

"Come on Lane. I think you might really like Pauls' friend Patrick. He's like super successful, he's the CEO of a tech company..."

I feel my spirits lift ever so slightly. I already know there's no chance I will be even remotely interested in this guy sexually, but at least he should be interesting to talk to.

"Shit." I yell as I read the rest of the email from Chris. Carl has already asked the electrician to come back next week, since they suspect that one of the units will need to be rewired completely. Electrical work isn't cheap, and this certainly wasn't in our budget.

When I first started working with Chris, I just assumed that if we needed more money for the renovation, his dad would give it to him no questions asked. Richard was one of the wealthiest men in all of Philadelphia. But Chris made it very clear that he was doing this project entirely on his own, and that there was no more money. It still blew my mind that he was able to save enough money to put thirty percent down on the purchase of all six homes entirely on his own. He was driven for sure. Which was kind of a turn on....

"You ok?"

"Yeah. I just have to do a little bit of work before the guys get here tonight. I'll be upstairs in my room if you need me."

I grab my laptop and head up the stairs, already thinking of ways to come up with the money for the electrical work that needs to be done. We'd have to find somewhere else to cut back.

"Ok, just make sure you're done in time to get ready. I'll pick out an outfit for you."

“Wonderful.” I tell her, even though I was very much looking forward to putting on a pair of yoga pants and an oversized sweatshirt. That's what I was planning on wearing over to Chris’. Something comfortable. I already could tell that Chris wasn’t the type of guy who would be impressed by a girl that spent an hour doing her make-up and that wore skimpy clothes. And it was already pretty clear that he wanted me bad. And it was pretty fun driving him crazy.

15

CHRIS

I check my email one last time as I turn onto my street. After I read the email that Carl sent me about the electrical work, I decided that I needed to go to the gym and blow off some steam. I spent over an hour running and lifting. I was sore and covered in sweat, but at least I felt better.

It was now seven thirty, which meant I had a half hour to shower before Lane came over. I hoped she was hungry when she got here and would take me up on my offer to stay for dinner. This might also be the perfect time to open the bottle of wine from my father that I had been saving for a special occasion. The idea of a night on the couch with Lane sounded beyond perfect. Even though she never wrote back to me to confirm eight o'clock worked for her, I feel it's safe to assume she is coming. She didn't say no after all.

My phone buzzes and I pull it out of my pants so quickly I nearly drop it on the sidewalk. I see my friend John's name pop up on the screen. I know why he is calling, and I don't really feel like talking to him. But I already accidentally hit the accept button, so I have no choice.

"Hey John."

"There you are. I was starting to wonder if you left town or something."

"No, I told you, I've been busy with this project."

"Perfect excuse to celebrate. Come on, it's Friday night. We haven't seen you in forever," John begs me.

"I know man, I can't tonight. I have something going on," I say as I put my keys into the lock and do my best to ever so subtly look though the window that is in the front of Lane's house. I see lights on, so there is a good chance she is home. But why hasn't she answered my email yet?

As I enter my house, I walk into the kitchen and look at the bottle of red wine on my counter. If Lane was somehow able to get our budget to balance again even after we paid for all of the electrical work, we both deserved a celebratory drink.

I hear the ping of an email from my phone and my heart hammers in my chest. The second I see Lane's name in the 'from' line of the email, I feel like I can breathe again. I scan it quickly to see if she is coming over tonight, but the subject line of the email is the same as the one I forwarded to her earlier from Carl. And there's an attachment. Could it be possible she already updated the budget?

I click on the attachment and wait for the spreadsheets to load. I scan the columns and see a line for electrical work. I keep following the numbers all the way down to the bottom of the sheet. My eyes almost pop out of my head when I see our newest total. Somehow, we were still under budget without tapping into our contingency money. We were still in very good shape, all thanks to Lane.

'You are the BEST :)' I write back to Lane.

Thirty seconds later, I hear a ping and see another email from Lane.

'Just doing my job. I am so grateful for this opportunity to work with you :)'

I feel a goofy ass grin forming on my face as I imagine Lane typing that message to me. Over the last week, Lane and I have been working remarkably well together. It was like she actually didn't hate me anymore. In fact, I was really starting to suspect that she actually liked me. And after seeing her latest email to me, it was pretty obvious I was right.

Except she never got back to me about coming over tonight. If she didn't want to come over, she would have said so, right? Maybe she forgot once she saw the email from Carl and was still planning on stopping by. Emailing her back again seems kind of pointless when she is right next store. It would be a lot easier if I just went over there and asked her.

Before I head out the door, I go into the kitchen and grab the bottle of wine from my kitchen counter. I look at the label once again. This bottle was a gift to my dad from one of his clients, and since he knew I liked red more than he did, he had insisted I take it. I was saving it for a special occasion, and now I finally had one. There was no one I would rather share this with than Lane.

With the bottle in my hand, I head outside. I know that Lane is home since she was obviously working and emailing me. And it is Friday night. It would make perfect sense if I knocked on her door, and told her that I wanted to thank her in person for all the hard work she had been doing for me. She'll probably tell me again how much she enjoyed working for me, and when I showed her the bottle of wine I have, it would be rude of her not to insist I come in and have a glass with her. It was a perfect plan.

I run up the stairs to Lane's door and knock three times.

The door opens almost immediately, and the second it does I see Lane. She looks even more gorgeous than usual. The sight of her with her long brown hair down around her shoulders is breathtaking. The way the red dress she is wearing hugs the curves of her hips perfectly makes me forget about everything else. It's like Lane and I are the only two people in the entire city right now.

"Lane, you look amazing."

Lane opens her mouth but doesn't say anything as she tucks one of the strands of her long brown hair behind her ear.

"Chris, what are you doing here?"

I hold up the bottle of wine.

"I just wanted to come over here and say thank you again. And if you weren't busy tonight, I thought we could..."

I see Lane's eye fly up from the bottle of wine and her gaze shifts over my shoulder. At the same moment, I feel someone approaching from behind. The crimson color rising in Lane's cheeks tells me that I should take my time turning around.

"Uh Lane." I hear a guy's voice from behind me that sounds as high pitched as a teenagers. I can already sense that this guy is a total tool. It's no surprise when I turn around that I see two guys dressed in skinny jeans and sweaters.

"Patrick." Lane forces a sweet smile on her face and looks at the scrawnier of the two guys. He pushes his thick black framed glasses up higher onto the bridge of his nose and stops at the bottom of Lane's steps. He takes one look at me, and then immediately looks back down at the ground.

"Hi Lane. Sorry we're a little early."

Lane looks at the guys at the bottom of the steps, and

then back up at me. Then she turns around and looks into her house.

"Chris, this is..."

"No it's ok." I put my hands up to stop Lane from saying anything else. She didn't owe me an explanation. If she'd rather spend her evening with these guys, then that was fine by me. "I was going to drop this off."

I extend the bottle of wine towards Lane. She looks at the bottle and hesitates.

"Please, I wanted to give this to you to thank you. Enjoy it."

I grab Lane's right arm and place the bottle of wine in her hand and fold her fingers around it. Lane bites her bottom lip, and from behind me I hear one of the guys clear his throat.

"You have a great night." I say to Lane as I turn to leave. She opens her mouth again, but says nothing. So I decide to save her any further awkwardness by leaving.

I throw an elbow into the ribs of the guy with the thick glasses at the bottom of the stairs. "Ouch." He grunts like a small child.

When I get back home, I slam the front door shut with so much force I worry for a minute it might have come off the hinges. I head straight into the kitchen and pour myself a glass of whiskey and throw it back. Then I move closer to the wall that I share with Lane and press my ear against it to see if I can make out any of their conversation. I hear what I am pretty sure is laughter. I try to imagine what they are all talking about. I feel my hands clenching into fists as I imagine Lane laughing at anything those two nerds would have to say.

Who were those guys and what were they doing at her house? I pace back and forth as I race through all the possibilities in my mind. Maybe cousins visiting from out of town? She was dressed way too sexy for that. It must be a double date with one of her roommates. But they weren't going out, they were all hanging out at their place, which usually meant....

"Fuck." I say as I press down on my forehead in an attempt to rid my mind of all thoughts of Lane. It's not healthy to be so upset. I need to get my mind off of her.

I hear music coming from Lane's house and more laughter. Rather than torturing myself any further, I turn my own stereo on full volume and pour myself another shot of whiskey. Then I run upstairs for a shower and promise myself I won't think of what it would be like if Lane was with me. It was like there wasn't anything I could do that wouldn't remind me of Lane. She was literally driving me crazy.

16

LANE

Talk about an awkward situation. Seeing Chris at my door right as Paul and Patrick showed up made me want to crawl into a hole and never come out. This was the first time I was ever literally lost for words. I must have looked like such an idiot standing there and not saying anything. But it's not like I could have just told Chris, 'it's not what you think, I am definitely not sleeping with either of these geeks, I'm just doing Ashley a favor.' Even though that would have made Chris feel better, it would have really made for a super awkward evening.

I feel my stomach twist into a knot as I picture the look on Chris' face on my doorstep. It sucked seeing him look so disappointed. I can't believe that the last time I showed up at his house after being out with Ashley, I thought it creepy when he told me he had been jealous at the thought of me sleeping with another guy. Now it didn't sound creepy at all. It actually made my nipples hard to think that Chris wanted to be the only one that got to fuck me.

I look into the small mirror above the sink in the powder room before I headed back to join everyone in the living room. Ashley had done a really great job on my hair. I so rarely ever wear it down, but when I do, it really makes a huge difference. And the dress she insisted I wear made me feel really sexy. I was glad Chris got to see me in it, but I wish I had the chance to tell him that it was too tight to wear panties underneath. The minute I think about what his reaction might be to hearing that my pussy was bare, I can feel a gentle breeze between my legs. It was a very freeing feeling.

"So Lane here actually works at a bank." I hear Ashley telling Patrick as I enter the living room.

I shake my head and try to focus on the conversation. But it's hard to listen to what they were saying and come up with polite responses when all I want to do is think what Chris would do to me if he knew I wasn't wearing any panties.

"Yeah that's right." I say as I take a sip of wine.

Ashley had insisted that we open the bottle of wine that Chris brought over. Apparently it was a very expensive and rare bottle. I always thought I didn't like red wine, but this one is unlike any wine I have ever had. And it was going down very easily. The slightly woozy feeling in my brain reminds me that I had better drink a glass of water after I finish my wine. Or even better, I should eat some food. Ashley did say the guys wanted to take us to dinner, somewhere fancy. That was the reason I agreed to let her get me all dressed up. It would be a waste to sit around at home in an outfit like this one.

"Wow, you're hot and smart." Paul says with a nasally laugh.

Patrick looks at him with his eyes wide and then down at my legs. I cross them in an attempt to cover myself. My skin crawls at the idea of him looking at me in that way. It feels rude.

"So did you guys decide what we're doing for dinner? I'm fine with anything, but I am a little hungry."

Paul looks over at Ashley who is sitting to his left on the couch. For some reason, they both burst into laughter. Paul touches the side of Ashley's face, and the next thing I know they are full on making out. Ashley practically jumps on top of Paul, and her skirt moves all the way up as she straddles his thighs. I know I should look away, and the second I do, my eyes land on Patrick. He is wiping his palms on his pants and also seems super uncomfortable.

"Would you like some wine?" I ask him.

He nods his head, so I walk into the kitchen. I grab a wine glass from the cabinet and fill it halfway. Then I pour myself another glass, all the way to the top until the bottle is empty. I take another long and slow sip, and regret the fact that I just offered a glass to Patrick. It seems like a total waste to share something this good with him. There's only one person that I want to share this with.

I walk to the back door in the kitchen that leads outside to our patio. I take a step outside, and breathe in the warm summer air. As I turn towards Chris' house, I see his kitchen light on. I go back inside and grab both of the wine glasses from the counter, and step carefully over the small shrubs that separate our yards. I take one deep breath before I go and stand in front of his door. I try to knock, but both of my hands are full. So I set one of the glasses down on the ground, just as loud music fills my ears. Why would Chris be playing such loud music? I knock as loudly as possible on the glass door, but I'm pretty sure he won't be able to hear me over the music. If I went around to the front door and the bell, Patrick would surely notice and find that rude.

I let out a heavy sigh as I do my best to peer inside and see if Chris is on the couch. Maybe I can get his attention by waving. I flail my free hand in the air, but there's no sign of him anywhere. I know I must look like a total idiot. I grab the other glass of wine and head back to my house.

I take one last deep breath before going back inside. I peek into the living room, and see Patrick all alone on the couch looking at his phone. Ashley and Paul must have headed upstairs. Whenever Ashley brought a guy home, it tended to get very loud. I can't think of anything more uncomfortable than trying to make small talk with a guy I'm not into while my roommates is making sex noises. *Ashley owes me big time for this.*

"Hey Patrick, what do you say we go grab some dinner? There's a cute sports bar around the corner..."

Patrick jumps to his feet.

"Yes, I would be happy to. Although, you look far too nice for that. Do you like French food?"

The truth was, I had never had French food. I couldn't even name a single French dish, other than French fries. But I knew if I admitted this to Patrick, he'd probably assume I was unsophisticated.

"Love it!" I say as I do my best to force a smile on my face.

"Great, our Uber should be here in two minutes."

Patrick opens the front door and steps to the side, waiting for me to exit first. I grab my purse, and head down the stairs.

As we're waiting, Patrick continues to look at his phone without saying a word to me. I just hoped the French restaurant we were going to has fast service. I have a good feeling talking to Patrick will be like pulling teeth.

17

CHRIS

Crap, I mutter under my breath when I hear Lane's door open just as I am unlocking mine. I turn the keys as quickly as possible in an attempt to open the door and run inside, just in case Lane comes out of her house and she sees me.

I know it's not the most mature thing I have ever done, but I have successfully avoided Lane all week. It hasn't been easy, since she's not only my neighbor but she works for me too. I have been very careful to not let the way I feel about her personally affect my work. I still answer every email she sends, but just a day or two late. That way she knows I haven't been just sitting around waiting for her to email me. I have a lot of other shit going on right now, and worrying about Lane and what she is doing accomplishes nothing. It's time to move on, and keep my eye on the prize. And that was the big fat payday I will be getting once these houses are ready for the market. Then I can move on, and out of this row house and as far away from Lane as possible.

I slam my door shut behind me and strain to hear what's going on outside. I hear footsteps, like someone walking down a flight of stairs, and then nothing. It looks like I dodged another bullet.

Just as I let out a sigh of relief, I hear a knock at my door. I do my best to not make any noise, and hope that whoever it is will go away.

"Chris is that you? It's Lane."

I know I have no choice, and I open the door. Lane is there on my step, in skin tight yoga pants and an oversized t-shirt. I look away to push down that feeling that is already rising inside of me. The one that tells me I should jump her bones, when I should be running like hell.

"There you are. I don't know if you saw my last two emails... I was a bit worried." Lane says as she looks down and clasps and unclasps her hands.

"Yeah no, sorry. I've just been really busy. But I'll take a look."

"Umm ok. Is everything going ok? You would let me know if there were any more issues right?" Lane looks at me with her eyes huge, pleading with me.

"Yeah, no it's all good. But I have to run, I told Carl I'd go pick out new handles for the cabinets."

I say the first excuse that comes to mind, as lame as it is. I just need to be away from her, so I can think again. And not feel like I've lost my damn mind each time I look at her.

"You're keeping the cabinets?" Lane stands on her tip toes and her voice rises.

"Yeah, it just made sense to paint them. So I should get going."

I pat my back pocket to make sure my wallet is still there, even though I know it is. Lane remains on my steps, just looking at me.

"You know, I actually really like picking out kitchen stuff. Would you mind if I came with you?"

I try to remember where the closest home improvement store is. There aren't any in the city, and the only one I can think of is over the bridge in Jersey near dad's house. That's at least a thirty minute drive with traffic. I think for a minute about telling Lane no, but the way she's staring at me with her big eyes makes my stomach flip. I know it would hurt her if I said no, and the thought of seeing her upset still bothers me.

"Sure. But I'm leaving now."

I hope Lane isn't like Larissa, my girlfriend in college, when it comes to getting ready to go anywhere. It always took her an hour to get dressed to go anywhere. Even somewhere as stupid as a hardware store would require a full face of make-up and a brand new outfit. I sure as shit didn't want to sit around and wait for Lane to get ready. That would only prolong this ordeal.

"Ok, let's go." Lane says proudly.

I feel my mouth hanging open when I realize that Lane is fine going to the store as she is. It seems so practical and easy. So unlike most women I know.

"My car is over here." I show her to where I was parked on the street. Even though every time I parked on the street, I discovered a new ding or scratch on my car, I didn't care. This car was ten years old, and had 150,000 miles. I just hoped it would last me the next few months. Once we were done with this project, I was going to have more than enough cash to treat myself to something nicer.

"This is your car?" Lane asks when I stop in front of it.

"Yeah."

I wait for her to tell me she just remembers that she has something else to do and run away. I'm sure Lane isn't the type of girl that is used to driving around in a beater. Maybe she's afraid of what her friends might think if they saw her in it.

"That's so cool you have a car. I miss having one, but I can walk most places."

Lane reaches for the handle and hops into the passenger seat. She reaches for the buckle, but it jams just as she is about to slide it into the clip. She reaches up and tugs, but it doesn't budge.

"Sorry, it can be a little temperamental." I reach across Lane, and my arm accidentally brushes right up against her breast.

"Shit, I didn't mean to do that." I say as I feel my cock twitch.

"No, it's ok. One of the hazards of having a big chest."

Lane laughs as she looks down at my hands.

"Ok, let me try this again."

I reach around her, doing everything in my power to avoid groping her again. But when I reach around her chest, I don't have enough room to grab the top of the seatbelt. I try a few more times, and Lane giggles.

"It's ok.Won't be the first time" Lane leans back in her seat, and her chest rises and falls as she takes in a deep breath.

I reach again for the seatbelt, and this time I don't stop myself as the inside of my arm presses up against her. Her skin feels so warm and soft, that I just want to bury myself inside of her breasts. What I wouldn't give to feel them on my face.

I grab the top of the strap and feed a little bit back inside until it releases. Then I pull hard until I have enough slack to reach the buckle. I slowly pull it across Lane's body, and marvel as the strap lands directly between her breasts causing them to part. Then I pull the waist band across her lap and slide it in until it clicks. I give it a final tug to make sure it's snug.

"Thank you." She says to me.

I throw my car into drive and take off down the street, keeping my focus on the road. I curse under my breath when the light at the end of the street turns yellow just as I approach.

"You know that guy last Friday, he was just..."

I reach for the radio and turn it on loud enough that I can't hear the rest of Lane's sentence. She didn't owe me any explanation and there isn't anything that she could say that would make me feel any better. Luckily Lane takes the hint and the rest of the ride she remains silent.

We make it to the hardware store in about twenty five minutes. As we walk inside I look around, and the place looks about three times larger than the last time I came here. They must have expanded. I see everything from paper towels to lightbulbs and lumber. All I want to do is run to where the handles are, picking the cheapest one out, and get the hell out of here. But it doesn't look like it's going to be that easy.

"Can I help you two?" A friendly salesperson wearing a bright yellow vest asks us.

"Uh yeah, we need new handles for kitchen cabinets."

"We have plenty of those. Come right this way." The salesperson takes off and motions with her arm for us to follow.

I have to practically run to keep up with the salesperson without falling behind. I focus my eyes on her, and don't even bother looking behind me to see if Lane is there. If she can't keep up, she doesn't belong here with me. I can't worry about her all the time.

"So everything on this shelf is half off, and if you don't

see what you're looking for, I can always check in the back." The woman says, waving her arms over a huge display.

I hear Lane squeal behind me. I turn around, and see her running right towards the large display at the end of the aisle.

"These are amazing!" Lane points to a set of white cabinets that have stainless steel handles that look just like all the other ones in here. There has got to be something identical to those in the half-off section.

The saleswoman smiles and walks over to Lane.

"Yes, these are from our designer collection. They were hand picked by those brothers who have that show on TV..."

Lane gasps and continues to run her fingers over the hardware.

"These are so cool! What do you think Chris?"

Both Lane and the saleswoman turn to look at me.

"How much?" I ask.

The saleslady hands me a tag with the price that is nearly five times what we had originally budgeted.

"Is that for a whole kitchen?"

Both women laugh again, and I fail to find anything funny about overspending. Why anyone would pay that much money for a single handle just because someone on TV put their name on the package was beyond me. Lane of all people should know better.

"We need twelve for each kitchen." I remind Lane, who is still staring at the cabinets as if they were some overrated piece of artwork in a museum.

"He sounds just like my husband." The woman says as she pats Lane's arm.

"No, I'm not her-" I scramble to correct the woman, but Lane cuts me off.

"Oh, you're right. Let's find something on sale."

Lane walks with her shoulders hunched to a selection of handles in a large bin, all with red tags. She digs for a few minutes, before finding a very sleek one.

"What do you think of this?"

"Perfect, we'll take them."

I walk over towards Lane to examine the handle further while the salesperson checks her inventory. As I'm turning the handle over in my hand, Lane reaches over and lays her hand on top of mine. I give it a squeeze.

"Let me guess, you guys bought a fixer upper as a starter home?"

I hear the saleswoman say from behind. I look at Lane, who has a goofy grin on her face. It looks like she's pleading with me with her eyes to play along. I don't give a shit what this lady thinks since we'll never see her again. I just care about getting out of here.

"Not exactly." I say.

"We're real estate investors." Lane says, standing up tall and proud as she tells the woman.

"A true power couple! And such a good looking one at that! I'm sure you hear that all the time."

Lane looks at me again with an even wider grin on her face. The easiest thing to do at this point is to play along, so I wrap one of my arms around Lane and she puts her head on my shoulder.

"Thank you." I say to the woman.

I feel Lane's arm wrap around the small of my back. The saleswoman disappears to begin ringing up our order, and I'm just about to pull away from Lane when I get a whiff of something on the top of her head. It's something that smells like a flower. It's so intoxicating and so feminine. I lean down towards her head to get a deeper whiff.

"Mmm," I say as I plant a gentle kiss on the top of her head. Lane pulls her head off my shoulder and looks me dead in the eyes with an intensity so fierce I drop my arms and take a step away.

"All set, here you go." The sales woman returns with a box containing all the handles. I pay and we head outside of the store. Lane stops halfway through the parking and inhales deeply with her eyes closed.

"Mmm something smells good."

"Yeah, that's Jon's place over there." I say pointing to the small building in the center of the parking lot. "He makes some awesome barbecue."

Lane places her hand over her stomach as it lets out a loud growl.

"Work was so busy today I guess I forgot to eat lunch." She says with a chuckle as her eyes remain fixed on the restaurant.

I open the trunk of my car and throw the box containing the new handles in and slam it shut. I want to jump into the driver's seat and drive all the way back to the city with the radio blasting and drop Lane off so she can go back home. But I am starving myself, and can't remember the last time I had really good barbecue.

"Want to get something to eat?"

Lane's face lights up, and I feel a little something in my gut knowing that I just made her happy.

"I'd love that."

As we set off across the parking lot towards the restaurant, I feel something on my forearm. I look down to see Lane wrapping her arm through mine. She looks up at me and smiles so sweetly, I can't even imagine pulling my arm away.

The restaurant isn't busy and we are seated right away. I

grab the draft list and study it intently until the waiter arrives. I recognize the face of the waiter immediately, but didn't have the heart to interrupt him as he gets right down to business.

"Good evening. So our special tonight..." Once he realizes it's me, he stops.

"Chris. Bro it's been way too long! How the hell have you been?"

"Good Jack, haven't seen you in forever."

I get up from the table and we give each other a hug. Jack and I exchange the usual pleasantries. Then I notice him starting at Lane.

"Sorry man, this is Lane."

Jack extends his hand to Lane and she shakes it with a puzzled look on her face.

"Lane, I used to work here back in college waiting tables." I explain.

Lane's eyebrows remain arched, as if the idea of me having a job in college doesn't make sense to her.

"Yeah, the place hasn't been the same without you." Jack jokes.

Lane finally cracks a smile.

"So what brings you guys out this way?" Jack asks.

"Business. We were shopping for some things we need for a renovation we're working on."

I explain quickly so Jack won't get the same idea as the woman at the hardware store. I know most of the time when a waiter sees two people out to dinner on a Friday night they probably assume they're on a date. I didn't feel like having that conversation in front of Lane tonight. Not with how weird she acted at the store, wanting to pretend like we were some sort of married couple. Girls are so impossible to understand.

"Very good. What can I get you guys to drink?"

Lane orders a glass of wine and I order a beer.

"So you worked here?" Lane asks as soon as Jack is out of sight.

"Yeah. It's really close to my dad's house. We used to come here all the time when I lived with him."

Lane studies my face with her lips pursed together as she nods her head. I don't know why she's having such a hard time understanding what I am saying.

"Is this where you grew up?"

Something about the way she asks her question makes me feel suddenly defensive.

"Uh yeah. And where did you grow up?"

"South Philly. Never lived anywhere else besides the city."

Lane sits up straight in her chair as she speaks and waits for my reaction. I don't give a shit where she was from, none of that has even mattered to me. I decide it's best to change the topic.

"Do you ever see yourself leaving? You know, living in the suburbs one day?"

Lane pauses and takes a long sip of her wine before answering.

"One day, maybe when I have kids it would be nice to have a yard."

I nearly choke on the sip of beer I just took. Lane's eyes wide and her cheeks turn red when she sees me coughing. She probably thinks her mention of the word 'kids' is what has caught me off guard, since most guys my age probably avoid that topic like the plague. But I'm actually pleasantly surprised to hear Lane mention having a family one day. Up until now, all she's ever talked about is her career and working. It was nice to hear that she had a softer, maternal side. It was also crazy how the more time I spent with her, the more sides to her I was seeing.

"But that will be a long time from now. Like years. I love the city, and the suburbs just seem so boring. And all the top financial firms are in the city."

“Gotcha.” I say with a wink.

“Would you like another, Lane?” Jack suddenly appears at our table.

“I shouldn’t...”

“Come on. She’ll take another.” I tell Jack, who hurries off to fetch Lane another drink.

“It's Friday night. Live it up a little.”

Lane moves her head from side to side, and I get a feeling Lane doesn’t do much relaxing.

“Unless you have somewhere to be later...”

“No, no one.”

My body tenses at her response.

“I mean nowhere.” Lane eagerly grabs the glass of wine from the table the minute the waiter sets it down and brings it up to her lips. She takes a long and deliberate sip, and all I can think about is what it would feel like to have her lips wrapped around my cock.

We spend the rest of dinner talking mostly about the project, and Lane also talks a little bit about her time in college, and how she met her roommates. We both order chicken and ribs. Lane surprises the hell out of me by picking up the whole half slab up and just going to town on it. She doesn’t even care when sauce gets on her face and she even licks her fingers when she’s done. It feels good knowing that Lane isn’t one of those girls that feels the need to impress me or act ‘ladylike.’ She just did what she wanted.

I settle the check with Jack when Lane uses the

restroom, and bring my car around to pick her up at the door. We even have a pleasant conversation on the ride back to the city.

After we get back into the city I park my car and jump out of the driver's seat and try to make it to the passenger door before Lane opens it herself. I'm just in time, and open the door wide and hold my hand out for her to grab onto as she exits. She grabs my hand tightly, and her chest lands on mine once she is on her feet.

"That was a lot of fun, thank you." Lane says looking up into my eyes.

"Thank you, it..."

Before I can finish, Lane's hand lands on the back of my neck and pulls my head downwards towards hers. The next thing I feel is her soft lips on mine and her tongue thrusting in and out of my mouth. I desperately run my hands up and down her body, doing everything in my power to pull her body up against mine and be as close to her as possible.

"Let's go inside." I say and pull her by the hand towards the door, not even giving her a chance to reply.

My mind races as I think about the last time Lane came inside my house. I feel as hard as a rock as I think back to how amazing everything started that night. That was until she got nervous and ran off. This time I was going to make sure she didn't change her mind. It was time she returned the favor, and we began to settle the score.

The minute the door is closed, I grab the hem of Lane's shirt and rip it off over her head. I stop when I see that she is wearing a sports bra, the kind that doesn't have a clasp and are a nightmare to get off. But I'm so desperate to see her magnificent tits that I can hardly see straight. So I grab the bottom of it, and keep yanking until I get it up over her head. I must have been pulling it harder than I thought, because when it's off and I look at Lane, a few locks of her hair have come out of her ponytail. They're surrounding her face and making her look even more irresistible than I ever thought possible.

Lane pulls the elastic out of her hair, and begins to smooth the loose strands back down. I grab the rubber band out of her hands.

"No, I like it down."

Lane shakes her head, and my chest feels heavy as I watch the long strands of her hair fall over her shoulders. She looks so wild and unkept. I smile as I imagine what her hair will look like when I'm done with her.

Lane runs towards me again and stands on her toes to reach my mouth. She moans as I grab the sides of her face and drive my tongue deeper and deeper into her mouth.

My cock is so hard it feels like it might rip the front of my pants at any second. I break the contact of our kiss and undo my belt buckle and drop my pants to the floor as fast as humanly possible. Lane looks down at my cock and bites her bottom lip. Then she pulls down her yoga pants, and I see bright red lace panties.

Lane's pants are still on her right ankle in a ball. She kicks her leg and her pants fly across the room. With only her red panties on, she sits back on my couch with her legs spread wide. I know what she wants, but this time, it's my turn first.

"On your knees." I tell Lane.

Lane's eyes narrow as she looks at me but remains seated on the couch.

"Now."

I gently grab her by the arm and pull her to her feet. Then I place my hands on her shoulders and watch as she falls to her knees. Seeing her obey me makes my hard cock throb. I need to feel it in her mouth.

Once Lane is on her knees, she grabs the front of my thighs with her hands and looks up at me with big eyes. I put my hands on the back of her head, and guide her towards my dick. She follows my lead, and once her lips are pressed up against my cock, she pauses.

I am just about to ram myself down her throat when Lane's tongue darts out of her mouth. She licks the tip of my cock like a lollipop, until it's covered in her saliva. Her tongue swirls over the head of my cock and my knees begin to feel weak as I imagine what's next.

Lane looks up at me one final time with a smirk on her face, before she takes my entire cock down her throat. She moans as it slides further and further down. Saliva drips down her chin. Her hand comes up and begins to stroke my shaft in a perfect rhythm. Her head keeps bobbing up and down quickly. I am amazed at how deep she can take me, and how she never gags even once.

My eyes feel like they are rolling back into my head as she continues. It's all I can do to maintain consciousness. The feel of her mouth is beyond anything I have ever experienced. I want this feeling to never end.

"Just like this?" She takes a break to ask me. I nod and guide her head right back to my cock.

"Yes, perfect baby."

Her lips touch my cock again, and I close my eyes as I wait for her to take me down her throat again.

"What did you just call me?"

"Nothing."

I should have known she wasn't the baby type. And neither am I. I have never used that nickname before in my life, but it just sort of came out on its own with Lane. And up until she objected, it sounded perfect.

I keep waiting for Lane's mouth, but nothing.

"What would you prefer I call you?" I ask, eager to do anything to get her to continue blowing me.

"I don't know. Just Lane I guess. Definitely not baby."

In my mind, I start to run through other nicknames that she might find more fitting. But I know better than to suggest any of them right now. None of that matters. All that I should be thinking about is finally getting my release from Lane.

"Ok Lane, you feel amazing. Now keep going. I'm so close already."

I grab the back of her neck, and bring her mouth right to my cock. She eagerly accepts it, and is even able to bob her head up and down faster. The feel of her little hand wrapped tightly around my shaft while her mouth moves up and down is too much. I know I don't have much time, and I already know where I want to cum. All over her huge tits.

I bend down ever so slightly until I can reach her breast. The last thing I want to do is interrupt Lane's movements in any way. Once I find her nipples, I roll them between my fingers. Her breasts begin to bounce as she continues to move, and I know I can't last much longer.

I groan and grab the back of Lane's head as it begins. Sensing exactly what I want, Lane waits until I start exploding in her mouth, then grabs my cock and brings it right over her chest. I scream out as my seed covers her. She looks down to watch it too, and smiles up at me once I'm finished. On shaky legs I find the couch and fall backwards. I reach for Lane who is next to me, still on her knees. With one arm I lift her up and onto my chest.

"How was that?" she asks with a giggle.

"Fucking fantastic."

I pull her close and kiss the top of her head.

"Now, it's your turn."

I spread her legs, and reach for her pussy. The red lace of her panties are so soaked that I can barely find her clit. My fingers continue to slip as I stroke her bud long and slow.

"Mmmm" Lane moans with her eyes closed.

I already can't wait for her to cum. My cock feels hard again as I watch her savor the feeling of my fingers. She reaches for one of my throw pillows, and brings it to her face to scream into. I grab it from her, and throw it on the ground.

"I want to hear you." I tell her.

I continue to circle her bud, and study Lane's face as she reacts to my movements. Then I take two fingers, and thrust them in her tight wet slit. I imagine what it would feel like to have my cock buried deep inside of her, and the walls of her pussy pressing all around it. It would be the ultimate pleasure to finally fuck Lane.

As soon as I say the word fuck in my head, I realize it doesn't sound right. Fucking is what I do to random girls that I meet drunk at bars. Lane is different in every single way. Getting Lane to sleep with me has been the hardest thing I have ever done. And I already know that once I do, it will be worth it. And it won't feel like I'm fucking her, but I'll finally be making love to a woman. Something I have never done before.

But before I make love to Lane, I want to see her cum hard. Even harder than the last time I was with her after we showered together. Harder than the time I ate her pussy in her living room. This had to be the most intense orgasm of her life.

I roll off the couch and onto the floor. I spread Lane's

legs wide, and she lets out a startled gasp as I put her legs up onto my shoulders. Then I bury my face into her tight, soaking pussy. My tongue goes right into her slit, and Lane bucks her hips wildly and wraps her legs all the way around my neck. It's like she's telling me I have no choice but to make her cum. And that's exactly what I'm going to do.

I hear Lane moaning as she does her best to be as quiet as possible. I keep moving my tongue in and out of her, doing everything I can to make her scream. Just when it sounds like she is about to let out a huge scream, there's a loud knock at the door.

Lane's eyes fly open and she tries to stand up. But I push her backwards.

"It's ok, don't worry about it."

I spread Lane's legs again but the pounding continues. Lane brings her legs together and sits up again.

"Who is it?" I yell.

"Hey Chris, it's Joe from unit five. Sorry to bother you, I tried Lane first but she wasn't home. There's some sort of leak in my kitchen..."

Joe is my seventy year old tenant, the last one still here aside from Lane and her roommates. I knew I should have made him leave when all the other renters did thirty days after I took possession of the houses. That was the amount of notice I was required to give them according to their leases. It was more than fair, and no one else really complained, besides Joe. He reminded me a lot of my own grandfather, and when he told me he hadn't been able to find anything at the end of the thirty days, I didn't have the heart to kick him to the curb.

Lane jumps up and runs to find her clothes on the floor. She hops up and down on one leg as she tries to get her pants back on.

"She's..." I start to tell Joe that Lane is here, but I stop when she runs over and smacks me on the arm.

"She should be home any minute. But I can come turn the water off."

Lane smiles and throws my shirt and pants to me. I put them on and stop in front of Lane. She opens her mouth but then points to the door, no doubt trying to hurry me along. But I need one last thing before I go. I grab her hair and pull her head back, and crush my mouth down on top of hers one last time. Lane's tongue swirls with mine for about thirty seconds before she pulls away and points to the door once again.

"Coming Joe." I tell him. Lane scurries into the kitchen to hide as I put my hand on the door.

Before I open it, I put my mouth right to Lane's ear and whisper, "The second we are done with this, I'm going to fuck you until you can hardly walk..."

I watch as Lane shivers and bites her lip. I vow in my head to get back here as fast as humanly possible. I throw the door open, and Lane hides behind it just in time.

"Thanks Chris. It's the strangest thing. I started the dishwasher before I went out today, and came back to like a foot of water all over the kitchen floor. And it's still just flowing everywhere."

I do my best to remember where the water valves are in my house. Joe's had to be in the same place. I want so badly to just shut it off and run back to Lane, but I already knew the moment Joe and I were gone Lane will probably run back to her house for her tools.

I follow Joe to his place, and run straight to the basement. I find the water valve, shut it off with a few twists and run back upstairs to assess the damage. But by the time I'm at the top of the stairs, I see Lane in her pink rubber boots with her tool box, some sort of vacuum. Her hair is still a wild mess. And I know beneath her yoga pants, her red panties are still soaking wet. It takes everything inside of me not to jump her right then and there.

"Sorry Joe, my roommates told me you were looking for me. Glad I got here when I did." Lane says, looking around at the standing water.

"Hey Lane." I say.

She spins around and looks at me. Her cheeks redden ever so slightly, and she switches her gaze back to the kitchen.

"I turned the water off." I tell her smugly. I hope she feels proud that I remembered what she taught me.

"Great. Joe, I'll suck up the standing water for now. And tomorrow, we'll call a real plumber that can look at the sewer line. There has got to be a reason this keeps happening."

Lane bends over to pick up the vacuum in one hand and the tool box in the other, and almost loses her balance. I rush to her side, and grab both items and start walking towards the kitchen.

"Carl can take care of this. He patched mine up."

I feel Lane's hands on the tool box as she tries to wrestle it out of my grasp. I set it down on the floor so she doesn't hurt herself.

"We can't just keep patching things up and not fixing the root cause of the issue."

Lane uses air quotes when she says 'patching', and it's so darn cute I smile like an idiot. While Lane is adorable, I remind myself how hard headed she can be. I know there is no way I can convince her right here that what she is suggesting is very expensive and unnecessary. Finding out now with only a few months left of the renovation to go that we need to dig a new sewer line is a liability that I don't need. If we can fix the problem for now, without investigating any further, I have no legal obligation to disclose anything. And while Lane probably thought having the sewer looked at was noble, this wasn't a charity. I can't have every single possible problem evaluated by a professional. That wasn't the expectation in this business. And not to mention, it costs time and money. Two things we were running shorter on every day.

"Please stop with the sewer, or you're going to be in trouble later..." I whisper in Lane's ear in my lowest and most seductive voice.

I bring my left hand behind Lane and pinch her amazing ass. Lane spins around and smacks my hand away. Then she lifts up her right foot, and brings it down with all of her weight directly onto my foot.

Joe hears the commotion and turns around to look at us. He scratches his head as he looks back and forth between Lane and myself.

"You really think it could be the sewer?" Joe asks.

"No, I don't. Lane we'll discuss this at the next budget meeting." I say through gritted teeth, doing everything in my power to keep Joe from getting suspicious.

"But..."

I shake my head with my jaw firmly clenched at Lane, and finally she stops.

"Ok Joe. Let's get this water cleaned up, and we'll figure the rest out later."

Lane smiles sweetly at Joe, and I feel jealous watching a smug grin form on his face. Lane's power on men was undeniable. If only she knew the effect she had.

"Makes no difference to me. I have to be out in a month anyway." Joe says with a shrug.

Lane comes up behind Joe and places a hand on his shoulder.

"Have you found a place yet?"

Joe looks down at the ground and shakes his head.

"Seen a lot of real nice ones. But they all want first and last month's rent up front. And a security deposit. Who has that much cash just sitting around. I'm on a fixed income!"

Lane pats his shoulders, and I feel something twisting in my stomach. Joe was the original landlord Howard's childhood friend, I recall him telling me when we first closed the deal. Joe has lived in this row home for thirty years. As much as it sucked forcing him out, this was a business. I had an investment to protect. And what Joe didn't know was that I was taking a small loan from my state teacher's pension fund for him to use as a down payment on his next place. It should only be a few more days till I get the check. Leaving an elderly man on the streets was bad publicity for sure. Giving him the money to get out was a wise business decision, I told myself. And it would help me sleep a whole let better at night.

"I can help you look if you'd like. Heidi has this realtor that is great."

Joe looks up, but I can't bring myself to make eye contact.

"Thanks Lane. But they all want so much up front..."

Lane wraps her arm around Joe's shoulder, and pulls him towards her side for a hug. I watch as the hug lingers for ten seconds, then twenty. It's starting to feel a little creepy, so I clear my throat.

"Let's get this water cleaned up." I plug Lane's vacuum in, and look for the power button. Just when I think I've found it, Lane rips it out of my hand.

"I've got this. Why don't you go home."

"No, I want to help."

"I don't want your help." Lane stands on her tip toes as she says. Her nostrils actually flare as she stares me down until I back away.

"Lane says she has it. You'd be surprised at what she's capable of. Tiny but mighty is what I always call her." Joe says, patting her on the shoulder.

Not wanting to cause a scene, I reluctantly leave. As soon as I get home, I text Lane to come over once she's done so we can finish what we started. An hour goes by, and no Lane and no text. Around midnight, I decided it probably best to get to bed. I spend the night tossing and turning, and torturing myself thinking about what I'd be doing if Lane was still here with me. I make a promise to myself that one day I will feel what it's like to fuck her.

18

LANE

I check the time on my computer screen one last time. I've spent the last five minutes sitting at my desk with my cursor hovering over the send button on the email I drafted this morning to the city inspector. I scan my message once more, and debate for the one hundredth time if my message sounds too harsh.

Just as I am changing the subject line to something less dramatic, I hear a knock on my office door. I look up and see my boss Nick in the doorway, and I'm thankful for the distraction.

"Hey Nick, come on in. I was just working on an email. Would you mind taking a look and telling me what you think?"

I turn my computer screen to the other side of the desk, and watch as Nick's mouth moves as he reads it. A few sentences in, his eye brows arch and he stops.

"What is this about? Your other job and the renovation?"

"Yes. Sorry I should have mentioned that. You see Chris..."

Nick holds up his hand to stop me, and I feel my

cheeks redden. My boss has been exceptionally kind over the last month when it came to listening about this project. And as interesting as it's been, Nick is also a busy guy. I'm sure he came in here to discuss something to do with banking.

"Sorry Nick, I can finish this later. What did you come in here to discuss?"

Nick pulls out the chair on the opposite side of my desk and takes his time settling in.

"So, do you have any meetings this afternoon?"

I take a quick look at my calendar, even though I already know it's empty.

"No, I actually kept my afternoon free. I figured I'd make some cold calls, check in with some of my top clients. You know, see if they have any referrals for me."

Nick looks down at my desk as I speak. I know that over the last month, I really have been slacking at work. It was just that banking seems so boring now compared to real estate. My heart just wasn't in it anymore. But I owed it to Nick to try harder. I feel a sudden sense of guilt knowing that I put him in the awkward situation of having to come talk to me about my activity. Nick looks so uncomfortable, literally squirming in his seat.

"Lane, your numbers last month dropped a lot. And since you don't have any meetings coming up, it would be very hard for you to make this month's goals. And we're already almost halfway through..."

"You're right. I need to buckle down and focus. I promise you, I'll make some calls today, and have my entire calendar for next week full."

I close out the email screen I was working on, and pull up my cold call list. The thought of dialing random numbers, waiting for someone to answer and most likely yell at me when I told them why I was calling makes me want to groan out loud.

"Lane, are you sure you even like banking?" Nick asks me, leaning in as he speaks.

I laugh, probably a little too hard.

"It's ok. I mean, for now."

Nick shakes his head, and I know that wasn't the answer he was hoping for. But I don't have it in me to lie to him. Not after all he's done for me.

"Lane, I'm going to do you a favor."

I sit up straight in my chair, eager to hear what he has to say. My mind races through the most likely possibilities. Maybe a raise, a promotion. Anything that would help me devote more time to the renovation and my real estate career would be most appreciated.

"I'm going to give you one month's pay, and time for you to find what it is that will make you happy. Since banking isn't it."

My jaw drops. Last time I checked, firing someone didn't count as a favor.

"No. Please don't. Having a job makes me happy. And I need this..."

"I promise you, one day you will thank me. You need to follow your passion. And the rewards will come."

I open my mouth to beg him again, but Nick stands from his seat and buttons his suit coat.

"Just make sure to forward any current matters to the team and myself, and leave your laptop here. We'll take care of the rest."

I nod, and wipe away a tear that suddenly escapes from one of my eyes. I know if I try to speak, I won't be able to stop myself from sobbing. I have never been fired from anything before. I'm not even sure what was going to happen. But one thing was for sure, if I wasn't going to be working here anymore, I wanted to get as far away from here as possible.

I slam the lid to my laptop shut, grab my purse and run to the front door. It was just after lunch, but given that I was just fired I don't think it's too early for a drink. I stop at the first bar I pass, grab a seat and text Heidi and Ashley both in our group message. Twenty minutes later, they are both by my side, listening to how unfair my life was.

"So you had a bad month. But you also had like two amazing years before that." Ashley says as I sip a margarita.

"Exactly. I busted my ass for that place. Even though I hated it." I close my eyes and shake my head as I think about how hard it has been doing a job that I hated. It was like every hour I spent there since I started working for Chris was time I could have been spending on the project, and therefore a waste.

I close my eyes as I imagine how good it would be to one day work in real estate full time. I would work like a dog, and I would truly be unstoppable. The only thing standing in my way was the amount of cash it took to get started. As I think of how much harder it will be to save enough to buy a property now that I don't have a job, I feel so discouraged I could cry. I try my hardest to think of something to make myself feel better. It wasn't my fault my parents were broke, and they couldn't just give me the money I needed, like Chris'. What a lucky bastard. I hope he knows just how good he has it.

"She'll have another." Heidi informs the bartender.

The thought of another drink and forgetting my problems for even a little while makes me smile. I grab the margarita the second it's set down in front of me and take a huge sip. I tell myself it's ok to get tipsy, or even drunk. I have plenty of time ahead of me to sit around and think about what my next move is going to be. Right now, I deserve to feel good.

Over the next two hours, I drink four margaritas. A personal record. When I can't drink another drop, the three of us decide to head home. The room spins when I stand, and for some reason, I find this hysterical and laugh so loudly everyone else at the bar turns to look at me. Ashley appears at my side, and grabs my arm.

"And remember Lane, you still have a job. You are a project manager. I know Chris thinks you're doing a great job."

The sound of Chris' name does something to my body. I feel a sudden rush of adrenaline. As we get closer and closer to our house, all I can think about is whether or not he might be home. I've completely lost track of time, but it's still light outside.

"Come on Lane, let's get you some water, and something to eat." Ashley says when we arrive in front of our house.

Ashley tugs at my arm when I stop abruptly. My eyes scan Chris' house for any sign that he might be home.

"You guys go ahead, I have to do something." I take one stop towards Chris', when I feel two sets of hands pulling me from behind.

"Lane, no. You're drunk." Heidi says.

I stand on one foot and attempt to touch my nose to show them both I'm fine. But as soon as I lift my arm, I almost topple over. I have never had a great sense of balance, I'm sure that would have happened even if I was sober.

"That's why I have to go and talk to him now."

Heidi and Ashley both look at each other with puzzled looks on their faces, and back to me.

"Just don't worry. I'll be right back."

Before either of them can say anything else, I make a run for Chris' and pound on his door with my fist. I know there's a good chance my roommates might show up at any minute and try to convince me to go back home. Which would probably be the smartest thing to do, but something inside of me is telling me I need to see Chris.

I pound on the door again, and just as I am raising my fist to pound again, the door flies open. My fist lands directly on Chris, whose eyes are as wide as a baseball. The look on his face makes me burst into laughter again. I double over and clutch my stomach.

"Lane, are you ok?" Chris asks as he grabs me by the arms and tries to help me stand upright.

"Oh yeah, I'm good. Ok, I had a few drinks. But that was only because..."

I debate in my mind whether I want to tell him I was fired or let go, because I still don't know what the fucking difference is. So I just blurt it out.

"I was fired." The minute the words are out, a huge sob escapes my throat. My body trembles as I give into the feeling, and allow the tears to finally flow free.

"What? Get in here."

I feel Chris' arms wrap around my body as he pulls me into his house. I bury my face into his chest so I don't have to see the look on his. He must think I'm a total failure. I'm jobless, drunk and crying. Why did I think coming here was a good idea again?

"My boss said he could tell I didn't like my job anymore. And that I've been working too much on your project."

I pound my fist into Chris' chest to emphasize my point. It was kind of his fault I lost my job. I just hoped he understood the sacrifices I made for his project and his career.

With my help he was going to be making a lot of money, and I'm going to be homeless and broke in a couple of months. This must be why the rich always seem to get richer, and people like me remain stuck.

"Lane, your boss is an idiot. You are amazing at what you do. I've never met anyone who is as smart and hardworking as you are. I mean that."

I feel Chris' hand under my chin, pulling my face upward so that I have no choice but to look him in the eyes. As soon as what he has just said registers in my brain, I feel the tears in my eyes stopping.

"I guess in a way he's right. I don't want to be a banker anymore. I want to work in real estate, like you do."

"Well that's what you should do." Chris says, like I'm an idiot for not just buying my own properties years ago. As if it would have been as easy for me as it was for him.

"It's not that easy, Mr. Money Bags. It's not like I have a rich father that can just write me a big fat check whenever I ask."

"Wait, what?"

I jerk my head so quickly that Chris' hand falls from my chin. I walk all the way around him and towards his couch. Once I'm in front of it, I close my eyes and fall backwards as I exhale loudly.

"Lane, are you sure you're ok?"

I open my eyes and am not surprised to see Chris standing in front of me.

"I will be. Life is hard, you know. For people like me."

Chris runs his hand through his hair.

"People like you? Lane, what are you..." Chris stops as his hand drops from his head. It takes everything inside of me not to yell at him for being so oblivious. How can anyone be so out of touch with reality that they can't even see how much harder life is when you don't come from a loaded family? Surely he knows that he is one of the very lucky ones.

"Oh, wait. Rich father. You think my father is Richard Dunekirk?" Chris' eyes narrow as he stares at me.

The word 'think' echoes in my brain. My face feels like it's on fire as I realize that I am wrong. How could I have been so stupid? Of course Richard isn't the only one in the city with that last name. I guess because they both worked in real estate I jumped to the conclusion. I close my eyes as the humiliation washes over me.

"Well, I did..."

"We don't even spell our last names the same way. His is with an e."

"Ugh." I moan out loud, feeling stupider with each passing second. I saw the way Chris spelled his last name every time we emailed each other. How stupid was that of me?

I squeeze my eyes tight and hope that if I keep them closed long enough Chris will go somewhere else, and save me the embarrassment of having to face him. Thirty seconds go by, and I still don't hear anything to indicate he is going anywhere. I finally open my eyes, and see his face. His expression is flat. He doesn't look angry, or offended, even though he has every right to be. The fact that he's so understanding and compassionate only makes me feel even guiltier for having judged him so unfairly. It was like I didn't really know him at all. The Chris I thought I knew was a completely different person than the man standing in front of me.

I rub my temples as I come to grips with what this all means. The real Chris was not a spoiled and privileged heir to a real estate dynasty like I had assumed all this time. The real Chris knew what it meant to work hard, and go after his dreams. Which means that he is a lot more like me than I could have ever imagined. It was starting to make a lot more sense why we worked so well together, and got along too. And it also explained why no matter how many times I told myself that he was bad for me, something inside of me kept pulling me back to him. I had always assumed it was just my pussy, but maybe it was something more than that. Something deeper.

I look up at Chris again, and he cracks a small smile. He reaches towards my face, and tucks a loose strand of hair behind my ear. I shiver from the slight contact. Now that I know the real Chris isn't bad for me at all, it was finally time to give my body what it has wanted for so long.

I take in a deep breath as I mentally give myself a bright green light. It was now very much safe to proceed full speed ahead. And my body was screaming at me to slam the accelerator hard.

"I hate seeing you so upset Lane. But it's all going to be ok."

I leap to my feet, and throw my arms around Chris. I grab the back of his neck, and bring his lips down on top of mine. I can hardly breathe as I desperately kiss him, and promise myself that this time I will hold nothing back.

Chris eagerly returns my kisses, running his hands up and down my back as I suck his lower lip mercilessly. I pause for a moment as my brain bombards me with all the dirty things I want to do to him.

"I want you to fuck me." I whisper in his ear, then I nibble on his lobe.

Chris' body tenses, and his hands land on my upper arms. He holds me completely still, and looks deep into my eyes.

"Are you sure?"

I feel my shoulders slump when I hear his less than enthusiastic reply. Talk about killing the moment.

"Uh yes, at least I was."

I lean in to kiss him again and try to recapture some of the passion that was so strong just seconds before. But Chris stops me.

"I'm not sure I can Lane."

I place my hand over my heart, which feels like it may explode inside of my chest. I force myself to take one ragged breath after another, and pray I can survive this crushing disappointment. I'm just about to make a run for the door when I feel Chris grabbing me by my ponytail. He pulls by hair downwards until my face is level with his.

"Believe me, I want to, more than anything. But, you're kind of drunk. And that is not how I want our first time to be."

Our first time. His words make me crave his body even more than I ever thought possible. I know I have to convince him I'm perfectly fine.

"No, I'm just tipsy. Watch this."

I attempt to balance on one leg, and put my finger on my nose. But the second I shift all of my weight onto my right foot, I start to totter. I put my foot down, and am just about to try again when Chris grabs me by the arm.

"No, give me another chance. I swear, even sober sometimes I can't do this."

Chris lets out a laugh, and I burst into laughter as well. I laugh so hard my belly starts to hurt and my eyes begin to water. I do my best to stop, but each time I look at Chris, I laugh even harder. Maybe I am a little drunk.

"Come on, let's get you something to eat."

"Can we get pizza? Or maybe ice cream." I practically jump up and down at the idea of a big slice with pepperoni.

"Yeah, I know a great place around the corner."

"Great."

I throw my purse over my shoulder and head out the door. Just as I hear Chris closing the door behind me, I feel his fingers pinching my backside.

"You'd better eat fast, so I can get you back home."

We both take off running down the street. Chris leads me to a small place that sells pizza by the slice. I order two with pepperoni and a Diet Coke. We grab a small booth, and Chris surprises me by sitting on the same side as me. I eat my first slice in silence, far too hungry to focus on conversation. With every cheesy bite, I feel my head becoming less foggy.

After I finish my first slice, I look around the table for my second. When my eyes meet Chris' he's just staring at me with a blank look on his face.

"What, do I have something on my face?" I ask as I grab a fistful of napkins from the dispenser on the table.

"No, I just like the fact that you eat."

"Are there girls out there that don't? I was always told all humans have to eat... you know... to survive."

Chris looks down at his own half eaten slice and erupts into laughter. I let out a polite chuckle, even though I still don't understand why he finds me eating funny.

About ten minutes later, I finish my pizza and my entire Coke. I feel much better, and now all I can think about is getting back to Chris' place and finishing what we started.

Chris reaches for my hand as we exit the restaurant. His fingers intertwine with mine, and he even brings my hand up to his mouth for a soft kiss. I smile so hard at the simple gesture that my cheeks begin to hurt.

"Feeling better?" He asks.

"Much."

I pick up my left leg, and have no trouble balancing on one. Then I effortlessly bring my finger up to my nose as my feet remain absolutely steady.

"See?" I ask him.

As soon as I pull my finger away from my nose, Chris plants a kiss directly on it. I probably sound like a damn cat purring as I savor the feeling of his soft lips on me.

The street lights begin to turn on as we approach our block. Everything seems much clearer in my head as the pizza finishes soaking up all the tequila that was left in my stomach. It feels good to be able to think again. Except when I start to think about the fact that I don't have a job. I start to groan in my head, but I end up doing it outloud.

Chris stops walking and steps in front of me with his hands on my shoulders.

"You're not thinking about your job again, are you?"

"No, because I don't have one."

I try to start walking again, but Chris' hands hold me in place.

"Yes you do Lane, you're still my project manager. I seriously can't finish this project without you. And once we're done with these houses, I'm going to buy more. And I'd love for you to work with me on that project as well. And all the ones after that."

I scan Chris' face for any indication that what he just said was some sort of cruel joke. Or maybe he said it just to make me feel better. But once again, he looks absolutely truthful.

"That is, if you aren't already buying up properties yourself. I would hate to get into a bidding war with you."

Chris winks, and I laugh for like the millionth time

tonight. Even though I still had a lot to figure out, I feel my worries starting to fade. Knowing that Chris respects me and believes in me makes me think that there are other people out there that might feel the same. And that maybe one day it might be possible for me to actually make it big, just like I have always dreamed of.

"You would really want to hire me again?"

Chris reaches for my hand again, and wraps both of his around mine.

"I wouldn't say hire, more like be partners."

My mouth falls wide open. *Partners.* I keep repeating the words in my head, over and over and over. My heart swells with praise as I envision what it would be like to work on a project that I owned a part of. I also imagine the thrill of holding my future in my own hands. And as scary and uncertain as real estate was, knowing that Chris and I would be doing it together makes me even more excited.

"Yes, I'd love to be your partner!" I say as I jump into Chris' arms.

The second his arms wrap around my body and I feel the hardness of his chest, I remember exactly where we left off in Chris' house. I grab Chris by the hand, and yank him in the direction of his front door.

"Come on, let's go home."

We both take off running. Chris' hands tremble with anticipation as he puts his key into the lock. The second the door closes behind us, I squeal with delight.

"I meant it before, when I said that I wanted you to fuck me." I whisper seductively to Chris as I kick off my shoes.

"Good, because I want to..." Chris comes up behind me, and I feel his hands on my ass.

I wait for him to finish his sentence, and when he doesn't, I know that can only mean one thing.

"Ok, well if you're still having second thoughts, I'm not going to force you." I smack his hand away from my ass, and move out of his reach.

"No, its just I've fucked girls in the past. Like random girls. But this is different Lane, because it's you."

My feet feel frozen under me. I stop to take in what he just said. It was true, in a way. As I think back to all the times in the past when I thought about sleeping with Chris, I never really thought of it as 'fucking'. I search my brain for a suitable synonym.

"Ok, do you want to make love to me?" I blurt while stroking my neck with my fingers.

The minute I say it, Chris' jaw drops. I want to kick myself for saying the 'L' word to a guy I've never even been on a date with. I wouldn't be surprised if he turned and ran away from me right now. Which would be even weirder since we're in his house.

"No, I didn't mean love. I meant, make..." babies is the only other term that comes to mind, but I know much better than to say that word. What the hell is wrong with me? I can't blame this on the tequila anymore. It was like just being around Chris makes me act like a drunken idiot, even when I'm sober.

"No Lane, I want to make love to you. More than anything I've ever wanted in my entire life."

Chris lunges for me and our mouths collide. His tongue devours mine as his hands begin to unbutton my shirt. It feels like an eternity before he undoes the first one, so I start at the bottom of my shirt to help him out. I do my best to undo the buttons as fast as humanly possible while still maintaining the contact of our kiss.

"Please make love to me." I whisper.

The next thing I feel is Chris' hands on my ass lifting

me up. I squeal as my legs instinctively wrap around his waist. I feel weightless as he effortlessly takes off for the stairs.

Once we make it to his room, he throws me down onto his mattress. I sink into the down comforter and bite my lip as I watch him pull his shirt off over his head. I watch as his stomach muscles flex as he throws his shirt onto the floor. His biceps look as big as a tree trunk. Even the slightest movements cause his muscles to ripple.

I throw open my own shirt and hear the sound of a button popping off. I must have missed one or two in my hurry. But I don't care, the only thing that matters now is being naked. I want there to be nothing between Chris and me.

Chris' cock stands up straight once it's finally freed from his boxers. It's so long and hard, that for a minute I worry it might not even fit inside me. But I know that I damn sure want to try. I reach for it, but Chris pushes me gently backwards back onto the bed.

"No, I want to make sure you're good and wet for me."

I close my eyes as his hands find my pussy. He rubs his fingers over my swollen bud as heat shoots through my entire body.

"Oh my god," I scream.

"Just keep your legs open." He tells me, using his elbows to spread them wide.

His fingers swirl inside of me, and I feel myself gushing all over my inner thighs. As good as this feels, I know that I want more.

"Please Chris. Please." I beg.

I hear Chris laugh as he climbs on top of me. He runs the tips of his massive cock around my slick opening. I thrash and wiggle underneath him. The anticipation is driving me absolutely crazy. I wrap my legs around his waist and do everything possible to pull him into me.

"Tell me what you want, Lane."

My eyes open so wide it feels like they might fall out of my head. He knows what I want, but I'm prepared to do whatever it takes to get it.

"Stick it in me."

"You can do better than that." He says with a wicked grin as he brings himself to the entrance of my pussy and stops.

"Pound me."

"That's better."

With that, Chris drives himself into me. The feeling of his rock hard cock inside of me is such a shock to my body that at first, I can hardly move. Chris remains still, giving my pussy a chance to adjust to the feeling of being so full. After a few seconds my body has acclimated and I want more.

"You're so fucking tight Lane." Chris says as he moves around gently inside of me.

"Maybe you're just really big."

Chris moans and moves his hips backwards, pulling his cock out ever so slightly, right before he drives it back inside of me.

The sensation is so overwhelming, that all I can do is scream. I scream so hard my voice starts to sound hoarse.

"Are you ok?" Chris asks as he kisses my forehead.

"More please." I beg, sounding more hoarse with each word.

Chris wraps his arms around me pulling me up and into his chest. I wrap my legs tighter around him and all the sudden, I feel my body being lifted.

The next thing I know, Chris is walking across his bedroom floor with me firmly wrapped around him. His cock is still inside my pussy, so I hold on tightly with my legs. I feel the coldness of my back pressing up against the wall. Chris presses me up against it harder, burying himself even deeper inside of me.

"Don't drop me." I say once I realize that he's going to be doing me up against the wall.

"Never."

I close my eyes and move myself up and down as I grab onto his shoulders. I feel like a rag doll as he effortlessly bounces me up and down, driving his cock in and out of me. He moves so quickly that I almost forget where I am. The pleasure overtakes me and I feel an orgasm building inside of me. I scream as it comes close and closer, until I finally explode in a wave of pleasure.

"Cum for me baby."

My body goes limp in Chris' arms. I no longer have the strength to move, but Chris continues to hold me. He rams himself in and out of my body in a perfect rhythm. The feeling is so intense that I want it to continue forever. I already know that I never want to leave Chris' arms. His grip on me is so tight, that I never once feel like I might fall. I can't imagine the amount of strength and energy it takes to do what he is doing now. But he keeps on going and going.

Chris' pace increases and he begins to groan. I can tell by the way his entire body tenses that he is close.

"I'm on the pill. You can cum inside me." I scream.

My own words catch me by surprise, so I open my eyes to make sure I didn't scare Chris. When our eyes meet, his are locked on mine. He licks his lips as he nods his head.

"I have a huge load for you." He says, and he thrusts long and hard into me. I feel the wetness spewing from his cock as he pulls me in closer to his body.

When he's done, he carries me back to the bed where we both collapse. I can feel sticky sweat covering his skin as he pulls me onto his chest. But I don't care. I put my ear to his chest to listen to the rapid beat of his heart.

"That was amazing."

"Yeah that was a first for me, having you cum inside me." I say as his seed trickles down my inner thighs.

Chris grabs me by the back of my head and forces it upward until I am looking him dead in the eyes.

"I want to be the only guy that ever cums inside of you."

The thought of any other guy doing what Chris just did to me makes me shiver with disgust. Even though I had never planned on letting Chris do that, it just felt so right. And the fact that he was the first and only guy to ever do that to me made my nipples harden.

"Deal," I say with a laugh as I give him my hand for a shake. Chris grabs my outstretched hand and kisses my palm.

"No, I'm serious. I want to make love to you all the time, and be the only one that gets to, ever."

"So we'd be partners in business, and in life."

Chris smiles as he strokes the top of my head with a tenderness that I never could have guessed he possessed.

"You could say that. But you are amazing, Lane. I want to do this right. I want to take you out on dates... treat you like a princess."

I lay my head back into the pillow as I savor his words.

"And when we're done with this project, I want to spoil you rotten. I'll take you to any restaurant you want, buy you a new wardrobe, whatever you'd like."

I smile so hard my cheeks begin to hurt. I know better than to kill the mood by saying this out loud, but I don't really like fancy restaurants. The portions are always so small, and the food takes forever. Even though I know my wardrobe needs some work, I do have Ashley's closet at my disposal. But hearing Chris say that he wants to spoil me was everything. This is the happiest I have ever felt in my entire life.

"Well, I'd rather you just save your money. So we can get started on our next project sooner."

I sit up and grab the sides of Chris' gorgeous face. He plants a huge kiss directly on my mouth. His hands move to the sides of my face, and he lightly strokes my cheeks.

"Pretty big day for me, getting a girlfriend and a business partner."

I sit up straight when I hear that word.

"So I'm your girlfriend?"

"We can work out the details later sweetheart. I'm exhausted." Chris says as he stretches his arms over his head and every muscle in his chest and stomach pops.

"Sweetheart?" I say, as a huge smile stretches across my face.

"Uh yeah sorry, if you don't like that one-"

"No, I do."

I lean over and give him another kiss on the top of his head. Chris closes his eyes, and looks so peaceful. I can tell he's going to be asleep in no time.

"Ok, I'd better get going."

I go to stand, but Chris grabs me by the arm and pulls me right back into bed next to him.

"You're staying right fucking here tonight. Part of the whole girlfriend thing."

I smile as I lay against his chest. I have never been anyone's girlfriend before. I used to think that girls who went around looking for boyfriends were silly and unambitious. But of all the things I've accomplished in my life, hearing Chris call me his girlfriend is probably the most satisfying.

"And Lane, I mean it when I say I don't want you to worry about a thing. You're my girlfriend now, and I'm going to take care of you. I don't want you to worry about a job or money, or anything like that. Once this renovation is done, I'll have plenty of money to take care of you."

My mouth falls open as he speaks. The truth is, I was without a job and should be doing nothing but worrying until I found another. But knowing I have a boyfriend like Chris actually makes it possible for me to relax. I curl up along his side, and put my ear to his chest to listen to the sound of his heart beating. *Everything is going to be ok*, I tell myself. Chris and I are going to knock this project out of the park, and take on the world of real estate together. There's no telling what we will be able to accomplish together. Everything is finally falling into place.

Thinking about all we have ahead of us is making me too excited to sleep. I sit up straight in bed, and am just about to ask Chris if he'd like to watch a movie when I hear snoring.

I try to lay down again just as I remember that my roommates will be worried if I don't come home tonight. I sneak downstairs to grab my phone from my purse. I text Ashley and Heidi both a message.

'Long story ladies, but I'm spending the night at my boyfriend's. I'll explain in the morning. Love you!'

Then I tiptoe back upstairs, and climb back into bed next to Chris. And even though I'm overcome with excitement, once I lay down next to Chris, it doesn't take long for me to fall into the most peaceful sleep of my life.

19

CHRIS

I tiptoe across the floor of my bedroom, trying to be as quiet as humanly possible and not wake Lane. Just as I'm halfway across the room, an uncontrollable urge to go back and take one more look at Lane in bed comes over me. I take two steps back towards the bed, and see that she is still sleeping like a baby. Her brown hair cascades across the pillow, and both of her hands are tucked under her cheeks. I take one more step closer so I can watch Lane's chest rise and fall as she breathes. Never could I have thought watching someone breathe would be so captivating.

After a few minutes of just staring at Lane, I check the time and know that I need to head downstairs. I hear the crew arriving in their trucks outside, and I always like to touch base with them before they get started for the day. Up until last week, talking with the crew just felt like work. But, for the last five days, I've had Lane by my side each morning. And not just for practical reasons. Sure, it's been such a huge time saver having her right there whenever Carl has any questions. She always has an answer, and I don't have to try and email her while she's at work and wait for a reply. Lane losing her job was the best thing that could have happened. It's such a comfort knowing that I have a partner in life, and in work. Especially one as smart and sexy as Lane. We are an unstoppable team, and I need to make sure that Lane is by my side every morning for the rest of my life.

Except for this morning, I want to let her sleep in. She looks so peaceful curled up in my bed that it would be a real shame to wake her up. So I turn once again and head for the bedroom door. Two steps in, one of the floorboards creak, causing Lane to stir in bed. I stop where I am, and hope that she will go back to sleep.

"What, who's there?" Lane asks in her sleepy voice as she rubs her eyes.

"Just me sweetheart. You can go back to sleep, I was just going to talk to Carl."

Lane pushes the blankets off of her body, and the sight of her dressed only in a white tank top and thong gives me an instant hard on. I still can't believe that I am lucky enough to have Lane in my bed every night. Never could I have thought I'd want to spend all day and all night with one person before. I always thought I'd get sick of anyone having them around so much. But with Lane, it was amazing. I just couldn't get enough of her.

"Just give me five minutes to get dressed and I'll come with you." Lane says as she hoists her legs over the side of the bed.

"No you should stay in bed."

I walk over to the side of the bed to give her a kiss, but the moment I see her hard nipples, I know I have to have her. I reach down between her legs, and sure enough, the lace crotch of her panties are soaked.

"And what were you dreaming about last night?" I

whisper in her ear and I begin to stroke her through the lace.

"I don't need a dream to get wet sleeping next to you."

Fuck. My cock throbs as I continue to finger Lane's pussy. Lane throws her head back, just as we hear the front door downstairs opening. The guys were here and going to start working. Lane looks at me with her eyes wide.

"It's ok, they can get started without us. Think you can be quiet?" I ask Lane.

She bites her lip and nods her head, indicating to me that she knows exactly what to do. This has become a favorite game of ours over the last week; I try to get Lane off while she tries not to make a sound. She took it very seriously, and up until this point she has never made a peep. Little did she know that I was determined to make her lose control and scream at the top of her lungs. I didn't give a shit what anyone heard. Lane was my girlfriend now, and no one was going to tell me when I made her cum. I owe it to her to give her whatever she wanted, whenever she wanted.

"How's that?" I ask Lane as she begins to buck her hips wildly.

"Mmmm." She moans with her eyes closed.

My cock twitches again as I watch her concentrate. I know it wouldn't be much longer till she exploded, so I pick up the pace, moving my fingers faster and faster.

Lane moans again, but as quietly as a mouse. So I pull her hair until her ear is up against my lips.

"Keep it down." I tease her, knowing how much it will turn her on.

Her pussy gushes even more, and I keep stroking her bud. I can tell she's right on the edge when we hear Carl.

"Boss you up there?" He yells up the stairs.

I look at Lane and I am about to stop when I see she is

very close. I know there's no stopping her now. She bites down on my shoulder which muffles her screams as she explodes.

"Good girl." I whisper as I stroke her hair.

Lane lays back in bed as she catches her breath.

"Be right there Carl." I give Lane one last kiss before I run into the bathroom to wash my hands and head downstairs.

"Sorry boss, didn't mean to wake you." Carl says when I enter the kitchen.

"No, worries. What are you guys working on today?"

"New light fixtures came in, so we'll get to installing those."

I nod as Carl fills me in on what they have planned for the rest of the week. While I don't understand everything, I am just relieved that never once do I hear him say anything is backordered or behind schedule.

Carl told us last week that there was a very good chance we might be finished in a month, which is an entire month ahead of schedule. I was sure that after all the problems we faced early on that we would never finish in time. But with Lane by my side, we had really picked up our pace. Getting these houses on the market early would save us a lot of money. Which was a very good thing, since I was running very short on cash. With Lane as my girlfriend, I knew I had to treat her right. During our first week as an official couple, I took her to dinner three times and even sent her to get a massage. Even though it wasn't cheap, I knew once the houses were sold I'd have more than enough cash to take care of her in style. Which is what she deserved.

"Morning." I hear Lane's chipper voice as she comes down the stairs.

"Hi Lane." Carl says.

Lane flashes him a smile as she heads directly towards me. She stands on her tippy toes and gives me a kiss on the cheek.

"I was thinking of going to spin this morning. That is, if you guys can manage without me for an hour."

"Yes, go enjoy. We'll be fine."

Lane smiles as she gets her water bottle and heads out the door. I spend the next hour browsing house listings to get an idea of what we should list the houses for when they're done. Then I hear a knock at the door.

"Dad." I say when I see my father.

"Hey Chris, I had a showing down the street and wanted to check in. Seems like everything is really coming together."

My dad looks around, and I can tell from the way he nods his head as he looks that he is pleased.

"It looks like we might finish ahead of schedule."

"That's excellent for your first project. That shows you have great management skills."

My dad reaches for my hand and shakes it. As much as I love seeing him proud, I know I can't take all of the credit.

"You know Dad, it's really Lane you should be congratulating. She's really been the one who has kept us on track."

"I'd like to meet this project manager of yours."

I continue to shake my dad's hand longer than necessary as I debate sharing my big news with him.

"Well actually, I've been meaning to talk to you about Lane. She's more than just my project manager. She's actually my girlfriend."

I feel myself standing tall as I tell my dad the good news. I haven't called anyone my girlfriend since college when I dated our school's biggest party girl named Larissa. That didn't exactly turn out well, given how different our goals were. I was going to school to get a degree, and Larissa was there to have a good time and land a husband. I wish I had listened to my dad sooner when he tired to warn me about dating Larissa, but I was twenty-two and stupid.

This time, things were very different. Lane had goals, maybe even ones loftier than mine. She wanted to work hard, and she inspired me to work harder than I ever thought possible.

I just hoped my dad would understand. I look at him, eager to see his reaction. He presses his lips together as he tilts his head to the right.

"Girlfriend?" He finally asks.

"Yes."

Dad walks over to me and puts his hand on my shoulder.

"Chris. I know it's natural at your age to desire female company, but right now is not the right time. Look how far you are. You've worked too hard now to risk getting distracted."

I feel my hands balling into fists at my sides. It was beyond infuriating to hear my dad refer to Lane as a distraction. Although, I sort of understood where he was coming from.

"Dad, I'm not a college kid anymore. I know what the stakes are-"

"I know you think that Chris. But I also would have never guessed in a million years that when you were a junior in college you would have gone to a concert the night before your final exams and slept through them all. You knew how much I was paying for you to go to school, and to have to pay for another full semester because you were too hungover..."

I turn around so I don't have to face my dad. Missing my

finals and failing an entire semester of college was one of the lowest points in my life. I still feel the shame as if it were yesterday. I had studied like a mad man the entire week before my exams, and I know if I hadn't been hungover I would have aced them all. But the night before Larissa called me all excited that her favorite band was playing at a bar downtown. She begged me to take her and promised me we'd be home at a reasonable time. I thought she understood how important my grades were to me. And the fact that she had her exams the next day as well made it even easier for me to believe her.

But after a few beers and shots, that night went from just a concert to an all out bender. Larissa had a power over me that I still can't explain to this day. I actually felt completely out of control when it came to her, like I physically couldn't say no. Whenever I tried, it never went well. But after failing an entire semester and being placed on academic probation, I finally had the balls to break up with her. I didn't feel anything as she sobbed and begged me for another chance. The whole thing was so awful that I vowed I would never make that mistake again.

"Dad, what I did was inexcusable. I don't know how many times I can tell you that I'm sorry and that I've learned my lesson. But Lane is different. She works even harder than I do."

With my back still turned to my father, I hear him walking towards the kitchen. Next thing I hear is the sound of cabinets opening and closing.

"These look nice, almost brand new. Smart decision to paint these instead of getting new ones."

I walk towards him.

"Yes. It was Lane's idea. A whole lot cheaper than new cabinets."

My dad looks closely at the handles that Lane and I picked out together. I start to think back to that night, and how Lane wanted to pretend like we were a married couple for the sales lady. And how dinner that night was the easiest conversation I have ever had. It was still hard to believe how far we'd come in such a short amount of time. I now have a lifetime of doing errands and eating romantic dinners with Lane. I shake my head as I once again try to wrap my brain around the fact that Lane is finally mine.

"So when can I meet this Lane?" my dad asks.

"She'll actually be here soon. She just went to the gym."

I reach into my pants pocket to check the time on my phone. I grin like an idiot when I see Lane's name flash on the screen. Even though its only been an hour and a half since Lane left my place this morning to go to spin class, I already can't fucking wait to see her again.

I hastily unlock my phone to read my message from Lane.

'Stopping for coffee, want your usual? :)'

'You're the best! Yes, and hurry your tight ass home.'

I feel bad the minute I press the send button. It was crazy of me to tell her to hurry. The last thing I wanted to do was make her feel suffocated. I just hoped my feelings for her weren't too much.

'Be there in five :)'

I tuck my phone back into my pocket while Dad and I head outside just as Carl is grabbing some tools out of his truck.

What the fuck, I think to myself when I notice the same woman in a black hooded sweatshirt that keeps showing up and just staring at the construction crew. This is getting out of hand. When the woman catches me staring, she adjusts her baseball cap, and a bunch of weird gray and pink hair falls out. She didn't look that old, but maybe she was just a confused old lady. I decided it's best to ignore her for now.

"Good news, if the new doors come in next week, I think we'll be able to finish by the end of the month." Carl says, as he pats me on the back.

"That is great news. Getting these houses on the market before the holidays will help them sell fast. I've already taken out a full page ad in the real estate section of the paper for the week we list." My dad tells me proudly.

"That's a great idea dad. We need to generate as much interest as possible."

I take a deep breath as I imagine how good it will feel to finally be finished. Even though Dad was pretty confident that we were going to make a great return on my investment, there was still time for something to go wrong. The faster we got this wrapped up, the better. I still spent far too much time at night awake worrying about all the things that could still go wrong. And what it could end up costing me.

Just as Dad and I turn to go back into the house, we both turn as we hear the sound of a vehicle approaching. We are both facing the street just as two men wearing hard hats and vest approach.

"Excuse me, which one of you is Chris Dunkirk?" A guy with a large stack of papers asks.

"Me." I say, as he puts the thick stack of papers in my hand.

"We're with the city. We received a tip that your sewer lines may not be up to code. I'm sorry, but we have to shut you down until we can investigate."

My heart hammers in my chest as adrenaline fills my veins. *Shut us down.* Did that mean we couldn't keep working? We couldn't afford to fall behind schedule. Not when we were this close.

"No, there has to be some sort of mistake. Carl, take a look at this." I say, throwing the stack of papers into Carls' hands.

He flips through the first few pages and runs a hand through his hair.

"Sorry boss. They're with the city. What they say goes."

"Surely we can still paint while you conduct your investigation. Painting has nothing to do with the sewers." My dad asks the inspectors with a hopeful look on his face.

"No, you have to stop everything until we finish."

I kick a rock on the ground in front of me with entirely too much force and let out a string of expletives.

"How long will this take?" I ask.

"A week tops. We have to dig up the line so we can perform a full diagnostic."

I do my best to focus as the inspector continues, even though I'm not sure about anything he is saying. Lane will know, I try to reassure myself. She'll know exactly what to do. She had been bugging me non stop about the sewers since she started. I'm sure she'll get a kick out of the fact that they are finally being looked at.

"Ok, just go ahead and get started." I say to the inspectors as they head into the first unit that was formerly occupied by a woman named Lindsay. I never got a chance to meet her, apparently she was pretty pissed off when I gave her thirty days notice to vacate. She left as soon as she could, probably to spite me. Little did she know that it actually helped me to have the unit vacated sooner.

I watch in a daze as Carl tells his crew to pack up. They fill their trucks with their equipment and climb in. Carl hands me the stack of papers, and its all I can do not to rip them in fucking half.

I flip through the papers, desperate for some answers.

Who the hell would place a tip to the city? And why would the city just believe them? A week was a long time to waste. And they probably wouldn't even find anything. Unless... what if Lane had been right all this time? What if there was something wrong with the sewer? I feel dizzy as I think about what that might cost, and the extra time. We were already losing a week.

I continue to flip through the papers frantically, almost ripping the staples out as I turn the pages. I stop when I see a copy of an email on the second to last page.

'To whom it may concern.'

I scan the body of the email since my brain is on overload. I almost give up until I see the last line of the email.

'Best, Lane.'

Lane tipped off the city. The thought of being betrayed by someone I thought had my back is a literal punch to the gut. I double over as the magnitude of what this means sinks in. I try to look down at the paper again to see if I read it wrong, but my hands are shaking too hard.

"Hey there, stud." I hear a familiar voice and stand up.

As I turn around, I see Lane in her sweaty workout clothes with a cup of coffee in each hand. She stops at the corner as she looks around at Carl and his crew. The color drains from her face when her eyes land on the car that reads City Inspectors.

"Chris, what are they doing here? Where's Carl?"

I watch as Lane's massive chest rises and falls. At least she feels guilty seeing what she has done. But it makes me sick to my stomach the way she has the nerve to ask me what they were doing here. As if she didn't damn well know.

"You!" I point my shaking finger in Lane's direction. "This is all your fault."

I take a step towards Lane, and she takes two steps backwards dropping both coffees.

"Let's calm down, I'm sure there's a reasonable explanation. I'll go talk to them."

Lane attempts to walk around me and towards the house, but I grab her by the arm.

"Like hell you are. You've done enough."

Lane's eyebrows arch as she looks down at my hand on her arm.

"What do you mean? I know this is bad, but we can handle it,"

We. I let out a small chuckle when I hear the word. There is no more 'we'. Lane made it perfectly clear when she ratted me out to the city that we were no longer a team. I am now all alone again, in my business and in my life. The way it should have been all along.

Lane goes to take another step and I tighten my grip on her arm.

"Let go of me Chris. You're scaring me."

I drop her arm like it's on fire and it falls to her side. No matter what she did, she didn't deserve to be scared of me. I hate the feeling of rage building inside of me. It's so intense, it's like I might lose complete control at any second.

"I don't want to hear another word from you ever again Lane. You need to go back home, pack your shit, and vacate my house within the next thirty days."

Lane's eyes widen and her lower lip trembles. Even though she is a filthy liar that just screwed me over royalty, the sight of her on the edge of tears still causes my throat to feel tight. I need to get as far away from her as possible just to be able to breathe.

"Chris, please don't do this. I have no idea..."

I walk closer to Lane, and she almost falls backwards trying to maintain some distance between us.

"Shut your filthy fucking..."

"Chris, that's enough."

I hear my dad approaching from behind. He is the last person on the planet I want to face right now.

"Dad, sorry. Lane was just leaving."

Lane looks to my father and back at me with her eyes still wide.

"So this is Lane? Nice to meet you." Dad extends his hand and Lane looks at it with her eyes full of tears.

The look of confusion on my dad's face makes me feel sorry for him, since there's no way he can possibly have any idea what is going on.

"It's ok dad. You were right. Let's go."

I turn and head back to my house with my dad close behind. As I slam the door, I'm pretty sure I hear Lane sobbing. *It's ok,* I tell myself. *She is a lying bitch. She deserves to cry.* No matter how many times I repeat this is my head, it's not helping the massive knots in my stomach.

"What was that about?"

My dad finally asks once we're inside.

"Lane was the fucking one who tipped off the city. Here," I throw the stack of papers containing Lane's email on the kitchen table. My dad's mouth moves as he reads it.

"Why would she do such a thing? She works for you."

"Exactly. I don't have a fucking clue."

I yank so hard on my hair that I wouldn't be surprised if I ripped it all out of my head as I pace back and forth across the kitchen floor.

"Well let's not dwell on the past. Let's move forward. First thing you need to do is formally terminate her, and give her a written notice to leave in thirty days."

"You're right." I have to hand it to my dad for being able to remain so calm and composed. I wouldn't even have blamed him if he went into an 'I told you so' rant. But instead, he has kept his focus and is actually helping me do what needs to be done. Starting with getting Lane out of my life for good.

I grab my computer, and begin typing an email to Lane notifying her that she is relieved of all duties. Then I forward her the same letter I sent to the rest of my tenants informing them that they had thirty days to vacate. Right after both are sent, I add Lane's email address to my junk folder, ensuring anything I receive from her won't appear in my inbox. Then I block her number from my phone.

I lean back in my kitchen chair and let out a huge sigh of relief once it's all done. Dad comes up behind me and pats me on the shoulder.

"I'm sorry son for what happened. But it could have turned out a whole lot worse. At least it's over now, and you can focus on what you need to do."

"That's right. No more distractions. I'm going to finish this project no matter what."

I reach up and pat my Dad's hand. He is the only person in this world who will have my back no matter what. And he is all that I need. I am going to achieve what we set out to do no matter what. No more distractions this time.

20

LANE

I turn off the TV as soon as I hear Ashley's keys in the door. I glance up at the clock and jump up when I realize it's already after five and I still haven't dressed or showered. In fact, all I've done today is watch trashy TV and eat pizza in my pjs. Which isn't really all that different from what I did yesterday or the day before. At least I don't think it was. It's hard to say for sure since all of my days seem to run together.

"Hey, you ready?" Ashley asks as she looks me up and down and shakes her head.

"Sorry, I'll be dressed by the time Heidi gets home."

I run up stairs, throw on some sweats and search for a clean t-shirt in the massive pile of laundry that is on top of my bed. I feel a sense of disgust rising in my gut as I look around at the mess. I had never in my entire life let my room look like this. And you would think that given how much free time I'd have over the last week I would have had time to do laundry, or at least pick up all the dirty dishes in my room. But I've had zero motivation to do anything. Each time I try to do anything productive, my body literally aches and I end up in a puddle of tears. Even just thinking about what a waste of space I've become causes my eyes to sting.

I shake my head and force all of the negative thoughts from my brain. This isn't a time to sit around and feel sorry for myself. We had exactly twenty days left to find a place to live. If we didn't do that, we'd end up on the streets. Then I'd really have something to cry about.

"Ready." I say in my most enthusiastic voice. I even manage a smile when I see Heidi is home.

"Hey, this came for you in the mail today. Looks important, it's from a law firm." Ashley says, holding a plain white envelope in my direction.

I stare at the piece of mail, wishing I had some sort of x-ray vision and I could read the letter without having to open the envelope. What if Chris had hired a lawyer to sue me? He was the only person I could think of who would want to do such a thing. I feel a lump forming in my throat trying to cut off my oxygen supply.

"Here, let me," Ashley says as she rips the top open.

I stare at her, feeling as though my feet are glued to the floor. Ashley unfolds a single piece of paper, scans it, before smiling and handing it over to me.

"You won't believe this!" she says.

My eyes open so wide that it feels like they might fall out of my head.

"Looks like you'll be receiving some money from that doggie boutique you invested in. The one that went bankrupt."

I snatch the letter from Ashley's hand. I need to see this for myself. When I received the news last year that the business I had invested most of my savings in was filing for bankruptcy, I thought I'd never see a penny. But according to this letter, I would be receiving a check in about a week. Once all of the assets have been liquidated.

"See a silver lining!" Heidi says.

I stare at the letter, grateful to finally have some good news. Maybe I'd get enough money out of the settlement to at least stay a float for a few months. Or even better, if I got my full investment back, maybe it would be enough to buy an investment property of my own.

The thought causes me to crack a smile. I know I should be more excited, but I can't even muster up enough enthusiasm to smile fully. It's like my brain is no longer able to believe anything good can actually happen to me. That is, without something else going terribly wrong.

"We'd better get going. Lindsay warned us that the bus to Manayunk usually runs late." Ashley says with a heavy sigh.

I try once again to give myself a pep talk, but nothing about looking at a rental in Manayunk makes me feel better. I just hope this place looks as good as it did in the pictures our realtor sent to us. Even though the location was less than ideal, it was a four bedroom house that was available immediately, and within our budget. We were lucky to at least have an option. Everything about it was promising, except the fact that it was in Manayunk. That meant we'd be surrounded by college kids, and we'd be forty five minutes from downtown and any decent bars or restaurants. It was like we were being sent off into exile.

"What bus number are we taking again?" Heidi asks as we head down the street.

"I think the sixty-four. And that takes up to Market Street where we transfer to the thirty-two. And that lets us off about four blocks from the house." I remind my roommates of the instructions I so carefully memorized from

Lindsay. The one good thing about the location of the house we were seeing was that it was on the same street as Lindsay's. We'd get to be neighbors again.

We finish walking up to the corner, and wait for our first bus which ends up arriving ten minutes late. Which causes us to miss our next bus. When we finally arrive, we are fifteen minutes late. Luckily our realtor is still there waiting, and so is Lindsay.

"Sorry about that, we finally made it!" Ashley yells as she runs towards Lindsay with open arms.

"Wow, I love this new look." Heidi says as she runs her fingers through Lindsay's new pink highlights. The rest of her hair is mostly still blonde, but also has a fair amount of silver highlights. Which sounds like a bit much, but somehow it really works on Lindsay.

"Thanks lady! I actually found an awesome salon just around the corner. Manayunk isn't all bad!"

My roommates and I smile sweetly at Lindsay as we follow our realtor inside the house. It is a single family house with four large bedrooms and a big front porch. There is even a small yard off the kitchen in the back. The front of the house looks a little more run down than it did in the pictures, but I do my best to keep an open mind as we follow the realtor inside.

"As you can see, the living room is very spacious. And here is the dining room." our realtor says as we look around.

"A dining room? We hardly even had room for a kitchen table in the city." I say, doing my best to focus on the positives.

I turn towards Ashley and Heidi, who are both looking inside the hall closet with their arms folded across their chests. The realtor shows us the kitchen which is full of new stainless steel appliances and has granite countertops.

It's almost nice enough to make me want to learn how to cook.

"Let's go upstairs." Ashley follows close behind me as we make our way up. All four bedrooms are equal in size, and best of all, they each have a walk in closet.

"Ok, this is a plus." Ashley says as she walks into one of the closets.

"You could actually fit all of your clothes in here. Instead of having to keep your off season stuff in the basement."

I look at Ashley, expecting her to appear as excited as I feel. She closes the closet door and flashes a smile that seems forced.

"So ladies, what do you think? I know you don't have much time, and the owner has three other showings today. So if you like it, you'd better move fast." The realtor asks once we are back downstairs.

"I think we'd be stupid not to take it. Right ladies?"

Our realtor looks at Ashley as she opens the front door.

"Let's talk outside."

As we walk back to the front porch to discuss, we hear a bunch of yelling. We look to the yard next store, and see about ten guys in their early twenties setting up a long plastic inflatable slide. Then they fill it with beer from red plastic cups as the first guy gets ready to take a running leap and slide down it.

"Hey ladies, you want to come join us?" They yell from across the yard, followed by a bunch of hollowing.

"Ugh no thanks." Ashley says with her nose upturned.

The hollering continues as we turn our backs to the guys, and do our best to pretend we don't hear them. As if that was even possible.

"You get used to it." Lindsay says as she rolls her eyes. "So anyway, what are you guys going to do?"

I look at Ashley who turns to Heidi. Both of them just stare at each other silently with their lips pressed together, as if they are waiting for the other to speak first.

"Well, I just don't know what else we can find in our price range that's available..." Heidi finally says.

"Really? You guys like this place?"

"No, but if we all get to live together, that's what matters." Ashley says as she attempts to wrap her arms around my shoulder.

I'm just about to jump up and down when I realize what they are doing. They are offering to give up their lives and all the comforts of city living for me. And while it is incredibly sweet of them, it would be selfish of me to take them up on it. I care far too much about Heidi and Ashley to let them give up everything just because my life is such a mess. It was all my fault that we only had twenty days to move out. And I was the only one without a job and very little savings. Ashley and Heidi could both afford to live in the city in a fancy building, and maintain a social life. The only thing holding them back was me.

"No. You guys don't belong here. I think it makes more sense that I move back home with my parents. You know, until I get back on my feet."

Ashley and Heidi's mouths drop open.

"Lane you can't do that..." Ashley says.

"No, I can and I should. It makes the most sense. You guys should stay in Center City. It's close to your jobs and it's where you belong. You would be miserable out here." I say, gesturing next door as one of the guys takes a running leap down the beer slip and slide while the rest cheer him on.

I look over at Lindsay who is staring down at the floor. I feel a knot forming in my stomach.

"Sorry Lindsay, I didn't mean..."

"No, it's ok. I get it." She says with a heavy sigh.

"Sounds like you guys have some thinking to do," our realtor says.

"Yeah, what do you say we all grab a drink? Lindsay, know of a good spot around here?" I ask, practically salivating at the thought of a big glass of wine.

"Sure do. No shortage of bars around here."

The four of us set off down the street and find a cute little pub about a block away. It's dark inside and not very crowded. We grab four stools together in a corner far away from the other people at the bar.

"So are you finally going to tell me what happened with Chris? I'm dying to hear." Lindsay asks the minute we are seated.

I take a deep breath in an attempt to hold back the tears I already feel forming in my eyes just from the sound of his name. I know that talking about it again is going to hurt like hell. But I hate leaving Lindsay out of the loop.

"He sort of fired me. Some inspectors from the city just showed up one morning while I was at the gym. They said they wanted to take a look at the sewers, and Chris just started screaming like a maniac that it was all my fault."

I feel the same familiar twisting in my stomach as I relieve our last awful moment together. I close my eyes and try like hell to maintain my composure. I have done enough crying in the last week to last a lifetime. But just thinking back to that morning and how it had started off so perfect was like a punch to the gut. I had never felt so happy in my entire life. I woke up that morning with an amazing boyfriend and job that I cared about immensely. I should have known that it was all too good to be true.

When I finally open my eyes, I am horrified to see

Lindsay snickering. There is nothing even remotely funny about what happened to me.

"Lindsay, are you ok?" Heidi asks, looking as confused as I feel.

"Yeah no. I'm just happy to hear that he finally got what he deserved. Whoever notified the city deserves an award, right Lane?"

Lindsay holds up her hand for a high five, and all the hairs on the back of my neck stand up.

"How do you know that someone notified them?" I ask as my voice begins to tremble.

"I don't know… I mean, I just assumed." Lindsay puts her hand to her mouth as another round of laughter escapes from her throat.

"It's not funny. Lindsay, what do you know about this?" once Lindsay is able to compose herself she looks back over at me. "Lindsay, tell me."

I grab her by the shoulders and shake her lightly to show her I'm serious. Every second that goes by without her saying a word makes it harder for me to breathe.

"Ok fine. I was the one who placed the tip. I emailed them, and I kind of…" Lindsay bursts out laughing so hard that she isn't able to finish the end of her sentence.

"Lindsay you did what?"

I jump up from my seat, no longer able to sit next to someone who could be so conniving and untrustworthy.

"I wrote an email, just letting them know it might be worth looking into."

I pull on my hair and let out a scream that sounds equal parts primal and pathetic. Everyone at the bar turns and looks in my direction, and I don't even care. I have much more important things to worry about now than looking like a crazy person in front of a bunch of strangers. And my behavior over the last week probably qualified me as a legitimate insane person anyway.

"Come on, it was your idea! That's why I signed the email with your name. How was I supposed to know you'd be mad at me?"

My name. It suddenly all makes sense why Chris blamed me. My first thought is to run all the way back to the city and knock on Chris' door and explain to him that it wasn't me. Maybe he'd pull me into his arms and tell me it was all ok. We could go back to exactly the way things were before the inspectors came.

But before I can get my hopes too high, I realize that even though I wasn't the one who wrote the email, I was the one who told Lindsay about the sewer line and put the idea into her head. It was all my fault. And even if I did tell Chris that I wasn't the one who wrote the email, he would still be pissed that I told Lindsay about the sewer line. I'm still the one who is responsible for crushing the dream he worked so hard for. There was no way he'd ever forgive me.

I grab my purse and throw it over my shoulder.

"Come on, let's get out of here." I say to Heidi and Ashley who both jump up from their seats.

Lindsay tries to grab my arm as we head for the door, and I almost punch her in the nose so I can run as far away from her as possible.

"Come on Lane, he deserved to be caught. He should have had the sewer line looked at when he first bought the houses. And you know his dad will just write him a big fat check and he'll be fine." Lindsay says as she waves her hand dismissively in the air.

"No, his dad won't. Because he isn't Richard Dunekirk. His dad is a realtor from New Jersey, and he raised Chris all on his own. Chris and his dad have worked their asses off so that he could have the chance to buy those properties. Being a real estate investor was his dream, and now..."

I feel Ashley's hand on my shoulder as I bury my head in my hands. I finally give in, and let the sobs overtake my body.

"Lane, I did you a favor. Look at what's happened to you. You went from being one of the most ambitious and hard working women I have ever met, to just being someone's girlfriend. Is that really what you want for the rest of your life? To never work again and spend your days sleeping with Chris?"

I lift my head from my hands and look Lindsay directly in the eye. My first reaction is to yell at her, call her every horrible name I know. But when I stop to think about what she just said, part of it hits home. It was true that meeting Chris changed my entire life. Meeting him cost me my job, and reshaped every future dream I had for myself. And as much as I want to blame Lindsay for taking that all away from me, I know I am partly to blame. It was far too risky putting my entire future in Chris' hands.

"Let's get out of here." Ashley says as her and Heidi usher me out of the bar. We walk a few blocks until we find an empty bench to sit on.

"You really liked him, didn't you Lane?" Heidi finally asks.

"I don't know, I think so. Yes." Finally acknowledging it out loud only makes me cry harder.

"I know, it hurts now. But it never would have worked out. Sleeping with your boss never ends well. It's really complicated to separate work and your sex life." Ashley says as she rubs my shoulder.

I start to imagine what would have happened if I had never slept with Chris. What it would have been like if I was just his project manager. We'd still be working on the renovation together, and in a few short weeks we'd be listing the houses and celebrating. But in a very different way if we had never crossed that line by sleeping together.

We'd have just shaken hands once the deal was closed, maybe toasted with some champagne. And when it was over, had we never slept together and fallen for each other, I would have just gone back to my life. A life without him. Somehow thinking of this alternate reality wasn't making me feel any less empty.

"So lesson learned, next time, no sleeping with your boss, no matter how hot he is?" Heidi says.

"No, next time I won't take a job with someone I'm attracted to."

Heidi and Ashley look at one another, but say nothing. I slip into silence as I think about what would have happened if I had rejected Chris' offer that morning when he came to my door and asked me to be his project manager. What would have happened if I had instead just kissed him? That's what I wanted to do ever since that morning I first laid eyes on him at the bank. But instead of just giving into my desires and seeing where they could have led me, I did everything in my power to talk myself out of being attracted to Chris. I told myself that he was just some entitled rich guy who would never know what it meant to work hard and to have big dreams. And I was so incredibly wrong.

If I had just slept with Chris, and not agreed to work for him, I would have gotten to know him without all of the other complications. Even if there was some way to go back in time and do it differently, sleeping with him right away would mean that I would probably still have my boring job at the bank and I would never have discovered my passion for real estate. But there's a chance I'd still have Chris.

The thought is both comforting and painful at the same time. So I give myself permission to hold onto this fantasy. I only hope the small amount of joy I feel from imagining what could have been will be enough to get me through the next few weeks. Because if I continue to feel as miserable as I have over the last week, I'm not sure I will ever be able to get back to the old Lane. And it's a real shame, since the old Lane was sure as hell a lot more pleasant to be around.

21

CHRIS

I hear a car outside, and pull so hard on the cord to open the blinds that cover the widow in the front of my house that I almost pull the whole thing down. It's a good thing I catch myself just in time and stop, because these things cost a fortune. The last thing I needed was one more expense.

My eyes land on a car driving down my street, but it's not the one I am looking for. It's just a regular black sedan, being driven by someone who has no fucking clue where they are going. I curse some more under my breath and go back into the kitchen to wait.

It's been over ten days since the city inspectors first showed up and shut down our renovation. They said it would take a week tops to do their investigation and let us know if anything needed to be addressed. Wondering was literally driving me insane. I can hardly eat, and sleeping was almost entirely out of the question. The minute I lay down at night, my mind runs through every worst case scenario. If the city did determine we needed to dig a new sewer line, it would be expensive. There was no way I'd get my hands on that kind of cash and finish in time. Every month I held onto the houses, I was losing money covering the mortgages.

And even if I did find a way to raise the money, I would have no clue how to find someone to do the job. I wasn't even sure what digging a new sewer meant. If I did have to hire someone, they'd have all sorts of questions that I wouldn't know how to answer. I would need a new project manager, and it was far too late now to hire another one. And I knew in my heart of hearts that whoever I hired next wouldn't hold a candle to Lane. And it would also cost even more money, which again I didn't have. There was no point in even thinking about hiring someone to do that kind of work, since it was out of the question.

I sit back down at my kitchen table, and try to look through the rest of the comps my dad had sent over. He was confident everything with the sewer would be fine, and that we would be finished in no time. He wanted to have the entire listing ready to go.

Part of me feels better seeing him so confident. But I almost can't shake the feeling that even considering the worst case scenario is too much for him. I'm not sure my ego would ever recover from being shut down this close to being finished. The thought of ever trying something like this again when there was a chance I could fail is way too nerve racking to even consider. Being a real estate investor is nothing like I imagined it would be. Because in all the times I dreamed of being here, I never thought failure was an option. How naive I was. Maybe I should just go back to teaching.

I lean back in my chair and take another deep breath. If only I had someone to talk this over with, someone who knew what I was going through. I put my hand on my knee in an attempt to steady my leg which seems to be bouncing up and down on its own. Being this jittery was making it impossible to concentrate on anything. I decide to get up and pace, when I hear a loud knock on the door.

"Boss you in there?" I recognize Carl's voice almost immediately. And while I'm happy he's here and I now have someone to talk to, I really wish it was the inspector.

"Hey Carl." I say as I open the door.

I take my time looking up and down the street as Carl walks into my house. I spot Carl's truck with all of his equipment, and feel immensely hopeful that he showed up expecting to work today. He, like my dad, was convinced the inspector would be giving us the green light today to continue.

"Sorry, I still haven't heard anything. They promised they'd be here at eight this morning, and it's almost..."

I pull my phone out of my pants pocket to check the time.

"Ten after eight. This is ridiculous." I slam the front door shut.

"I'm sure they'll be here any minute. I'll get everything unloaded so we can start the minute they give us the go ahead." Carl says with a confident smile.

"It's been ten days Carl. That can't be good."

"They work for the government. Everything moves at their slow as shit pace since they know they have us by the balls."

Carl goes back to his truck and I watch him from the porch. I practically jump when I hear a car turning onto our street. Sure enough, it's a while pick-up truck with the words 'City Inspector' on the right side. I have to stop myself from running down the street and banging on his car door like a mad man. I promise myself I will act calm, and wait on my steps as it takes what seems like twenty minutes to parallel park his truck.

"Chris." The inspector says crossing the street. "How are you this morning?"

I let out a laugh. What the fuck did he except me to say?

"Depends on what you're going to tell me."

"Ok, so I'll get right to it."

The inspector places his clipboard under his chin as he uses both hands to pull up his pants. He gives them a few good tugs.

"So, I ran the report past my boss this morning. "

I don't care, I want to scream. Why is he dragging this out? Did he decide to work for the city because he enjoys tormenting people? It must be a power thing. This is the only way to get people to give a fuck what he had to say.

"And." I say, nodding my head and doing everything possible to get him to hurry up.

"Well, I have good news and bad news. Which do you want to hear first." He says with a sickening smirk on his face.

My heart hammers in my chest. It's all I can do not to grab him by his fat neck and squeeze it till his face turns red.

"Good news first." Carl announces as he comes up beside me.

"Well, good news is the sewers are old, and backed up. But you should get another fews years out of them with a good cleaning before they need to be replaced."

I close my eyes as Carl pats me on the back. *I was right all along, and Lane was wrong.* I want to walk right over to her front door, tell her the news and gloat in her face. But I knew that if I saw her, I wouldn't feel better at all. I'd feel as miserable as I did that morning when the inspector first showed up, and told me that not only was my project in jeopardy, but I had been stabbed in the back by the one person I trusted more than anyone in the world.

"That means it's back to work. Told you, boss!" Carl runs to his truck, just as the inspector starts again.

"Not so fast, I still have to tell you the bad news."

The knot that has been in the pit of my stomach all week-long twists until I'm pretty sure I'm going to throw up all over the sidewalk.

"There was a small crack in the foundation. That's going to need to be repaired until you can do anything else."

The inspector undoes the clip at the top of his board and removes the large stack of papers. Unable to take the suspense any longer, I turn my back to him. I hear the papers shuffling, and I'm pretty sure Carl is now leafing through them.

"Boss, it's not that bad. I know a guy who can get this fixed for us in no time."

I close my eyes as the reality of what I know I need to do sinks in. I want so badly to find another way out of this, but I know I can't. I have fought for as long and as hard as I possibly can. It was time to admit defeat. There is only so much a guy would take.

"No, it is bad. That would cost money, and I'm completely tapped out."

"Well, until the foundation issue is fixed, I can't authorize any more work here."

I turn to look at the inspector who is once again trying to hoist his pants up over his gigantic stomach. Once they are up, he tightens his belt with a grunt.

"He's right boss." Carl says again.

"Then we have to stop. We'll just list the houses as is, and disclose the foundation issue. We've made enough improvements that I should be able to recoup what I've put into them. And I can move on."

I tug on a fistful of my hair until pain shoots all the way through my scalp. The physical pain is a distraction from the cluster fuck that is going on inside my head. It feels like I may explode any second.

"Your call, boss. I guess I should pack up then?"

I look over at Carl's car once more, at all the supplies for the last few small jobs we were going to finish before listing the houses. One more fresh coat of paint, and some new light fixtures. They were to be the icing on the cake, the small touches that would show the buyers that the houses were move in ready. They were going to help dad sell the houses in no time.

But I couldn't put another penny or another minute of work into these houses. It was time to cut my losses.

"Yes. We're done here."

I turn and walk towards my house and slam the door. I don't want to give that fat fucking inspector the satisfaction of knowing I was defeated. Now everything that I had done over the last five months was all for nothing. We'd have to list the houses as 'investment opportunities', and the only type of buyer who would be willing to take a gamble would be a seasoned investor with a big fat portfolio and a lot of cash. Someone who had enough money to fix the foundation, and was smart enough to see the huge payday that would follow, all from doing a very small amount of work. The same staggering profit I would have made had the fucking city not shown up and put a halt to everything.

I do my best to remind myself that there is still a chance I could break even, and walk away with what I came into this deal with; my down payment. It would be enough to move on to something safer. Safe was exactly what I needed now. Maybe a long-term rental. Nothing flashy, but a property with good bones. I'd start small collecting a few hundred bucks every month and continue to save every penny until I could add to my portfolio. In another fifteen years, maybe I'd have enough to actually live comfortably. If I watched every penny, and I didn't have such miserable luck the next time.

But the more I think about it, the more I realize that safe just doesn't excite me. Safer projects aren't as profitable. But they were less risky. I had already gone big, and had nothing to show for it. It was time to do the smart thing, no matter how much it sucked. Even if it crushed my soul.

I'm just about to pour myself a drink, even though I'm well aware it's way too early when I hear another knock on my door. All I want is to be left alone, so I almost ignore it completely until I hear my dad's voice.

"Chris, is that Carl's truck? Where is he going?"

I bring my arms up behind my head and take a deep breath before going to the door. I know I owe him an explanation.

"Dad, it's over. There's a problem with the foundation."

My dad practically pushes me out of the way to get into the house.

"The foundation? What the hell were they doing looking at that? It has nothing to do with the sewer."

"I don't know. But I'm done. I don't have anything left to fix that, or pay another month of mortgage payments. We have to sell everything as is."

I wait for him to argue with me, but instead he smiles.

"It's ok Chris. We will have these sold in no time. I've got the listing all finished, all we need are pictures."

"Great, let's get someone to photograph the units."

"Yes, but first things first. I already made you an appointment to get a new headshot. I thought we could do it to celebrate once we got the clean inspectors report-"

I bring my fist up and am just about to punch a hole in the fucking wall, until I realize how bad that will look at the showings.

"But we still need one." Dad continues, holding up his hands to let me know I need to calm down. It's amazing how he can keep his cool at a time like this. If there was ever something to be pissed about, this was it.

"A headshot of me? Why?"

"Real estate is a people business. You are your own brand. It's important. And it will help you sell fast."

The thought of anyone seeing the listing for a bunch of half-finished houses with my name attached and a picture was a bitter pill to swallow. I just hope that if I ever do anything else in real estate again, no one will know about this failure. But, if what my dad was saying was correct, and it would help us sell faster, it was a small price to pay.

"Fine, where do we need to go?"

"I'll drive. Just go upstairs, put a suit on and shave."

I run my hands over the stubble on my chin. I usually shaved daily, especially when I was with Lane. Her skin was so soft and delicate, that the last thing I ever wanted her to feel was the roughness of my stubble.

But over the last week, it all just seemed so pointless. I have been on auto-pilot, doing only the things that were critical to surviving.

"Fine."

I run upstairs and take a long shower and shave. I put on my lucky suit, the one my dad gave me when I first graduated from college. It still fits like a glove, and looks impeccably sharp. It was nice for a minute not to look as miserable as I felt.

My dad drives back to New Jersey, to a photography studio of some woman named Amy.

"Amy is the best. She does all the headshots, and most of the pictures for my listings."

I don't even answer him, and we walk inside in silence. My dad checks us in with the receptionist, and I head to the bathroom to look at myself in the mirror one last time. I try unbuttoning my suit jacket entirely and putting my hands in my pockets, doing my best to act natural. But somehow, I still look uncomfortable as hell; like I'm waiting for the dentist to call my name, rather than a real estate investor ready to show his latest renovation project off to the entire world. Even though I was a total failure, I didn't want the entire world to see that in my picture. I needed to project confidence and success, even if it was total bullshit.

As I think back to how I originally imagined this moment, it feels like I have a knife stuck in my rib cage. I thought I'd be celebrating, maybe taking a trip to Atlantic City, going out all night with my friends. I didn't think I'd be right back to square one. Wondering what I was going to do with the rest of my life.

"She's ready for us," my dad says, as he appears behind me in the mirror and pats me on the shoulder.

I shake my arms, and try to remember how I normally stand when there isn't a camera pointed directly at me. Just knowing that this picture will appear on a full page in Philly's largest newspaper makes me forget.

"Let's get this over with."

My dad furrows his brows, but knows better than to say anything to me. I have been a real ass over the last ten days. He didn't deserve to be treated this way, but no matter how hard I try, I can't help myself. I feel like I'm constantly on edge, ready to explode at any minute.

"Amy, I'd like you to meet my son Chris." My dad says as he leads me to a tall blonde in a tight red dress and heels holding a camera with a very long lens.

"Chris, I've heard so much about you from your dad. It's so good to meet you."

Amy extends her hand and looks me over from head to toe and she waits for me to shake it. I decide to do the same, and start at her heels, and look up and down her toned legs.

"Amy has been doing my headshots for years. And when she is able to fit it into her very busy schedule, she even does some of the pictures for my listings. The way she captures natural light is really amazing."

Amy's cheeks redden as she waves her hand in the air.

"Oh stop."

"Where do you want me?"

"Right this way." Amy points to a white backdrop in front of a large light that almost blinds me the minute I look into it.

I walk over to a spot with blue tape on the floor, and stand facing Amy.

"Ok, let's loosen up a bit. And can you try to smile?" she asks, pointing her camera in my direction.

It's so hard for me to force a smile on my face that my cheeks actually strain from the effort.

"Come on, you can do better than that."

I shake my arms at my sides and try to focus. Amy's heels click on the wooden floor as she walks over behind me.

"Relax. This should be fun for you. With a face like yours, getting a good shot will be a piece of cake." Amy says as she begins to rub one of my shoulders.

I know she's trying to get me to relax, but the feel of her hand on me causes me to hunch my shoulders. Amy stops, and walks around the front of me.

"I don't bite, I promise. Unless you like that sort of thing." Amy says with a wink.

It didn't take a genius to see that Amy was flirting with me. And instead of being flattered, I only feel even more annoyed. It was awfully bold of her to just assume I was single, because I sure as shit don't feel that way. All I can think about is what would Lane think if she knew what was going on? Would she be pissed to see another woman putting her hands on me? It was totally obvious that she wanted me badly, but part of me still felt proud that I wasn't even tempted in the least. Which was stupid, since Lane is no longer my girlfriend, or anything to me. But for some reason, imagining Lane feeling jealous does something to me. In some sick and twisted way it makes me feel better. Like Lane deserved to be angry, to know what it felt like to see someone else have what she wanted. The thought of Lane seeing me with Amy was oddly comforting.

"Sorry boss, you tell me exactly what you want me to do," I say to Amy, as I shoot her my best crooked grin.

Amy's entire face lights up, and she brings her camera up to her eye and begins clicking away.

"The camera really loves you." she says as she moves around me getting various angles.

"Well, it has good taste I guess." I say, hoping what I just said didn't come off as too cocky. I usually felt my flirting game was on point, but today, it feels like I am forcing myself.

"Your dad also mentioned you might need some pictures taken of your house, that you have a big listing coming up. I'd love to see your place."

"Yeah, are you free tomorrow night?" I almost kick myself for suggesting she come at night. That probably sounded much more like a date than a photo shoot.

"Yes, although, I need some daylight to do the outdoor pictures. But don't worry, I can stay as long as you need me," she says with another wink.

It was somewhat of a comfort to see that Amy knew what she wanted and wasn't being subtle. The thought of actually sleeping with her does nothing for me, but I keep thinking about what it would do to Lane if she somehow saw Amy while she was over. She'd get the wrong idea for sure, and hopefully be seething.

"Great, how's around seven?"

"Perfect." Amy says as she squeezes my arm and nods her head in approval at my biceps.

"Are we done?" I ask when Amy lowers her camera.

"If you want-"

"Good." I head directly for the exit, not even stopping to tell my dad we're done. I just needed this all to be over, so I can move on with my life and put this nightmare behind me. As unlikely as that seems, the hope of forgetting is what's keeping me going. I sure as hell can't spend the rest of my life feeling like this.

22

LANE

I take one last deep breath as I try to mentally prepare myself to knock on my parent's front door. Even though their house in South Philly was only about four miles from where I had been living in Center City, it felt like a totally different world.

As I look at the flower boxes under the front windows of my parents' row home, I can almost see my mom lovingly watering her flowers each day. My mom always took such immense pleasure in these two small window boxes. Since they could never afford a place with a yard, this was the only garden my mom had ever had. Such a shame since she loved tending to her precious flowers.

I'll never forget the look on my mother's face when she first saw the patio on my very first place in the city. Knowing that my mother was actually jealous of what I had made me feel like I had really made it. I had done better than my parents had, and escaped South Philly. I had thought that place and my job at the bank was just the beginning of my journey into greatness. Little did I know I'd end up losing everything.

"Lane, why didn't you ring the bell? Were you just going to stand out there all day?"

The front door flies open just as I am about to knock. I see my mom standing on the other side with her arms wide open.

"You said you needed to talk, is everything ok?"

I hate the look of fear I see in my mother's eyes. I guess it was a bit unusual that I called out of the blue and asked to stop by. I should have known that it would be pretty obvious to her that I didn't have any good news to share.

I give my mom a hug, then head inside and collapse onto their old plaid couch with a heavy sigh. A cloud of dust fills the air. I'm pretty sure my parent's couch is older than I am. It probably had about fifty pounds worth of dust mites living in the cushions.

"Everything is fine, sort of."

My mom squints as she studies my face. I know there is no fooling her.

"Well, I actually wanted to ask you guys something. I have to move out of my place in a couple of weeks, and I'm trying to save money for a new business venture."

"You are starting a business? I feel like I'm sitting next to Bill Gates!" My mother says proudly as she pats my knee.

"Yes. I want to invest in real estate. The last few months I've been working as a project manager."

"Is that what you do at the bank? It sounds so fancy."

My mother squeezes my knee with excitement.

"No, I was a personal banker. I don't do that anymore."

I decide to continue before either of them can ask me any questions about losing my job. That is the last thing I want to talk about now. Well, second to last. There is one thing that is even more painful and raw, and that is talking about Chris.

"You see, my business partner and I sort of had a disagreement. So it's time I strike out on my own."

I lift my arm, and swing it through the air in an attempt to look more confident than I feel. I still don't want my parents to know that I am a complete failure. It's best to just be as vague as possible, until I can turn the mess that is my life around.

"I hear about these types of things all the time. Very common in the business world." my father says.

"Lane, you are so smart and hard working. I know you will be just fine on your own." my mother reassures me with a big smile.

"The thing is, I need to save up enough money for a downpayment. To buy a place of my own that I can renovate and sell to someone else, for a lot more money." I explain.

"You mean you want to be a flipper?" my dad asks.

"It's called real estate investing. Lots of people have done it, and made serious money. It's a real thing dad."

I practically stomp my foot on the ground, like I'm a little child having a temper tantrum. It was no surprise they didn't understand, having never worked in the business world themselves. One day, when I made it big, they'd get it. It was time to push all negativity aside if I was going to ever have a chance of saving up enough money to buy a property.

"You would know better than me. How long will it take you to save up this money?" my dad asks as he flips through the newspaper.

"That's what I wanted to talk to you about-"

My mother turns her head towards me so fast I hope she didn't pull a muscle.

"Lane, you know money is tight for us."

"Yes, I wasn't going to ask you for any. I'm actually waiting on a payout from another venture of mine. But in the meantime, think I could stay with you guys for a while? You know, save some money on rent?"

I do my best to force a smile on my face so my parents won't realize the desperateness of the situation. It's better they think I view living with them as a good option, rather than a last resort.

My mom looks to my dad, who lowers his newspaper briefly before going right back to reading it intently.

"Sure honey, this will always be your home. In fact, we were actually considering getting a roommate. We actually have a few repairs we need to make. And given your expertise, maybe you could help us with that. You know, instead of paying rent?"

My mom scoots towards me on the couch until our thighs are touching. When my eyes meet hers, they are full of what looks like excitement. I don't want to burst her bubble by letting her know that I was planning on living here rent free, given that I had no source of income at the moment.

I feel the tiny glimmer of hope that has kept me going over the last week dissipate. This was a stupid idea. Even though I still had no choice but to move back in with my parents, the right thing to do was to pay them rent. I am too old to mooch off of them. It wasn't their fault I was a total failure.

But as I run through the details in my mind, I realize that paying rent means that I will have to get another normal job, most likely at a bank. Saving enough to invest in real estate on my own will no longer be even remotely possible. It was time I let go of that dream. Maybe that would free up enough space in my brain to do what I needed to do, and that was survive.

"Funny I was just looking at the real estate section here, isn't this your place Lane?"

My dad hands me a section of the newspaper, and the minute my eyes land on the picture of Chris, it feels like my heart has stopped beating.

The picture of him takes up almost a third of the entire page. It's a full body shot of Chris in a suit, leaning up against a wall with his arms folded over his massive chest. On his face is what most people could classify as a smile, but I know he's holding something back. I knew him well enough to know what it looked like when he was actually happy. His whole face would change when he genuinely smiled, even his eyes would look different. In this picture, it looked more like he was just trying to be polite.

I put my hand over my chest in an attempt to steady my rapidly beating heart and reach for the paper. I pull it out of my dad's hands so fast I worry for a minute I may have given him a paper cut.

"That's your place isn't it Lane?" my dad asks again.

"Yes."

I stare at the page, unable to tear my eyes away from the picture of Chris. All I can think about is how this might be the last time I ever see him. And my mind is going crazy imagining what he is doing right now.

How did the inspection go? Is he going to be able to finish on time? What kind of offers are going to come rolling in? What I wouldn't give to be able to ask him these questions.The relation that I might never know how the renovation turns out washes over me like a rip current. It's all I can do to keep myself upright and breathing as the waves come crashing down on my head.

"Do you know that man? He's very easy on the eyes." my mom asks, looking at the picture in my hand.

As I fight back the tears forming in my eyes, I am stricken by the irony of what my mom just said. Looking at Chris was the furthest thing from easy on my eyes. Each time I look at his handsome face, my eyes sting and beg for me to cry more tears.

"Yeah, he was my landlord. He bought all six units from Howard when he moved a few months back. I sort of worked for him, and..."

I look at my mom and try and gauge her reaction to see if it's worth continuing. I have never talked to my mom about a guy before. She probably thought I was still a virgin.

"What? You guys slept together?" my dad asks, causing my cheeks to burn as if they were actually on fire.

"No. I mean... yes."

I'm just about to apologize to my mom when I see her smiling as she looks back to the picture of Chris.

"But it was more than that, we dated."

"Dated?" my mom asks, with extra emphasis on the 'ed'.

"Yes." I admit, looking down at my hands that are folded in my lap.

"You dated a guy this good looking and he's successful. What the hell happened?"

"We sort of had a misunderstanding. About work."

My mom and dad look at one another, and my mom scrunches the corner of her mouth and narrows her eyes.

"These things happen. I'm sure you two can work it out."

"I don't think so, it's very complicated."

My mom makes a funny face at my dad, who chuckles.

"You hear that, she doesn't think we understand how relationships work. We've only been married for thirty-four years."

I laugh as I look at my parents. Thirty-four years was a long time. As I think back to all of the things my parents have faced together, I realize that it might be worth listening to what she had to say.

"Every relationship has its challenges. It's easiest to hurt the ones you love the most, because love is all about emotions. Mostly good ones, but also a lot of bad ones."

I stop to think about what my mother just said. It made a lot of sense. If Chris knew that it was Lindsay that tipped off the city and not me, it probably wouldn't have affected him the way it did. Sure, he would have been pissed, and still would have had to deal with the consequences, but he wouldn't have felt so betrayed. And I could have been there, by his side, helping him deal with whatever needed to be done.

The thought of Chris dealing with the city inspector, and having to hire someone to dig a new sewer line makes my chest feel heavy again. He shouldn't have to do it all alone.

"I know he's hurt very badly. But it wasn't me. Do you think if I told him the truth he'd believe me?" I ask my mom, fully aware that I left out many important details. She probably has no clue what I'm talking about. And I don't even care if she knows the whole story, all I need is for her to tell me I have a chance.

"Do you love him?" she asks, looking me dead in the eyes.

Love. Even though Chris and I referred to what we did in the bedroom as making love, neither of us had a chance to say the actual words to one another. So admitting it to my mother felt like a lie. Even though in my heart of hearts, I wanted to scream at the top of my lungs that I loved him. I also promise myself that if I am ever lucky enough to get another chance, I will make certain that I don't waste any more time telling Chris how I feel. The desire to finally tell Chris that I love him fills my veins with adrenaline.

"I care for him, deeply."

I jump up from the couch and begin to pace the small living room.

"Well honey, life is too short. Go to him, explain that you're sorry about whatever happened, and I'm sure you two will be just fine. Everyone has these arguments."

I feel a burst of excitement as I think about what my mom just said. It is true that every couple has had their problems. And while I have no idea if Chris will believe me or not when I tell him it was actually Lindsay who notified the city, I know that I have to try. If I don't, I will regret it for the rest of my life. There was no way that Chris didn't miss me. There was no way I could have made up in my head the way he felt for me.

"You're right mom. I should go talk to him."

"You go ahead dear."

I throw my arms around my mother before heading to the door.

"And when do you think you'll be moving your stuff here?"

"I'll call you later. After I talk to Chris."

The thought of seeing him again and telling him the truth is both parts terrifying and reassuring. But until I tried it was almost impossible to think of anything else.

23

CHRIS

The doorbell rings, and I take one last look around my house before going to answer it. Something about one of my throw pillows still doesn't look right. So I pick it up and quickly attempt to fluff it before setting it back down on the corner of the sofa. I just hope the extra pillow was enough to make up for the fact the house still wasn't quite move in ready.

"Be right there Amy." I yell as I walk to the front door.

I throw it open wide, and greet Amy with a smile. She is dressed in another form fitting dress and four inch heels. The camera bag on her right shoulder makes it look like she may topple over at any minute.

"Here let me help you."

I grab her bag and set it down on the coffee table. Amy opens it up, pulls out her camera, then unscrews one lens and replaces it with another.

"Love what you've done to this place." Amy says as she looks around.

Once her eyes land on the scuffed up old paint job and

the missing light fixture in the ceiling, her eyes open wide. She quickly forces a smile on her face.

"The lighting this time of day will be perfect for the outside shots. Mind if I start there?"

"Wherever you'd like."

Amy smiles as she saunters across the living room floor. I watch as she intentionally sways her hips from side to side with each step. I force myself to watch her, but all I can think about is how hot Lane looked when she walked like this. It looked so effortless when Lane did it, like she walked that way every day. And with Amy, it didn't seem natural. More like she was trying to put on a show for my benefit.

"Can I get you a glass of wine?" I ask as she heads through the back door.

"I don't normally drink on the job."

"Glad you're making an exception today."

I grab two wine glasses from the cabinet. I chose a Cabernet that I have been saving for a special occasion. When I bought it, I told myself it would be perfect to share with Lane when we finally closed on the sales of the houses. Not that I needed wine to make being with Lane feel special. It would have been so perfect seeing Lane's excitement had we sold the houses for the amount my father originally told us we could get. That was if we had finished the job, and actually had something to celebrate. Now, when the houses were finally sold, rather than celebrating, I'd be trying my damnedest to forget this whole mess ever happened.

I look in the backyard and hear the click of Amy's camera. She moves around the yard and crouches down as she tries to get just the right angle for the back of the house. The look on her face is of sheer determination. I decided to take the wine into the living room and wait inside until she is finished. The last thing I want to do is interrupt. We need as much help as possible making these houses look good.

Just as I sink into the couch, I hear a knock on the front door. It's most likely my dad. I should have known he wouldn't be able to stay away today, since he knew that Amy was taking the pictures. As much as it is kind of annoying that he keeps trying to micromanage everything, I know how important it is to get these houses on the market. So I jump up from the couch to let him in.

I swing the door wide open, and the sight on the other side of my door is almost enough to give me a fucking heart attack. I have to blink about fifteen times just to make sure I'm not hallucinating. After I shake my head a few times, I am able to confirm that Lane is actually standing on my porch, right in front of me.

"Hey, have a minute?" she says as she plays with a section of long brown hair that is hanging down around her neck.

The hammering of my own heart in my ears is so damn loud I can't even hear myself think. I know I need to tell her hell no, and to get as far away from me as possible. I've already told her this, and made it perfectly clear that I want nothing to do with her. Yet, here she is, on my porch once again looking just as stunning as she ever has. The sight of her in her stretchy pants and sheer white t-shirt gives me a flash back to how good she looks naked. What I wouldn't give to pull her into my arms, rip off her clothes and take her right up to my bedroom. Maybe I could screw her hard and rough, punish her for what she did to me. That would serve her right if I used her like she used me. Except I know that if I did that, she'd want to talk afterwards.

And I know that once she starts talking, I'll see the Lane I used to know. The one that had my back and shared my dreams. I miss that Lane so damn much. But I can't forget that Lane is gone. The real Lane is a backstabber, and cares more about proving a point than anything else. She can't be trusted. I need her out of here before I fall right back into her trap. She's already fooled me once, and if I'm stupid enough to let her get close enough to me again, I might not survive her betrayal a second time.

"Uh, actually, this isn't a good time." I tell her as I exhale loudly to slow down my heart which is beating much too quickly.

Lane fidgets with her fingers and presses her lips together. I know I should slam the door shut, but instead I stand there like an idiot with it wide open as I stare into Lane's brown eyes. I wait for her to turn around and leave, but after about thirty seconds she ducks her head and sneaks under my arm and right into my house.

"We need to talk. About that email and the city..." Lane says as she walks into my living room and stands in front of my couch.

I squeeze my eyes shut, as I beg my mind to block out everything she is saying. I don't want to think about that day when everything in my life went to shit. Dwelling on the past wasn't going to help me at all. The only thing that I can do now is learn from my mistakes. And the biggest mistake I ever made was thinking I could trust Lane.

"Lane, it's ok." I say the only thing I can think of that will get Lane to stop talking.

And sure enough, she stops mid sentence and narrows her eyes at me.

"What?"

"It's all water under the bridge. In fact, the sewers were just fine, the inspector said."

Lane opens her mouth to say something else but stops when she spots the two glasses of wine on the coffee table.

"Yes, so if you came to apologize, thank you, but you don't need to. Everything has worked out just fine."

Lane's gaze remains glued on the two glasses or wine, and her mouth hangs open. Just then, Amy comes inside. I am so relieved to see Amy and for the distraction that I actually throw my arm around her shoulder.

"Hey Amy, this is Lane, my neighbor. She was just leaving."

Lane's lip trembles as she looks up at Amy. I look at Amy, and do my best to beg her with my eyes to play along. She somehow seems to know what I am asking, and reaches up and puts her hand on top of mine.

"Hi Jane."

Lane's eyes pop wide open.

"It's actually Lane." I say, unable to stop the laughter I feel beginning in my throat.

I'm pretty sure Amy heard me just fine. It's almost scary how good women can be when it comes to messing with each other.

"Yeah I guess I should get going."

Lane begins to walk backwards to the door and crashes into the corner of the coffee table. One of the glasses tips over, and the wine spills all over my new cream colored wool rug.

"Oh my god, I'm so sorry." Lane reaches for the glass, but I grab her by the wrist and stop her.

"No, you've done enough. Just leave, now."

The hurt in Lane's eyes is like a sucker punch to my gut. As much as it sucks having to hurt a woman I once cared so much about, I know that I have to do it. It's the only way I can make sure she never comes back. I'm not sure I can stay strong again if she ever tries again.

"Ok, but I really need to talk to you." Lane says as her voice begins to crack.

The more upset she gets, the more I feel my resolve fading. I know I need to do something to get her to run out the door and never turn back. So I decided to up the ante.

I take my arm that is still wrapped around Amy's shoulder, and begin to run my fingers through her hair. She begins to purr like a kitten.

"Babe, you take that glass. I'll go get another."

"Thanks babe, red is my favorite."

Amy smiles at me adoringly. I had a very strong feeling she was the type that liked to be called babe. It feels good to be right.

I look to Lane, whose nostrils are flaring as she exhales loudly. Seeing her pissed was a lot easier to handle than seeing her hurt. It was starting to feel like I was finally winning my battle to get over Lane.

"Bye Lane."

I let go of Amy to grab the wine glasses from the table. I put the full one in Amy's hand, and I raise the empty glass of wine in the air as Lane runs out the front door. The minute she's gone, it finally hits me like a fucking freight train that this will probably be the last time I ever see Lane. At least I hope. And as much as I want to feel relief, I still feel so enraged at the entire situation. And at myself for being so stupid.

I feel Amy's hands on my backside, and I jump like I've just been hit by a bullet.

"What?" she asks.

"I'm sorry. I just remembered I have to do something. Take as much time as you need, I'll be upstairs."

I run up the stairs before Amy even has a chance to answer. I'm not ever sure if she'll be too pissed off to finish taking the picture we need for the listing. I know I should care, and go back and make sure she does. But all I can think about now is being alone. It's a feeling I'm all too familiar with.

24

LANE

As I make my one hundredth trip down the stairs carrying a cardboard box full of my clothes, I pray I am able to get the rest of the boxes out of my bedroom before my arms fall off.

"Are you sure you have to leave now? We have two more weeks, you know." Ashley says as she unpacks a bag of Chinese take-out on our living room coffee table.

The smell of my favorite moo shoo reminds my body of just how hungry I am. But sitting down and eating would take up far too much of my precious time. And even though I know I am hungry, the underlying sense of nausea I have had in my stomach all week makes even my favorite meal look very unappealing.

"I'm sure. I just don't want to spend another day next to him. If I have to see him with that woman one more time..."

I drop a box containing my winter clothes next to the front door. I feel like kicking it for some reason, even though my clothes haven't done anything wrong. As much time as I've spent blaming myself for everything that went wrong with Chris, I know that it can't possibly be all my fault. Chris was the real asshole. The biggest mistake I made was letting myself fall for him so hard and believing I meant something to him. He clearly no longer cared about what happened with the city inspectors. They didn't even find any problems with the sewer. As he said, it was all 'water under the bridge.' And even though he wasn't mad about that, he still wanted nothing to do with me.

I still can't wrap my head around how he was able to move on so quickly. Even the thought of another guy was enough to make me want to throw up. It will most likely be years before I will be able to even think about dating again. Or maybe never. It all seems so pointless to emotionally invest in a guy when they can change their minds in an instant for no good reason. And if I ever did get over having my heart broken by Chris, the last thing I would ever do was take another risk like this. No one could survive this type of pain twice in a lifetime. It was far too much.

"Come on Lanc, this is our last night all together as roommates. Can't we all eat dinner together?" Heidi says with her eyes wide.

The look of disappointment on Heidi's face stops me dead in my tracks. I have been so busy being mad at Chris and about the disaster that is my life that I haven't even stopped to think about the fact that this was our last night all together. Tonight was the last time all three of us would sit on this couch and eat take-out food in a house we all lived in. The realization hits me like a crowbar to the shins. Maybe I've been in denial because the thought of living without my two best friends was far too much for my already overloaded brain to handle.

As I look over at Heidi and Ashley on our couch, my mind begins to replay all of our best times together as roommates like some sort of cheesy home movie. It was almost impossible to fathom that after tonight, I would never come home and see them. Ever since we graduated from college, they were the ones I came home to every single day. They were the ones that were there the day I had my first real job interview. I still remember the way they asked me for every detail and listened so patiently to my very lengthy answers. They were also the first ones I told when Chris asked me to be his girlfriend. They were there for me during the bad times too, like the day I lost my job at the bank. Whenever I was stressed or exhausted, they always had my back. Life without them was certainly not going to be the same.

Ashley grabs a carton of food from the paper bag and makes a big plate of all my favorites.

"Just try a little. I even got you extra duck sauce." She says with a huge smile.

I take the plate from her and simply nod. I am afraid if I try to speak now, I might totally lose the small shred of my sanity that I have left.

"Oh my god I just realized; didn't we get take out from here the first night in this house?" Heidi says as she looks down at her plate of fried rice.

"That's right! We ate on the floor on paper plates while watching a movie on Lane's laptop!" Ashley says as she smacks me lightly on the leg.

We all slip into silence as we think back to that first night. We moved into our row home on a rainy Monday evening. Ashley's parents had generously donated their old living room furniture to us, and her brother decided it was better to wait until it stopped raining to bring it over. But we were all so excited to move into our new place, that we still came with air mattresses and sleeping bags. It was the most exciting sleep over of my life; complete with Chinese food and of course, a bottle of wine. We all stayed up till almost two that night, just talking about how awesome adult life in the city was going to be.

I can still remember Ashley and Heidi talking excitedly about all the guys they were going to meet. And all I could think about that night was my career and making it big, and how jealous that was going to make everyone back in South Philly.

Boy was I ever wrong about how my life was going to end up. How humiliating it was going to be to face everyone back home once I moved back into my parents house. Talk about a failure.

I shake my head to rid my brain of as many negative thoughts as possible. I decide to instead focus on something positive; how incredibly lucky we all felt that first night in our house. That night, we were all just so excited to be living in the city that nothing else mattered to us. We had more fun that night with take out food on the floor than most people have in a mansion full of furniture.

"How perfect that this was our first meal together, and now it's our last." Heidi says as she drops her fork onto her plate.

"Stop it guys. I'm only moving two miles away. We're still going to see each other all the time."

Ashley and Heidi both look down at their plates full of food.

"And I have an interview next week... at another bank. Who knows, maybe I'll have money for a place of my own soon."

Heidi smiles and picks up her fork.

"Really Lane? If you get the job, we're looking at a high rise this weekend. Maybe they have a three-bedroom available."

"That's great for you guys. But even if I got this job, it

would still be too expensive for me. And I need to save money."

My brain feels like it might explode as I try to think of what my plan should look like for the rest of my life. I used to enjoy daydreaming about my future so much, but now, it just all seemed so useless.

"Speaking of saving money, I can't believe I didn't give this to you yet." Ashley jumps up from the couch and runs into the kitchen. She returns a few moments later with an envelope and a big smile on her face.

"It's from that same attorney that was handling that dog boutique bankruptcy. Maybe it's your check."

Ashley holds the envelope a few inches in front of my face. When I don't reach for it, she begins to wave it in the air to make sure that I see it.

"Ok thanks."

I grab the envelope and slide it between the folded flaps of one of my cardboard boxes near the door. Then I pick up my fork and try to take a few bites of my dinner. It tastes like sand in my mouth. I can barely swallow it. All the stress of the last two weeks has made even eating my favorite food feel like a chore.

"So tell me about the high rise you guys are looking at." I say, doing my best to focus on the positive.

Heidi's face lights up and she flails her arm excitedly as she tells me all about the building. "It has a doorman, a rooftop pool and a full-service gym."

I look to Ashley to see if she is as excited as Heidi, but she's still staring down at her plate.

"What Ash? You still want to see it right? The pictures look amazing, and it's right by your office."

"No, it's perfect, except..."

Ashley's cheeks redden as a huge grin appears across her face.

"What is it then?" I ask her.

"Remember Paul?"

It takes me a few moments to make the connection. Paul was the guy who brought his friend, Patrick over for that super-awkward blind date at our apartment. That was the night Chris showed up at my doorstep, and mistook Paul's friend for something much more than he was. I still feel a flutter in my stomach as I remember how jealous Chris was when he saw Paul at my doorstep. Just the thought of me with another man made him so angry, because he wanted me all to himself. How quickly he changed his mind about that. Now he was the one with another woman. I almost scream out loud as I imagine what Chris and his girlfriend are doing right now, or what they did after I left after that awful night I tried to apologize to Chris. Even though when I went over that night, I wasn't entirely sure he'd be able to forgive me, I just wasn't expecting for him to have moved on so quickly. It was like he forgot all about me and everything we had. He must be so used to woman lining up to have sex with him, that sleeping with me was no big deal to him. And here I was, thinking I was special.

"Yes. How has that been going?" Heidi asks leaning in closer to Ashley to hear the details.

"Well, he's been super busy with work, and so have I. We haven't been seeing a lot of each other the last few weeks. And when I finally told him that I wanted to be more of a priority, he asked if we could get dinner tomorrow night..."

Heidi's jaw drops and she puts her hands on Ashley's shoulder.

"OMG, you don't think he's going to..."

Ashley holds up her hands to stop Heidi.

"I'm not sure, but I don't want to jinx it."

All three of us listen as Ashley tells us about the restaurant Paul has chosen, and what she plans to wear. This could be a huge moment in Ashley's life, and I'm just so happy to be a part of it. I'm so engrossed in our conversation, that I almost forget that Dad is stopping my tonight to take a car load of my boxes over to his house. It takes three honks of his horn for me to finally realize he's here. I hired movers to come tomorrow for my furniture, but they charge by the hour. So I'm trying to move as much as possible by myself.

"Oh crap, that must be Dad."

I tell my roommates as I jump up and look out the window. Sure enough, my dad's old station wagon is double parked in front of our house with the flashers on. I look up and down the street for a parking spot, and of course, there isn't a single one. I know we have to get his car loaded up quickly, before he gets side swiped or ticketed.

"I'll be right back." I say, grabbing one of the boxes that I stacked by the door.

Dad hops out of the car and opens his trunk. I see Mom's head popping out of the passenger's side. I do my best to smile sweetly, even though I'm annoyed that she's taking up the front seat. I could have fit three boxes up there if she hadn't come.

"Let me." Dad says, reaching for the box.

I want to tell him no since he has a bad back. But I have a very strong feeling he will insist on helping.

"Thanks, I have a few more inside. I really appreciate your help."

My dad is just about to say something when we hear a car behind us honking their car horn very loudly.

"Close your door asshole," the driver yells out of his window.

Dad looks back to the driver's side of his car, and we both see his door wide open. He was in such a hurry to help me that he must have forgotten to close it. I'm just about to give the driver the finger, when I hear a familiar voice.

"Enough with the horn." Chris says as he bangs onto the side of the other car. Dad closes his door and the other driver speeds away.

My cheeks feel like they are on fire as I look down at the sidewalk and pray that Chris will run into his house without saying anything to me. The last thing I need right now is to make awkward introductions. I'm so close to being out, and never having to see Chris again. Was it too much to ask to not have to run into him today?

I hear footsteps moving in my direction, so I turn my back and head towards my house to grab another box. I'm all the way to the first step when I hear it.

"Lane, I had no idea that was you."

I nod and am just about to run up the rest of the steps when I hear my mother's voice.

"Hello there, you know Lanie?"

As much as I want to run, I know I need to save my parents the embarrassment. They deserve better than having to talk to the man that broke their daughter's heart. So I turn around and walk to the car window that my mother is sticking her head out of. I step right in front of her, shielding her from Chris as he begins walking in her direction.

"Mom, this is my landlord. I'm sure he's heading back home now."

I turn and look at Chris with my arms over my chest. Then I shift my gaze to his front door to give him the hint.

Instead of just leaving, he walks over and stands directly in front of me. He's so close by the time he stops walking that I can see his chest rising and falling with each breath he takes.

"So nice to meet you. You must be Lane's parents."

Before my mom has a chance to answer, I cut her off. Even though I know it's super rude, I'm sure that once I tell her all the details she will be grateful I spared her from having to talk to someone so despicable.

"Yes, these are my parents. They're helping me move. I should be gone by tomorrow, so don't worry."

The tension between us is so thick I could cut it with a knife. We both stare into each others' eyes, as if we are both trying like hell to win some sort of blinking contest.

Just then, Heidi and Ashley come out each holding one of my boxes. I am so grateful for the distraction I practically skip towards them. I take a step to the right to walk around Chris, just as he decides to move in the exact same direction as me. I look him dead in the eyes so he knows just how serious I am. He holds my gaze and takes a deep breath before finally taking a step backwards. I practically run to Ashley and Heidi.

"We thought about hiding these, so you wouldn't be able to leave us."Ashley says as she sticks out her lower lip. Heidi puts her hand on Ashley's shoulder, and as much as I want to reassure them again it will all be fine, I also don't want to give Chris the satisfaction of seeing the toll this has taken on everyone. He would probably get some sort of satisfaction out of knowing that he not only destroyed my life, but my roommates as well. Even though they were completely innocent in all of this.

"You're moving out now?" Chris asks.

I chuckle as I try to imagine how he could possibly be surprised.

"Yeah, my landlord gave me thirty days..."

I walk over to Heidi and take the box from her and walk it over to my dad's car. Ashley follows me with the one she's holding, and we both load them in. I take my time, and pray that when we return to the sidewalk, Chris will have enough sense to leave. But of course, he's still just standing there, like he's watching some sort of sad show. So I just do my best to pretend I don't see him.

I look past Chris to Heidi, and notice her shoulders trembling. Her hand is up over her eyes, and I'm pretty sure I hear deep sobs.

"Heidi, please don't cry. It's all going to be fine, I promise."

Heidi takes a few minutes to compose herself before answering.

"I know, I'm just going to miss you so much. I wish we had just signed that lease in Manayunk. We could all be starting a brand new adventure together."

I hug Heidi as tightly as humanly possible as I imagine what it would feel like if we were all moving somewhere together. I squeeze my eyes as I feel tears threatening to escape from my tear ducts. I hear Chris clear his throat, and what sounds like his footsteps heading back towards his own house.

"Manayunk might not be so bad after all. We could all go to Lindsays' cool new hair salon. You know, I think I might be able to pull off pink highlights almost as well as she does." Heidi says with a laugh in between sobs.

I stroke Heidi's hair and smile as I try to picture her with the same pink highlights as Lindsay. While they do look awesome on Lindsay, I know Heidi is kidding. It would be a sin to mess with her gorgeous chestnut locks. I close my eyes and wait until Heidi stops crying to let go. When I feel what I think is Ashley's hand on my shoulders, I open my eyes and am horrified to see Chris directly behind us.

"What did you just say?" Chris asks Heidi.

We break our hug to look up at him. Heidi has a look of shock on her face, and I'm pretty sure the look on mine is super pissed off. Chris has a lot more nerve than I ever could have imagined, interrupting my last few moments with my roommates. Why was he pretending like he had any right to be here?

"What?" Heidi asks as she dabs her eyelashes with her fingertips.

"You said Lindsay, and something about pink hair. Was that the girl who used to live next to you?"

Heidi stares at Chris without saying a word. I'm sure she is trying to figure out why the hell he would care what Lindsay did with her hair. We both shoot him dirty looks, when Chris grabs me by the shoulders.

"Lane, I need to talk to you. Now."

"No." I say, pushing his hand off my shoulder as I let out a grunt of disgust. "We're kind of busy here, just leave us alone."

My dad approaches from behind.

"Lanie, everything ok?"

Chris smiles at my dad, doing his best to convince him everything is ok. But my dad knows me well enough to know that I am extremely uncomfortable.

"These the last of the boxes?" he asks as Ashley comes back outside with another.

"Yes. Let's go."

My roommates and I give each other one last lingering hug outside of our house. I hear Heidi starting to cry again, and the last thing I want to do is leave her upset. But I can still feel Chris' eyes burning into my back like a laser pointer, as he stands behind us on the sidewalk like a total creeper.

"I'll be back tomorrow, when the movers come." I reassure my roommates, as I make my way to my dad's car.

There's just enough room for me in the backseat, along with about three of my boxes. I open the door and take one last deep breath.

"Lane wait..." I hear from behind me as I begin to climb into the car. The sound of his voice once again stops me in my tracks, but I know better than to turn around. He made his choice, and while it feels good to know he is actually capable of feeling sorry for what he did, I don't need his pity. Sure things are bad now, but I am going to turn it all around. When I finally land another job, and save enough money to buy a property, it will be all the sweeter after surviving this. This has to be rock bottom, and the only way to go from here was up.

"No." I say in my most stern tone as I climb into the backseat.

"Dad go." I order my father with my eyes closed. I don't open them until I'm sure we're far enough away that I don't have to risk seeing Chris again. Tomorrow I'll be out for good. And Philadelphia was a large enough city that the chances of having to ever run into Chris again were fairly slim. I reassure myself that it's almost over but somehow, it does little to comfort me.

"Hope you packed yourself an overnight bag. You know, in case you don't feel like unpacking all these boxes tonight." My mom says from the front seat.

I feel like kicking myself for not thinking of that. I pry open the flaps of the cardboard box next to me, and see only throw pillows and a few books. All I need is a toothbrush, and maybe a change of clothes until tomorrow.

"I'll be fine." I say, pushing the contents of the box back inside. The flaps are almost shut when I see a white envelope sticking out of the right hand corner. I realize that I must have thrown the letter from the attorney in here after Ashley gave it to me.

I grab it from the box, and my hands tremble as I debate whether or not I should open it now. It will most likely be a very small amount of money, I tell myself. I've already had enough bad news for a lifetime. I finally decide there's no point in waiting any longer.

I stick my finger along the seam, and pull until the entire top rips open. I grab a folded sheet of paper, and as I am opening it, a check slips out. The inside of the car is dark, but we stop right next to a street light that illuminates the front of the check just enough that I can make out the amount.

I gasp when I realize that not only did I get the full amount that I invested back, but I also somehow got interest as well. I feel a bit of hope forming in the pit of my stomach, the first I've felt in weeks. Maybe things weren't quite as bad as they felt.

"You ok back there?" My dad asks.

"Yeah, I just got some good news."

I tell my parents about the doggie boutique I invested in two years ago, and how it went bankrupt as I skim the body of the letter from the attorney.

"I really thought I was an equity investor, but it turns out, it was set up as a loan with interest." I explain to my parents, even though they probably have no idea what I am talking about. It's sad I didn't realize I was loaning the boutique money, instead of investing it. It made a lot more sense now that I got anything after the bankruptcy.

"Wow honey that's great. Looks like you can get started on your new business venture sooner than you expected."

Even though I now technically have enough money to buy a small investment property, the thought of looking for one makes my head spin. As much fun as it's been being Chris' project manager, doing it all on my own was far more risky. If it didn't work out, I'd be left with nothing. This money was my last chance. My parents were already stretching themselves too thin helping me with a place to stay. I have no one else to fall back on, so it was time to be responsible.

"We'll see. Might be better if I just get another real job." I say as my dad pulls into a parking spot outside of their house.

"Welcome home Lanie." my mom says with a squeal.

As I look up at the house I grew up in, a bunch of memories come rushing back. Despite the fact that all of them are pleasant, my hand trembles as I put it on the car door. I would rather sleep in the backseat of my dad's car than go inside for some very odd reason. Maybe because that was the only way I could delay the inevitable.

25

CHRIS

As I watch Lane's dad drive away and she disappears from my view, I feel too stunned to move. I stand there on the street corner for at least ten minutes, trying to wrap my brain around what her roommate just said.

Lindsay has pink hair. She has to be the person I've seen lurking around the job site like some sort of spy from a crappy movie. Even though she used to live here, it was still really weird for her to have that much interest in the renovation. It couldn't just be curiosity, she was clearly pissed about something. Was she mad enough about losing her house to tip off the city about the sewer and try to make it look like it was Lane?

As my mind races through the facts, it starts to look more and more likely that this was the case. Lane genuinely looked shocked when she saw the inspectors that morning. She was so excited the entire week before about the progress, that it never fully made sense to me that she would do anything to jeopardize our timeline.

I race back into my house and search frantically inside for the packet of papers from the city inspectors that contained the email that was signed by Lane. After emptying all of my kitchen drawers, I finally find it and flip to the email. I scan it again, and this time, I look at the sender at the top. 'L-ing-city-life' was the sender of the email. This was not the email address that Lane used when she emailed me. 'L 'could be for Lane, or Lindsay. I quickly fire up my laptop, create a fake gmail account with a different name and send an email to the mystery address.

'Lindsay, great meeting you the other night. Let's grab a drink when you get a chance, let me know when you're free."

My heart hammers in my chest as I hit the send button. I check my inbox every two minutes, hoping she'll see it right away. She'll either write back that I have the wrong person, or she'll take the bait and write back. Then I will know once and for all that it wasn't Lane who sent the email to the city.

The fact that there was a very good chance that Lane never betrayed me makes it almost impossible for me to sit still. I think back to how things felt that morning, when Lane and I were still a team. If Lindsay responds to my email, Lane and I could go back to the way things were. Except Lane seemed so pissed when I saw her. She wouldn't even talk to me. Would she forgive me if she understood? I pace the kitchen as I debate how likely that is.

I pour myself a shot of whiskey and throw it back in an attempt to silence all the conflicting voices in my head. They were loud as hell, and giving me a splitting headache. As the whisky burns in my throat, I take my phone out again and check my new fake email account.

The inbox is still empty, so I hit refresh. Then I see it. My hand shakes so hard I accidentally hit the delete button instead of open.

"Fuck." I scream as I throw my empty shot glass across the room. The sound of shattering glass fills the air. I look back at the screen, and notice a deleted message icon. I click it, and find the email inside.

'Omg heyyy!! I must have been hammered, I don't remember giving you this email address. But a drink sounds amazing! When are you free? :) -Lindsay.'

It was Lindsay. Fuck it, I don't care how angry Lane is, I need to tell her that I know. She deserves to know the truth. I grab my phone, pull up my contacts, and almost immediately I realize I deleted her number. *How could I have been so fucking stupid?*

I run next door and just as I am about to pound on the front door, I remember she is gone. I watched her climb into her father's car and drive off. I never even asked for a forwarding address since she never put down a security deposit. The thought of never seeing Lane again makes it almost impossible to breathe. *Was this really how it was going to end between us?*

No, she said she was coming back in the morning to get the rest of her furniture. The thought of having one more chance to talk to Lane finally causes my lungs to unclench, allowing me to breathe. I have until the morning to try and figure out what the hell I am going to say to her. I may only have one chance, and whatever I decide to say will be in front of all of her roommates, movers, and maybe even her parents.

I lay awake in bed most of the night trying to figure out how I can get Lane to forgive me. I try to think of what could possibly be going through Lane's head right now. She's known all along that she never sent that email to the city. So when I screamed at her and cut her out of my life completely, she probably thought I was the world's biggest asshole. If she has felt even half as lonely and empty as I have since the last time we were together, it wasn't going to be easy to win her forgiveness.

When the sun finally comes up, I am at least relieved that I no longer have to try and sleep. But I still have no fucking clue what to say to Lane. I spend the entire morning drinking my coffee and staring out the window, waiting for any sign of movers or Lane. When a big white truck finally pulls in front of her house, I know this is my chance. Adrenaline shoots through my veins as I run out my front door, and look frantically for Lane.

I watch as the movers fold down the back of the truck and scan the sidewalk for Lane. One of the men finally takes out his cell phone, and presses it to his ear as he waits for her to answer.

"Hi, we're out front." He says politely as he waits for a reply. "Not a problem, see you in a few minutes."

I decide it might be a bit too much if I'm outside the minute Lane arrives, so I go back inside to wait. A few moments later, I watch as her father's station wagon pulls up on our street, and Lane hops out of the back seat. With a cup of coffee in one hand, she walks towards the movers and greets them in her most chipper tone. Lane looks like a fitness model in her dark blue yoga pants, and an oversized sweatshirt that falls off her left shoulder. Her skin that is exposed is so soft and supple looking, all I can think about is kissing it. Her dark hair is piled up high on top of her head, with a few pieces falling around the back of her neck. I know this can't be the last time I see her.

"Lane." I scream a little too loudly as I run out my front door.

She turns around to face me, her eyes are wide and bloodshot. She takes a pair of sunglasses from the top of her head and lowers them over her eyes as she lets out a labored sigh.

"Chris, I don't have time for this today. I am trying to get everything out today..."

"I know, it will only take a minute... I have something to tell you."

I run towards Lane, who takes a step backwards with her arms up in front of her body.

"No." She says sternly.

"Look, I know that it was L-" I begin, right before Lane screams so loudly I can't even hear what I am saying.

"I said no."

All three of the moving men look over in my direction. I can tell from their stare just how much the tallest one would love to swoop in and rescue Lane from a screaming lunatic. I don't want to give him that satisfaction.

"Lane, I know-"

"Stop. When I came to your house wanting to talk, did you hear me out?"

I know better than to answer her question, even though she pauses as if she's waiting for me to reply.

"No. You were too busy with your new girlfriend. Well, now I'm moving on. And I am the one telling you that I don't care what you have to say."

Lane's words cut me like a razor blade. She was right. Maybe that night when Amy was over, and Lane came to my door, she was planning to tell me the truth about Lindsay. Had I just had the decency to hear her out, we wouldn't be here now. We'd still be in my bed, making plans for the future. And I wouldn't feel like the biggest asshole on the planet.

"Ok." I whisper.

Lane's eyes open wide, as if she wasn't expecting me to give up. But the truth is, I don't have any fight left in me. She was done, there was nothing I could say to convince her otherwise.

I turn and begin walking back to my house. I hear the sound of Lane's footsteps as she heads back to the door of her old place.

"If you guys could start upstairs with the bedroom furniture..." She says to the movers.

For some reason, my feet feel frozen to the sidewalk. I can't just go inside and never see Lane again. I feel compelled to stand there and watch. Maybe it's because I want to make sure the movers are able to pack everything for her, I tell myself. But whatever the reasons, I decide to stay right where I am until she leaves for the last time.

"You are far too pretty to be named Joe ma'am." One of the movers says as he looks back down at his papers as raises his eyebrows.

Lane blushes as she tries to figure out what he is saying.

"Joe?" she asks.

Just then, the front door of unit six opens, and out comes my other last remaining tenant aside from Lane's roommates. Joe takes his time coming down his front steps, waving enthusiastically to the men.

"Hi fellas, sorry I wasn't expecting you quite this early."

Lane runs over to Joe's side, and tries to help him on the last step.

"Joe, you're moving?"

"Yes, I found a nice place only ten blocks away. Lots of folks my age, and a swimming pool." Joe tells Lane, holding his head high and proud.

"That's amazing, I was so worried..."

"I was too. But Chris over there decided to give me back my original security deposit with interest. It was so long ago when I first moved in, that I must have forgotten all about it. Apparently I gave three months of rent upfront to Howard. More than enough to get me started at my new place."

Lane smiles sweetly up at Joe, who looks over in my direction. I wave back at him. Lane's gaze lingers on me, and slowly she lifts the sunglasses up and places them back on top of her head.

The movers follow Joe inside of his house, and come back out carrying a sofa. They make several trips back and forth, all the while, Lane remains at the bottom of Joe's steps just staring.

I take a step towards her, then stop. I look at her, and ask her with my eyes for permission. When she doesn't object, I take another step. And another, until I'm only about ten feet away.

"Joe never put down a deposit, did he?" she asks.

I shake my head and let out a laugh.

"No. But I knew he was far too proud to take money from me."

Lane stares at me as the corners of her mouth move. I'm dying to know what's going on inside that pretty little head of hers.

"That was... really nice of you."

"What was I going to do? Kick an old guy out on the streets. That would be bad business."

Lane smiles, and the sight of her looking happy does something to my gut. I feel like for the first time in two weeks I can actually breathe.

"Lane, I know it was Lindsay."

Lane's mouth drops open and her face turns pale. She puts her hand up over her mouth, as she exhales loudly.

"I know it wasn't you. I am such a fucking idiot for thinking you were capable of such a thing. I am so sorry."

Lane opens her mouth, then closes it again as she narrows her eyes. I can't tell if she's relieved that I finally know the truth, or if she's still mad.

Lane's head turns around as we both hear the sounds of another large truck approaching. I turn around just in time to see another moving truck pulling up in front of her house.

"Hi Miss, sorry we're late." A man says as he steps out of the truck.

"It's ok." Lane says to him, even though her eyes are still locked on mine.

The man walks towards us, and stops uncomfortably right behind me.

"You still want us to move your stuff?" The guy asks with a puzzled look on his face.

Lane looks at him briefly, then back at me as she bites her lower lip.

"No." I answer for her. "Lane, I'm sorry. I was a dick. You don't have to leave. You can stay until we settle. Please."

I look at Lane, praying she tells the guys she's changed her mind. She looks at her front door, and then back to the truck.

"I uhh..." she says in a trembling voice.

"Look, we got another job in Northern Libs, so if you don't need us..." the guy says as he scratches his head.

"No." Lane finally says.

The mover stares at Lane. He's probably wondering just as I am whether 'no' means, 'no I don't need you to move my stuff', or if she means, 'no don't leave.'

"So should we get started?"

"Yes." Lane says.

I let out a huge breath of air just in time to keep myself from passing out. As I watch the movers follow Lane to her front door, I feel like the entire block is spinning. *She was really leaving. It was over.* Knowing that there is literally nothing left to say, I head towards my own house and slam the door shut.

I fall backwards onto my couch, and squeeze my eyes shut. I wonder if I have enough whiskey in my house to help me fall asleep long enough to forget about Lane. But I doubt there's enough whiskey in all of Pennsylvania.

"Fuck." I scream as I punch one of my pillows on my couch so hard that feathers fill the air. I watch as one floats up high, and sways back and forth before landing on the floor. I look at the mess I've just made, and instead of being annoyed I have to clean this up, I'm just happy to be thinking about anything else besides Lane. That is, until I hear a knock at the door.

I punch the empty pillow once more before I run to the door and fling it wide open. My heart pounds in my chest when I see Lane standing at my front door. She's shifting her weight from side to side, just like she's done so many times in the past.

"What?" I finally ask after a few moments of silence.

"I wanted to say thank you. For what you did for Joe."

"Don't worry about it."

I put my hand on the top of the door and think about closing it. As rude as I know it is, I can't think of anything else to do.

"So I saw you listed the houses already. I thought that was still a few more weeks away. You still have some work to do, right?" Lane says as she sticks out her neck in an attempt to see the inside of my house. Her eyebrows arch when her eyes land on the feathers from the pillow all over the floor.

"No. We're listing as is."

"Why?"

"The city shut us down."

My hands involuntary clench into fist and I fight the urge to pound them into something.

"I thought you said the sewer was fine?"

"It is, but there's a problem with the foundation. And we're out of money."

Lane puts her hand over her stomach and hunches over slightly like she's just been punched in the gut.

"It's all my fault. If they hadn't come to look at the sewer..."

"No it's not your fault. I know it was Lindsay who emailed them. It wasn't you."

Lane puts her hands inside the large pocket of her sweatshirt and fiddles with something.

"But I'm the one who told Lindsay that I thought we needed a new sewer line. If I hadn't..."

"No. You couldn't have known she would do something so spiteful. Really. I forgive you."

Lane bites her bottom lip to keep it from shaking.

"You forgive me?"

"Of course." I stare directly into Lane's eyes so she can see just how serious I am. Seeing her so upset is causing an excruciating pain in my stomach. Like someone is twisting all of my insides with a rusty wrench.

Lane shakes her head, and looks down at the floor.

"Well, in that case..." She slowly begins to lift her head, and the next thing I know she is taking a flying leap directly towards me.

I'm so shocked that I almost bring my arms up and push her away. Luckily, I catch myself just in time and I am able to wrap my arms around her just as her lips land on mine. I close my eyes as the feeling of Lane's wet tongue on mine overtakes me. Her lips are so soft, and the sound of her exhaling is so familiar and comforting. I pull her into me as close as possible, and silently make a promise to myself that I will never lose her again.

"I am so sorry Lane." I place my hands on the side of her head and angle her head upwards until her eyes meet mine.

"I'm sorry too." She says.

"No, you have nothing to be sorry about."

I crush my mouth down on top of hers before she has a chance to say anything else. I put my hands under her firm ass and give her a pat. She takes the hint, and leaps up into my arms and wraps her legs around my waist. I carry her inside and close the door.

I walk across the living room and fall backwards onto my couch. I put Lane down right next to the pile of feathers.

"Yeah don't worry about that." I say as Lane looks at what's left of my pillow.

Luckily she doesn't waste any time asking me questions. Instead, her hands go directly to the buckle on my pants. The minute her soft hand finds my rock hard cock, I cry out in ecstasy.

"Yeah baby, just like that." I say, almost immediately realizing my mistake. I wait for Lane to object to the nickname, but instead she laughs.

"I've missed this." She says in a low voice as she looks at my fully erect penis.

"Believe me, I've missed it more."

I lean back and close my eyes as I feel Lane's mouth on my shaft. She kneels down in front of me and looks up at me as she takes the elastic out of her hair that was holding it up in a bun. She shakes the brown waves and shoots me a look so sexy, I'm afraid I might explode. Then she reached down for the hem of her sweatshirt, and in one smooth move rips it off over her head. Her tits look even better than I remember in her white lace bra.

"Wait." I grab Lane by the shoulders and bring her up to her feet. Then I throw her down on the couch next to me.

"Your turn. Spread your legs for me." I say as I crawl between her thighs.

"Oh god yes." She screams with her head back. "Right fucking there."

"Shhh." I whisper. "We don't want the movers to hear you."

Lane nods her head and continues to moan. She wraps her legs around the back of my neck, bringing me deeper and deeper into her pussy. Her juices run down my chin as I bury myself inside of her. I do my best to find her bud, and continue to run my tongue up and down it. Her hips begin to buck wildly, and I know it won't be long.

"Cum for me baby." I tell Lane.

She brings her hips up and down even faster. Then she screams loud, as her whole body trembles right before it goes completely limp. I pull myself up onto the couch and slide in next to her, putting her head to rest on my shoulder.

"The movers." I say.

Lane smiles even though her eyes are still closed.

"You told them to leave, didn't you?" I ask as I stroke a piece of her hair.

"Yes, because I thought you said..."

"I did, and I meant it. You can stay until the sale is settled. We've had about five showings this week, but I don't think any of them are going to make an offer. We may have to lower the price again."

Lane looks down and sighs. The last thing I want her to feel is pity. I used to think not finishing this project was my biggest failure, but now I know losing Lane was. Now that I have her back, I don't care if I lose all my money. With her by my side, I know we can find a way to make it back. And even if we spent the rest of our lives trying and never made a dime, I think I'd still be happy.

"Stop. It's ok, I promise you. We'll find something better." I put my hand up under her chin and raise her head up. Lane nods.

"I know, but you're so close. If you could just fix the foundation... and do another coat of paint..."

I press my index finger to Lane's lips to stop her.

"It's over, and it's ok. I have put everything I have into this already. I literally don't have another dime..."

Lane's eyes pop wide open and she jumps up from the couch. For a moment, I begin to worry she is so repulsed by my failure that she is going to leave. Maybe I jumped the gun thinking we were back together.

"Lane, don't go. Please."

Lane laughs as she grabs the sweatshirt she's wearing up off of the floor and begins to rifle through the large pocket in the front.

"No, I'm not going anywhere. And neither are you, until this is finished."

I am just about to ask Lane what the hell she means when she pulls a check out of a wrinkled white envelope and smacks it down on the coffee table. I scan the top to see who this check is from, and see the name of a law firm. I'm too busy trying to figure out where this check came from to notice the amount, until Lane's points directly at it. My eyes open so widely I can practically see my eyebrows.

"Lane, where did you..."

"It's from an investment of mine. And I want to make

another investment in us. I want us to finish these houses, and sell them for what they are worth."

I mentally try to calculate the figures that Carl gave me the other day to determine what it would take to finish the job. What Lane has is more than enough. But can I really take money from her?

"What? Is it enough?" Lane asks with a timid look on her face.

"It's more than enough, but are you sure?"

"More sure than I have ever been about anything in my life. I want to be partners again."

Lane sticks out her hand for a shake with a wicked grin on her face. When I don't stand to give her my hand, her cheeks redden.

"What? I just meant business partners."

I stand up next to Lane, and pull her hand into mine. Then I bring it up to my mouth and kiss the back of it.

"No, I want to be more than business partners. Lane, the fact that you are investing everything you have into us makes this the easiest decision I have ever made."

I put my hand on the back of Lane's neck and bring her lips to mine. I stroke the side of her face as our tongues connect and slowly move around one another. Lane lets out a gentle sigh of contentment into my mouth. At this moment, nothing else matters. I can feel every fiber of my body finally relaxing. I didn't even realize until this moment that I must have been walking around the last few weeks wound up as hell. I feel normal again now. This is how life is supposed to be.

A thought pops into my head. I need to ask Lane something immediately. There's only one way to make sure I never lose Lane again. And I need her to know just how serious I am about us. So I pull my mouth from hers to tell her, causing her eyes to open wide.

"Lane, we should get married."

"What?" Lane practically screams. "Are you serious?"

Ok, maybe that was a bit early. The last thing I want to do is scare her.

"Maybe not right away, but eventually." I say, doing my best to recover. Lane laughs, so I know we are probably good for now. "Right now, I need to make love to you."

Lane squeals in delight, and we both race upstairs. Once we make it to my bedroom, I take off all of my clothes as fast as humanly possible. I don't even realize until I'm done that Lane is standing there, watching me undress.

"Your turn." I say to her.

Lane slowly reaches around to her back and unhooks her bra, one clasp at a time. Then she slowly brings the white lace straps of her bra down her shoulders. Not able to wait another second, I reach for her bra and try to pull it down in the front to expose her gorgeous breast. Lane brings her arms back to the front and swats my hands away.

"Hey. Hasn't anyone ever told you good things come to those who wait?"

Never have I heard words so true in my entire life, I think to myself. But instead of answering, I bring up my hands in mock surrender and walk backwards to my bed and collapse. Lane was absolutely right. Waiting for her was anything but easy, but having her back in my life was worth it. Even if I had to go through the shit storm that losing her was all over again, I would in a heartbeat to have her.

I watch as Lane seductively moves her hips as she slides her pants down inch by inch. I lick my lips as I see the hot pink lace fabric of her thong. When she's finally naked in front of me, I stay exactly where I am on the bed.

"Ok ready." Lane says as she jumps onto my lap. Her legs straddle me as she ravages me with kisses all over my face and neck.

I stand up with her still in my arms and lower her onto the bed. She instinctively puts her hands behind her knees, bringing her legs up to her chest. The sight of her bare spread pussy makes my cock throb. I climb up on top of her and bring myself directly to her slit. I run my tip along her outer lips until I'm covered in her wetness. Then, I slide myself all the way inside. Lane gasps as I enter her, and reaches her arms up and around my neck. I throw my arms around her as well, pulling her into my chest as I continue my gentle rhythm.

"I love you so fucking much Lane." I whisper as I press my lips to her forehead.

"And I love you Chris."

A bead of sweat from my forehead feels like it's dripped into my eye. It makes my vision fussy for a minute. I go to wipe it away before Lane gets the wrong idea and thinks I'm crying.

I put Lane's head on my shoulder as I move my hips up and down. Lane wiggles her hips, trying to drive me deeper and deeper inside of her.

"Sorry babe, I'm trying to make this last a little while."

"No, I want you deeper. It feels so good."

I thrust hard and deep, knowing I have to give Lane what she wants. And the realization that I will have plenty of opportunities in the future to make love to Lane for years to come overtakes my entire body, forcing me to explode.

"I'm cumming inside of you Lane." I say as I bury myself inside of her as my cock pulses.

"Good." She whispers as she nibbles my ear.

After I blow my huge load, I collapse next to Lane on the

bed and pull her to my side, wrapping my arms and legs around her until she's engulfed. I need to be as close to her as possible right now. The need to hold her is like nothing I have ever experienced before in my life.

"That was amazing." She says.

"You're telling me."

I close my eyes as all of the sleepless nights catch up to me.

"So about this foundation problem..." I hear Lane ask.

I open one eye, and of course Lane sits up in bed and pulls up the calculator on her phone.

"Have any numbers for that? I'm just trying to figure out what we'll have left for the final touches that is."

I smile as I close my eyes again.

"Yes I do. But I'm exhausted. What do you say to a quick nap, and then we can take a look at the numbers?"

I hear the keyboard on Lane's phone click a few times, and laugh at myself for thinking Lane would really choose sleep over work.

"On second thought, let me grab what Carl gave me." I say sitting up.

"No, you look exhausted. You stay here and sleep, for as long as you need. I'm going to go grab my laptop. I'll call Carl since we need to discuss paint colors anyway."

I open my eyes as a smile overtakes my entire face. Lane was too good to be true.

"You are amazing. I am literally in awe of you."

Lane continues to type on her phone.

"I mean it, get some sleep."

Lane turns to me, and leans down and places a gentle kiss on my forehead. I know I should get up and review the budget with her, but something inside of me tells me it will be ok. *Lane has got this*, a voice inside of my head says. I lay back into my pillow with my eyes closed, fully confident that Lane will handle everything. I know that if I get some rest, we can finish this project. All of my problems that had been making it impossible for me to sleep for weeks are now suddenly gone. I close my eyes, and fall into the deepest and most restful sleep of my life.

EPILOGUE

LANE

Two Months Later

As I walk into Philadelphia's swankiest restaurant, the man at the host's stand literally does a double take as I enter. I almost look behind me to see what has caught his attention, until I remember just how smoking hot I am right now. I look down at the black silk, knee length dress I borrowed from Ashley for the occasion. It literally hugs every curve of my body. Then I brush a long curl off of my shoulder and bat my long false eyelashes at the man and watch as he tries to collect himself.

"Have a reservation with us tonight ma'am?" he asks with his mouth still hanging open.

"Yes, under Dunkirk." I say proudly.

"Looks like you will be dining at our VIP table in the wine cellar." The man informs me.

I've never eaten in a wine cellar before, or a VIP table for that matter. But I'm not surprised Chris went all out tonight. He did warn me when he first asked me to be his girlfriend that I was going to have to get used to him spoiling me once our project was done. And tonight, we were celebrating, what I hope is the successful completion of everything we have worked so hard for. Chris and his father were meeting this afternoon to hammer out the final details of a very good offer they received this morning. It has been less than twenty-four hours since we've re-listed all of the six units. That had to be good news. And the fact that Chris refused to tell me anything, and instead insisted I meet him here tonight has my stomach full of butterflies. I was never normally one for surprises, but I have a good feeling the news will make it worth the wait.

"Right this way ma'am." The host says gesturing for me to follow. I do my best to keep up as we walk all the way across the restaurant in my four inch heels.

We come to a private room with walls filled to the ceiling with expensive looking bottles of wine. My eyes land on Chris seated in the center at a small rectangular table, with crisp white linens and a candle illuminating from the center. Chris jumps up from his seat as I enter.

"Lane, you look..." Chris exhales loudly as he looks down, staring at my four inch pumps and all the way up to my hair that has been expertly curled by Ashley.

After I got back with Chris, I gladly moved back in with my besties. The last two months of being together has been everything. Even though I know it's all ending very soon, I am so excited about the future.

"So do you." I say as he leans in and kisses me on the cheek. Chris is dressed in his lucky suit, since he wore it to the settlement before dinner.

"So, I ordered a bottle of red. I know you usually prefer-"

I don't give a crap what we are drinking, I almost scream out loud. How could I possibly care about wine at a time like this? I needed to know how the deal went. The suspense was killing me.

"It's fine, just tell me! What was the offer?" I ask, leaning so far forward in my seat I almost slide off the edge.

Chris laughs and finishes pouring my glass.

"It was more than fair. I took it."

Chris slides a piece of paper in my direction. The number is drastically lower than the asking and takes my breath away.

"Why did you take this? There were five showings on the first day! We could have waited." I take a big sip of wine as my heart rate accelerates. I look over at Chris and am horrified to see him laughing.

"Well, the deal is only for four units."

That made much more sense. As I do the math, I realize that for four of the six units the offer on the paper was really really good. Over asking on a per unit basis. I should have known Chris' dad wouldn't let him be low balled.

"Ok, well that's better." I say as my heart rate returns to normal. "They didn't want all six?"

Chris slowly pours himself a glass of wine, and I see his mouth move as if he's trying to break some bad news to me.

"I've decided I am keeping mine. With all the great memories in it, I couldn't stand the thought of leaving it."

I clap my hands at the thought of Chris staying in his row home. I loved visiting him there. The last two months that we've been back together I have slept over there practically every night. It truly felt like home. The thought of someone else living there was hard to think about. Maybe that was the reason I still hadn't found anywhere else to live. My roommates and I still haven't looked for anything seriously, even though we all know our house could be sold at any time.

"And, as for the other unit."

Chris reaches into the pocket of his jacket, and for a minute I feel like I can't breathe. That is, until I see it's a key. I laugh at myself for thinking it was a ring. As exciting as a proposal would have been, moving into together was still a huge step. And he technically already proposed to me. Although, part of me still hopes he will one day do it properly with a ring. Maybe guys just don't think like that.

"The other unit I kept is yours Lane. And I want you to keep your house. With the money you gave me, you have earned it. It's the least I can do to repay you for all you've done."

I do my best to smile as Chris places the key in my hand. I already have a key, so I guess this was symbolic for him. It was a very kind gesture, as impractical as it was. I do my best to not think about how much my unit could have sold for, and what it would have meant for our next project.

"What?" Asks Chris.

"Thank you, it's very generous but..." I look down at my fingers as I swirl my glass of wine by the stem. And while what I am about to say is practical, I also know it probably sounds like the least romantic thing in the world. But I can't lie to Chris, he needs to know why I'm not jumping up and down. I just hope it won't hurt his feelings. But I owe him honestly.

"I spent most nights at your place anyway. And if we sold five units instead, we'd have even more money for our next project."

"So, you want to move in together to save money?"

I put my head in my hands to save myself the embarrassment of seeing Chris' reaction to my stupid statement.

"No, that's not the only reason..."

"Well I have a better one."

I feel Chris pulling my arms away from my face, forcing me to look up. He's looking down at his hand, which is holding up a massive diamond ring that is sparkling so bright in the candlelight that I am afraid it might blind me.

"If we were engaged, it might make a lot more sense to move in together."

I stare at the ring, completely unable to utter a single word as I stare at the magnificent princess cut diamond. And the gorgeous, caring and most generous man that I have ever met who is also willing to make me his wife.

As I continue to think of what to say next, it occurs to me that Chris still hasn't proposed. I don't want to jump the gun.

"What do you say?" He finally asks.

"To what? You didn't ask me anything."

"Well, the last time I did, you kind of turned me down, so forgive me for being cautious. A man's ego can only take so much."

My jaw drops as I try to comprehend how Chris could have actually thought I would have turned down a proposal from him.

"I never said no!" I say a little too loudly. Our waiter has just returned and stops abruptly by the door looking very hesitant. But I don't care if I am too loud, I need Chris to know.

"I didn't. In fact, I thought we were already engaged."

"Well, then if you accepted, this is yours." Chris holds the ring towards me and reaches for my left hand. Which I pull away.

"Actually, let's do this right. You ask, and I'll give you my answer. No more confusion." I tell him as I fold my arms across my chest and smile.

Chris drops to his knee and motions to our waiter who

sets two glasses of Champagne on our table and then hurries off. Chris grabs my left hand once he's kneeling, and places the ring at the very tip of my ring finger.

"Lane, you are literally the most amazing woman I have ever met. I knew from the moment you first ran right into me. The fact you made me work so hard to win you over only proves that you are probably too good for me. But I don't care, I'll spend the rest of my life trying to prove to you that I am worthy of you. Because everything in my life is better when you are in it. I couldn't have finished this project without you. You literally made my dream come true. Now let's spend the next forty years coming up with new dreams, and knocking them out of the park together."

A tear escapes my eye and trickles down my cheek. Chris slowly moves the ring up my finger and past my knuckle and then stops.

"Lane, this is where you tell me..."

"Yes!!!" I scream again as more tears roll down my cheeks.

Chris slides the ring all the way on my fingers and jumps to his feet. He pulls me into his arms as I feel my feet leave the floor. Once he sets me down, I pull my hand up to examine how the ring looks on my finger.

"I'm just wondering, if we got something a little less expensive, could we buy an even larger property next time?"

"Lane, we will be making serious money the rest of our lives. Now it's time to enjoy our success."

Chris grabs the glasses of Champagne from the table and we toast. Then we kiss, soft and slow. *Enjoy our success*, his words echo in my brain as I try to convince myself I have actually achieved what I have always wanted, and more. No more working my ass off at dead end jobs barely making ends meet while I wait for my big break. It was here in front of me, and my dream job came with the best partner I could ever ask for.

We were a success together, which was oddly much more satisfying than achieving success all on my own could have been. It was time to enjoy it! Not only today, but for the rest of our lives.

The End

COMING SOON - SAMPLE CHAPTERS

UNTIL HE CONFESSES

Prologue

Callie

I was nervous as hell.

Anna was too but she had managed to convince herself otherwise and so here we were, nervous, and briskly walking beside each other as we tried to locate the house. A few minutes later, and just as we turned the corner, we came upon it. iIt was impossible to miss.

The chatter from the few students loitering outside as well as the music immediately explained to anyone, just exactly what was happening within.

"Here we are!" Anna said as she grabbed my hand. "I told you it wouldn't be that far from the bus stop."

"Getting to the bus stop took twice as long as you said it would, Miss," I shot back. "You better hope Sandra is here otherwise we're screwed. I'm still a hundred percent sure she was bluffing."

"She wasn't," she said. "She knows she's our ride home otherwise we *are* screwed."

I smiled because if getting caught and landing in severe trouble with our parents was the outcome of this night, I was certain it would still be one I would remember.

"Let's go," I snatched my hand away from hers as we arrived at the door, and she gave me a nervous look.

"I thought you had guts," I mocked, and just as expected this spurred her entrance into the house.

The living room was packed, which made me wonder just how many people from our high school had been invited. It couldn't have been everyone so perhaps students from other high schools were also present?

This seemed to be the case because as I stuck close to Anna as we pushed our way through, there wasn't a familiar face to be found.

Especially Sandra's, the outgoing classmate who had invited us on what we still believed was a spur of the moment's excitement.

The information had been spread by excited whispers in class and huddled conversations in the hallway until eventually we'd had to ask Brett at lunch what the hell was going on.

"Party of the year," our friendly classmate from middle school had informed us.

"Simon's parents are going to be away for the weekend so everyone's going to be there. Students from all three grades I heard, and maybe students from other high schools?"

My subsequent question and concern had been simple but still remained unanswered.

"Is there going to be a chaperon or lifeguard there?"

Anna gave me a look that showed her regret at inviting me.

I didn't blame her as I didn't think I was too taken with the rowdy nature of parties.

It took me and Anna a few more minutes of filtering through more faces before we eventually stumbled into Brett lounging in shorts by the pool side.

He waved the moment we called out to him, so we headed over.

Just before we arrived two girls suddenly dove into the water and Anna was annoyed.

"Goddamn it," she cursed at the wet stains that appeared on her bright red, frilly blouse.

"I can't believe you're both here," Brett said.

"I can't believe you were invited," Anna said, and he gave her a vicious look. I was amused at the exchange, until I finally noticed the chubby boy lounging by his side. He was familiar as I had seen him around school, but we'd never had a chance to meet.

Tonight however, we waved at each other and said hello.

"I thought you said you were going to be surrounded by the ladies," Anna mocked Brett as my attention went to the students loitering all around in pairs, all cliques.

"We've been rejected," the other boy said. "So, we've settled for the stars and sipping martinis."

My gaze shot to the glasses they had in hand.

"Those aren't martinis," I contested. "I can see the bubbles."

"It's Sprite," Brett said and received a slap to the arm. "There's alcohol though, but it's only accessible to the seniors club."

"What the hell is a seniors club?" Anna asked.

"No idea," he replied. "But so far, I've been able to put decent hearsay and sightings together. There seems to be 'another' party upstairs that's for the cooler kids.

"And we're not cool?" I asked.

All three gave me incredulous looks.

"Wanna swim?" I smiled at Anna.

"Are you kidding? This entire circus can be shut down in a second. I don't need the added trouble of trying to find my clothes and a towel when I need to scram."

There was sense in her words, but as more and more people got into the water, my discomfort remained.

" I don't see a lifeguard anywhere."

"There is one," Brett said. "Why do you think we were able to get invited?" he referred to the friend sitting by his side. "I brought a guy from work. He's a senior and swimmer at Gunn High. I had to pay part of his fee out of my own pocket though to get him to come."

I was skeptical.

"Can he really swim and save anybody?"

"No idea but he sure looks like he can. Let's put it this way; I'd bet my money on him rather than that fake martini over here."

The boy jabbed into his side, and it made Anna laugh.

"Let's get a drink," I nudged her, and she agreed.

"We'll be back," we announced to the boys and headed back into the house.

By this time, our nerves had dissipated some and for a moment I even caught Anna's shoulders moving slightly to the music as we headed towards the kitchen.

"Don't get carried away," I told her. "We have to leave in an hour, or we're toast."

"Have fun," she shimmied even harder as she grabbed my shoulders to force me to move along with her.

"In this one night of the year, can you not be so uptight?"

I rolled my eyes, but in an effort to pull my shoulders out of her grasp, I ended up staggering backwards.

Anna's eyes went wide with shock, while my heart nearly flew out of chest at my loss of contact with balance and gravity.

My arms flailed out as I tried to grab onto any surface, but fortunately, I was shoved against a solid body.

My entire life in that moment, flashed before my eyes at how I had just been saved from probably landing on my ass and being the joke of this entire party and quite possibly the entire school.

"I'm sorry," I started to apologize as I turned around to meet the guy I had fallen against.

He was tall with brown curly messy hair and looked just as shocked as I was.

Anna immediately apologized as well.

I moved away from him but then something in his expression changed for the worse as he shot a look at the friend that was beside him.

And then they stood in my way.

I smiled and tried to escape but he kept coming after me. Until eventually, I frowned, stopped retreating and met his gaze head on.

"You're in too much of a hurry," he said. "The least you could do was say a few more words before leaving. I could have been severely hurt just now by how hard you bumped into me."

I watched him and felt my skin begin to crawl. He was attractive I realized, with a very cute little boy face on an almost adult's body kind of way. But there was just something so slimy about him that made me want to move even further away.

"I have access to the VIP floor," he said. "Come with me and I'll get you a real drink. And a private space for us to talk."

I could barely keep my disinterest off my face.

"No," I replied. "I'm fine right here with the fake drinks."

"Callie," Anna called from behind, her tone filled with disappointment. I shot her a dark look.

"Your name's Callie?" he asked. "Isn't that a boy's name?"

My gaze went to his hair.

"That's a lot of curls," I said. "Isn't that a girl's style?"

The guy beside him started laughing, but at the sharp look his friend shot his way, he soon hurried away.

"Come with me," he growled.

Anna stepped forward and latched onto my arm so that she could whisper into my ear. "Let's go with him. How bad could it be? There are other people up there, aren't they?"

I gave her an incredulous look and shook my head. Then I turned back to the boy, even more adamant that I didn't intend to go anywhere with him.

"No, thank you," I said and was about to turn away when he suddenly grabbed my wrist.

I was alarmed.

"What are you doing?" I snapped.

"You won't regret this," he said. "Trust me."

And then he began to pull me along, wrenching me from Anna's grasp. His hold on my wrist hurt and the harder it dug into my skin the more terrified I became.

"Let me go!" I said through gritted teeth, trying my best to keep my voice down so that it wouldn't bring unnecessary attention to us. However, he didn't listen.

Soon, we arrived at the bottom of the stairs, and he kept trying to pull me up with him.

Grabbing onto one of the banisters, I jerked my hand away with all my strength and in that moment, he suddenly let me go.

I fell hard on my ass and lost my breath. I also lost my

temper and before I could stop myself, I grabbed the opened can of soda on the floor and flung it at him.

"You fucking idiot!" I cursed and the liquid splashed everywhere! On his hair and face and clothes... the wall and a few more people around. They all swore at me.

I was shocked, my mouth instantly falling open.

"I thought it was empty," I said. "I'm sorry."

"Callie!" I heard Anna's alarmed call and could feel all the attention I had been trying to avoid gradually turned towards us.

"I'm sorry," I said again but something in his eyes made a cold chill run down my spine. He marched towards me. I felt helpless. All I could do was throw my arms over my head, a scream stuck in the back of my throat and ready to break free the moment I felt pain.

The strike I was expecting never came. Instead, there was a shout over me as I crouched down in a defensive pose to hide my face. A few seconds later I looked up to see the exchange that was intervening on my behalf.

There was another guy, completely dressed in black, much taller and dark haired. Although I could only partially see his profile, I could tell that it was stern as he faced the boy that had tried to attack me. I immediately felt saved.

He had caught the other boy's wrist and I watched as with one hand he pushed him so roughly away that my attacker staggered and fell against the steps.

People passing tried to soothe and calm the situation, however he ignored them all. He seemed furious.

"What the fuck is your problem?" he roared, giving the boy cowering on the stairs a lethal look.

"Don't touch her again," he said. "If you do, you'll pay dearly for it."

Then, without a single word further or even a glance at

me, he turned and continued on his way towards the back door.

We all stared after him until I realized that my attacker was still on the steps. He met my eyes. Despite his annoyance and embarrassment, he got up and stormed his way up the stairs.

Anna rushed to my side.

"Oh my God!" she exclaimed. "What was that? And who was that? I'm happy we didn't go for the other guy. This one's way hotter. Damn… I knew something good was going to happen with us coming here."

I couldn't believe her, but I also couldn't stop myself from staring at the boy as he headed towards the pool area.

"I need a drink," was all I could say, and Anna giggled by my side.

"There's some Sprite on the counter," she said.

I couldn't help but smile.

"Fake martini it is then."

"We could have gotten the real deal upstairs."

I ignored her and headed over to the counter.

After grabbing a can of Sprite, I watched amused, as she found a used martini glass close to the sink. After giving it a quick wash, she poured half of her can into it and then raised the glass up to me.

"Cheers," she said and stuck her pinkie out as she took a posh sip.

I did the same and although it was no martini, all the sugar and carbon dioxide hit all the right spots for me.

I couldn't help but look over my shoulder, still a bit shaken and on guard in case any other drunk crazy person came over to me. And in case that boy showed up again.

"Let's go back to the pool area," Anna came over, but of course I had to feign reluctance.

"No," I refused, but she refused to budge.

"Don't be shy. He's probably not here anymore."

"I don't know what you're talking about," I said.

She grinned.

"Your knight in shining armor."

I made a dismissive noise but was unable to work up a strong enough will to refuse when she started pulling my arm.

Back at the pool side it didn't take us long to find him because he was on the pool chair that Brett's chubby friend had occupied earlier, but rather than lying down he was seated and going through his phone. I was so struck that I didn't realize I was still moving towards them until we suddenly stopped.

"Hey!" Brett called out. "I wondered where you two went."

He then noticed Anna's glass.

"Ooh, you're a copycat I see," he said.

She laughed.

"Too bad Dan's not here anymore. He would have been glad to see that he cultivated a protege."

"Cultivated a protege?" Anna asked dryly.

I smiled but my attention was truly on the boy that had his head lowered and was for all intents and purposes ignoring our existence.

I was instantly turned off by how pompous he seemed but was unable to completely fault him for it, after all, he had helped me when I needed it and without a single ounce of fanfare. Perhaps it was just the way that he was, to do and say the needed and be on his way.

Brett soon noticed my attention and then tapped on his shoulder.

"Here's our lifeguard," he said. "Lifeguard, meet Anna and Callie."

He gave us both a glance, but I couldn't help but imagine or perhaps hope that his gaze lingered just a fraction of a second longer on me.

"We already met," Anna said.

As for me, I couldn't put together a single coherent thought or think of a word to say so I kept my mouth shut.

"You've met?" Brett seemed surprised. "Inside?"

"Yeah, he helped us out." Anna said.

"Anna," I hit my shoulder with mine.

She frowned at me before I cleared my throat.

"Yeah," I squeaked out.

Brett laughed and looked out across the pool.

"Too bad no one's drowning. Lucas, is there a way I can get my money back from you?"

Lucas gave him a dark look. I was amused but when the flush heated my cheeks, I quickly looked away to save face.

Something suddenly shattered behind me.

Startled I turned to see that a commotion had begun. All of a sudden, swarms of students were hurrying out of the house and towards us.

"Side gate! Side gate!" they yelled.

"Uh oh! Time to go." Brett jumped to his feet excitedly.

I grabbed Anna's hand.

"What?" I was confused and scared. "What's happening?"

"Their parents are probably back or something. Who knows. Be careful though so you don't get caught in a stampede. Wait things out."

Both boys rose to their feet, and we tried our best to go along with them.

"We haven't found Sandra," Anna complained. "How the hell are we going to get home?"

"Let's make it out first and ask that question later," I said.

"Isn't this someone else's house though?"

"I don't think they're home either."

"*God,*" she groaned.

The haste and panic were nightmarish. We crashed and stumbled into each other. Eventually though, we made our way to a side street and eventually we burst out onto the main road along with many others.

Anna was amused as we watched people fall all over each other, both drunk and amused and all I could do was shake my head at how lacking in dignity it all was.

"All for some fake martini's," I said with a sigh, and she laughed even harder.

"It was worth it."

"Well, it won't be, Anna, if we don't find our way back to your house in the next thirty minutes."

"What about Brett?" Anna asked. "Maybe he could help us out."

"Does he have a car?"

"I don't even know if he drives but I'll call him.

"You have his number?"

"Of course, I do. He's in our grade, you know."

"You know I don't talk to anyone."

"Exactly," she muttered as she tried to find his number. "And how's that working out for you now?"

We walked along the beautiful houses of the affluent neighborhood. I waited for the call to connect and listened as Anna spoke to him. She sounded excited and so when the call finally ended, I was hopeful for good news.

"He doesn't have a car," she said, and my spirits instantly deflated.

"But that Lucas guy does. They said they're going to turn back and watch for us, so be on the lookout."

I turned, my pulse immediately quickening.

"They're coming back?" I asked almost to myself, but Anna noticed and responded.

"That's what I just said... oh there they are!"

"Brett!" she called out and we watched as an old Camry pulled up to the sidewalk.

Brett leaned out of the passenger window and waved at us.

"Miscreant mobile," he said. "Let's go! Hurry up."

Anna laughed as she hurried over, but I refused to run faster than was needed.

Soon we got into the back and a spicy scent hit my nostrils.

My gaze instantly went to the rearview mirror, but all I could see was the side of his face as he pulled back onto the road and began to drive cautiously away.

"I'm starving," Brett said. "What do you guys say we stop by for some McDonald's? Lucas?" He didn't respond but Anna did.

"I'd love that."

I jabbed her with widened eyes.

"We need to get home."

"Oh please," she said. "I'm sure we're going to get caught anyway. We might as well have something to eat beforehand to give the night some meaning."

Brett laughed and tapped loudly on the roof just as the car accelerated.

Lucas gave him a stern look and I lowered my head to hide my amusement.

"Sorry," he said casually, but when I looked up, I nearly

lost my breath because he was staring directly and intently at me through the rearview mirror.

Lucas

Visiting McDonald's when it was almost midnight was the last thing I wanted to do.

Especially when it truly was out of my way to find one that wouldn't be closing in minutes.

"Why don't we just go to a proper dinner?" Brett suddenly suggested. "Make this a date of some sort."

At this I gave him a look and from his exclamation I was sure that he received looks from everyone else too. I wanted to gaze at the rearview mirror to see if she had once more tried to look at me, but I couldn't bring myself to. So, I kept driving until I heard her friend's voice from behind.

"That's not a bad idea." Followed by a yelp of pain. "*Ow*!"

I almost smiled then, and Brett laughed.

"So, it's a date," he said. "Who's my partner?"

He looked back ... all smiles but was immediately disappointed.

Silence filled the car and then I heard Anna's voice again.

"Me," she said, and I couldn't stop myself then from glancing at the rearview mirror. She didn't look at me, and an irresistible urge to taunt her rose within.

We soon found an open diner, I parked in the lot, and we all got out.

"My darling," Brett called, and I watched as he went around the car and threw his arm around Anna's shoulders. At first, she resisted, but amusement soon overcame her enough to finally give in. She slid her arm around his waist, and they basically hopped and skipped into the diner.

I went ahead on my own and truly couldn't help but wonder about why I was so aware of the girl behind me. I pushed the door open and couldn't help but hold it open for her. She looked at me for a moment and then quickly diverted her eyes as she hurried up to cross the threshold. I watched her from behind and was glad that I had taken the initiative.

She was dressed quite simply and not as though she was going to a party that had advertised itself as being raunchy and chaperon-free.

She had on a dress that had a flattering fit to her upper body but flared out from the waist. Over it she had thrown on an oversized denim jacket. Her hair was in a half up half down hairstyle that I couldn't help but admit fitted her immensely and then she had on off-white Converses with one of the laces coming loose.

I watched them to the point where I got so distracted, I began to wonder if I should call her attention to the fact that she could trip over it, that I almost bumped right into her when she abruptly stopped. Irritated with myself I stepped back quickly and headed straight to a booth by the corner.

The others came along and seated themselves around me. She was right across from me with her friend beside her while Brett was beside me.

"This place looks decent," Brett said as Anna pushed his hands off hers.

"Too bad I can't exactly vouch for their food since I haven't been here before. Has anyone been here before?"

"I have," she suddenly said, and it was the perfect excuse for me to look up.

"I came here with my parents I think, a few years ago. My dad's job is not too far from here."

"Oh, yeah," Anna said. "That's right."

"And?" Brett asked, and I watched as she stared directly at him as she replied.

"I really can't remember."

Anna laughed and so did I. Brett feigned offense.

"You suck," he said.

She smiled.

"I'm sure it wasn't bad though because if it was then I wouldn't forget. So, since I can't remember then it means it's passable and nothing stood out."

"That works too," he said. "Oh, the waitress is coming over."

She arrived looking exhausted with tendrils of hair escaping her bun. I kept my gaze on Callie as Anna made her order.

"Chili fries, burger, no tomatoes. Extra lettuce."

"Same for me," she piped up.

"Me too," Brett said.

"Make that four," I told the waitress.

She nodded and walked away, and the entire table was once again thrown into silence.

Awkwardly, the girls began to chat with each other while Brett turned to look at me with a stupid smile on his face.

I ignored him and pulled my phone out of my pocket. I listened to both girls and not till the food arrived did I look up, and at that time I wondered what it was about her that I was so intrigued by.

Perhaps it was because I had been impressed from the get-go of how she had handled that idiot that had been harassing her.

She almost wouldn't have needed my help until those last few seconds, and that sparked a little respect for her that was unusual for me. It was also all the more heightened by the fact that she seemed to be quite reserved.

Plus, there was also the undeniable fact that she was unarguably gorgeous.

Not in a blatant way, but in a way that made it impossible to look away.

Ah, those plump lips...

Brett tapped my shoulder and I turned to him with a frown to realize that my food had been placed before me. There was an unmistakable glint of amusement in his eyes, and it was quite worrisome to imagine what the source was.

I didn't even dare to look at her or Anna because something told me that I had been caught by all parties unashamedly staring at her lips.

Chapter 1

Callie

(9 years later)

"I'll never forgive you."

I snorted in amusement as I zipped my luggage shut, and then turned around to meet a scowling Anna leaning against my open bedroom door.

"Work is more important than dating."

"You took this shift to get out of this double date."

I didn't have any arguments there, but I wasn't about to admit to it either, so I grabbed my luggage, took one last look around my room to be sure that all was in order, then smiled at her.

"This is a special route and I'm not going to miss it for all the world. We're flying to London, and you know I'm usually never available when we have a London route. I'll be there for three days even and I'm planning on turning it into a little vacation. I'm sorry but that experience holds much more promise than a blind date."

"It's not exactly a blind date."

She stood in my way.

"Anna," I complained. "I'm going to be late."

"It's not a blind date. It's Bryan's coworker," she insisted. "Would I set you up with someone I wasn't absolutely sure you were going to hit it off with? He's wonderful."

"Really?" I asked dryly. "How many times have you met him?"

"At Bryan's birthday," she immediately replied.

I narrowed my eyes at her.

"That was almost six months ago. If he was so wonderful then why are you only just now mentioning this to me? You know why? Because he didn't stand out to you. Bryan probably talked you into it because he lobbied him or something."

"And what's wrong with that?" she asked sheepishly. "He's handsome and has a decent job. Come on, hon. Give the man a chance."

"Next time," I said, and put her determinedly out of my way.

"Callie," she implored as I hurried straight to the entryway. Before she could stop me, I slipped on my polished shoes, grabbed my purse, and was out the door.

"Callie!" she called out again as I was halfway down the hallway towards the elevator.

"Yes?"

"Bring me something nice from London, will you? And it better be special, worth disappointing me for."

I sent her a smile and walked away.

****

The moment I arrived at the airport and met up with the crew, we went through the motions of security checks and soon we were aboard the Gulfstream G700 that would be flying us across the Atlantic Ocean.

I was excited, more so than usual, due to the extra days I

had in the city before we had to return, and I planned to take full advantage of it.

I was one of two hostesses on this flight, and the other was a colleague I had flown with a couple of times, so I was comfortable. She too expressed her excitement of traveling to London again although she'd already visited several times before.

"It's a wonderful city but the rest time has always been too short," she told me as we sorted out the meals for our incoming guests and made sure that all was in place.

"I hope to go back properly but not through work. I'm going to take my husband with me and we're going to have two whole weeks to ourselves."

I envied her because two whole weeks was a stretch for me. I knew that I would get bored if I spent too long by myself and this disgusting lack of independence had been promulgated mostly due to the fact that I had spent the majority of my life so far, by a certain Anna Leewens's side. I could always sense her loss anytime she got into a relationship and since it was rare for me to be in one, she made it her sole mission to ensure that I wasn't lonely. It was amusing but I was aware for sure that I would miss her terribly if she ever had to leave for an extended period of time.

Especially since my dad passed away midway through college and I was left to my own devices and, of course, Anna's.

"Client is on his way," Julianne announced.

I turned around, adjusted my uniform and crossed checked the vibrant red of my lipstick in the lavish restroom mirror.

"Do you know who the client is?" she asked, as we

headed down the aisle together towards the open front door.

"No idea," I replied. "We didn't even get many details about their preferences. There are three people though. Two men and one woman. I guess we'll know who the boss is among them at a glance."

"Always," she smiled, and we went ahead to take our positions just as two jet black vehicles pulled up. Two people exited the town car in front while behind yet another two exited the SUV with one of them going behind to pull the door open for the other.

"Ah," Julianne sent me a look that made me smile. "The boss had been spotted."

The weather was wonderful. It wasn't too humid like it would have been in the middle of summer but was just perfectly mild and almost even cool as autumn approached.

I was in a great mood, but all of that soon came to a halt as the group of three started coming over. I couldn't help the note a familiarity to the boss behind. That walk. No, it couldn't be...

I watched intently; the professional smile plastered on my face slowly dissipating as they climbed up the short flight of steps. Thankfully I remained alert enough to greet the first two in front and introduce myself, but what a shock it was to feel the effect of the boss behind them on my entire being.

He was dressed casually, in a white dress shirt with the first two buttons undone and the sleeves rolled to his elbows.

His hair was slightly tousled, given the late afternoon breeze, but there was no one quite as unmistakably and devastatingly handsome as Lucas.

He stopped before me, then stared directly into my

utterly shocked eyes. If there was any surprise in him that I was standing right before him he didn't show it.

In fact, he gave me as much attention as one would a stranger in a crowded train, and then headed in to take his seat.

Julianne nudged me then, her eyes widened. "You didn't greet him," she said. "That's the boss."

I awakened from my trance. "What?"

"That's Lucas Marsh. The boss!"

Preorder the book here:
Until He Confesses

ABOUT THE AUTHOR

Thank you so much for reading!
If you have enjoyed the book and would like to leave a precious review for me, please kindly do so here:

Dream Crusher

Please click on the link below to receive info about my latest releases and giveaways.
NEVER MISS A THING

Or
come say 'hello' here:

ALSO BY IONA ROSE

Nanny Wanted

CEO's Secret Baby

New Boss, Old Enemy

Craving The CEO

Forbidden Touch

Crushing On My Doctor

Reckless Entanglement

Untangle My Heart

Tangled With The CEO

Tempted By The CEO

CEO's Assistant

Trouble With The CEO

It's Only Temporary

Charming The Enemy

Keeping Secrets

On His Terms

CEO Grump

Surprise CEO

The Fire Between Us

The Forgotten Pact

Taming The CEO Beast

Hot Professor

Flirting With The CEO

Surprise Proposal

Propositioning The Boss

Made in the USA
Monee, IL
02 June 2023

35184992R00173